KILLING THE BORDENS

LIZZIE BORDEN AND THE UNSOLVED 1892 BORDEN MURDERS

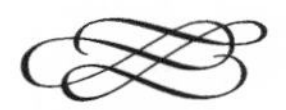

C. CREE

Killing the Bordens.

This is a work of fiction. While some characters, dialogue, and circumstances portrayed by the author are based on real people and historical fact, references to real people, events, establishments, organizations, or locales are intended only to provide a sense of authenticity and are used fictitiously. Characters, incidents, and dialogue are drawn from the author's imagination and are not to be construed as real.

ISBN (hardcover): 978-1-964439-01-3
ISBN (paperback): 978-1-964439-00-6
ISBN (eBook): 978-1-964439-02-0

Library of Congress Control Number: 2024913408

Written on Scrivener software and formatted using Vellum.

Cover design by Richard Ljoenes Design LLC.

First Edition
2024.08.16

CONTENTS

AUTHOR'S NOTE

The Bordens were real. Abby and Andrew Borden were murdered in Fall River, Massachusetts, in 1892. Lizzie Borden was suspected.

The Borden story is one of the most famous unsolved mysteries in American history. Thousands of pages of original case materials still exist, including witness statements, newspaper reports, trial transcripts, and lawyers' notes. The Fall River Historical Society maintains an extensive collection of documents, photos, and other evidence.

Since the murders, many novels, movies, and plays have been based on the Borden story. There was even an opera. These are often true to the premise but then tell tales inconsistent with the facts.

My goal with *Killing the Bordens* was to create the most historically accurate fictional telling ever written of the Borden story. Where possible I've used historical records and other related sources to understand and tell the story, including using direct quotes from police notes, legal journals, and transcripts.

Through years of research, many aspects of the events became clearer.

Killing the Bordens also reveals who committed the murders, how, and why.

Warning: This book involves disturbing topics, including but not limited to hatchet murders, blood spatter, corpses, and autopsies.

Note: For a character list, floor plans of the Borden house, and historical notes, see the end chapters. See www.ccreewriter.com for additional materials related to the Borden story.

CHAPTER 1

THURSDAY, AUGUST 4, 1892, FALL RIVER, MASSACHUSETTS

For most of the morning, neighbors and passersby on sunny Second Street went about their lives unaware. Dozens passed right by the Borden house, which was so close to the street that pedestrians could almost lean over from the sidewalk and touch it on their way to the paint shop, livery, diner, and doctors' offices. That day a newspaper seller worked up and down the street and men cut bricks in a yard behind the Borden place.

Sixty-nine-year-old Andrew Jackson Borden trudged up the hill from downtown at twenty to eleven, wearing the black wool suit and Prince Albert jacket he wore every day, regardless of season or summer heat. That morning he was ill, short of breath and weak as he returned home unusually early for his noon meal.

Widow Adelaide Churchill lived just north of the Bordens. She'd spent the morning making beds and cleaning the home which she, her mother, and sister ran as a boarding house. It was an ordinary day, hot and muggy, but not especially so for August.

At quarter to eleven, Adelaide went to the market one street over.

Walking back, she saw "the Borden girl," their twenty-six-year-old live-in maid, Bridget Sullivan, running across the street from Dr. Bowen's to the Borden home.

Adelaide wondered if someone was ill. She was well acquainted with the Bordens, her neighbors of twenty years.

Andrew Borden's money was in mills, real estate, and banks, and he cared mostly about his own affairs and property. When he met Adelaide on the street he'd greet her with, "How do?" and a tilt of his head. That was generally all.

Andrew's second wife, Abby, was sixty-four and stepmother to his two daughters, the first Mrs. Borden having died in 1863. Abby had few friends and people called her "fleshy" because of the weight she carried from sweetbread indulgences.

Older daughter Emma, a spinster, forty-one and just younger than Adelaide, was friendly enough and always proper. Adelaide found her bland and inscrutable.

Miss Lizzie Borden was also a spinster at thirty-two. With her close friends she was known as kind, generous, straightforward, and a good listener. She had an easy, contagious laugh. She could also be guarded and defensive. More emotive than the rest of the family, Lizzie's sharp tongue had gained her a reputation for being difficult, but she was also the only Borden who could laugh at herself.

If Adelaide were honest, only if pressed, she would have to say that she'd never quite liked any of the Bordens.

Adelaide set her bundles down in her kitchen and saw, out her window, Lizzie standing inside the Bordens' screened side door. Lizzie leaned against the door frame, rubbing her forehead in apparent distress.

"Lizzie, what is the matter?" Adelaide called out.

"Oh, Mrs. Churchill," Lizzie replied. "Do come over. Someone has killed Father."

Adelaide delayed only long enough to tell her mother there was trouble next door, and then hurried over. Lizzie sat almost frozen on the second step of the stairs just inside the door, her gray eyes wide.

Tragedy and death were common in those days. Adelaide's father had died twenty years before and her husband only a few years into their marriage. Her sister was also a widow.

But murder was not common, and Adelaide thought that maybe Andrew was only sick rather than dead or killed. Lizzie, who'd never lived outside her father's house, was prone to overreaction.

Adelaide touched Lizzie's arm. "Lizzie, where is your father?"

"In the sitting room," Lizzie said, her expression flat.

Looking into the kitchen and to the closed sitting room door, Adelaide listened and heard nothing in the hot, humid house. Was a killer hiding inside? She spoke more softly, "Where was you when it happened?"

"I went to the barn to get a piece of iron."

For what use, Adelaide did not ask. "Where is your mother?"

"She had a note to go and see someone who is sick," Lizzie said, "but I don't know if she is killed too, for I thought I heard her come in."

The Borden house was poorly built and carried sound. Abby should have appeared if she could. And where was Bridget?

Lizzie said, "Father must have an enemy. We have all been sick, and we think the milk has been poisoned. Dr. Bowen is not at home and I must have a doctor."

It was possible that Andrew had an enemy. Or enemies, thought Adelaide. Indifferent precision was Andrew's business gospel, including swift eviction of families who could not pay their rents. Perhaps a disgruntled former tenant had killed him and fled. A horse-drawn wagon on the street clomped and creaked by. "Shall I try to find someone?" Adelaide asked, too scared to look herself.

"Yes." Lizzie nodded emphatically.

Gathering her skirts and sprinting to the stables across and down the street, Adelaide found her working man. "Mr. Bowles, somebody has hurt Mr. Borden; go and get a doctor," she gasped.

"Yes, ma'am."

"Hurry and do not try for Dr. Bowen. He's not at home."

"Yes, ma'am."

The newspaper seller overheard some of the exchange and went to find a telephone. Adelaide ran back to the Borden house, where she found Lizzie in the same state, still in the entryway. "I shall have to go to the cemetery myself," Lizzie said vaguely.

"Oh, no," said Adelaide. "Lizzie, the undertaker will attend to all such things as that for you."

After that they waited in hot, stuffy silence.

Adelaide had been in the Borden house before, though not often. The old, narrow house, with its closed-in rooms, was hardly suitable for a man as rich as Andrew Borden. It had been a tenement house with two apartments when Andrew bought it in 1872 and he did not fully convert it to a house for one family, leaving a peculiar layout of small rooms and awkward doorways. The kitchen did not have a sink. Instead, a sink room hid near the side door. The Borden daughters could not host grand parties in the small parlor, sitting, and dining rooms.

The family slept on the second floor, with the parents' room at the back and Lizzie's, Emma's, and the guest room at the front, connected only by a door directly between the parents' room and Lizzie's bedroom. That door stayed locked. Andrew had the only key. Emma's room was off of Lizzie's. The front stairs led only to the front bedrooms and the dress closet. Mr. and Mrs. Borden's room in the back and Bridget's attic room could only be reached via the rear stairs.

The house sorely lacked comforts. It had no bathrooms, save for one toilet in the cellar and two cold-water-only sinks — one in the cellar and the one in the sink room near the kitchen. When the household did bathe, much to the daughters' frustration, they used pitchers and basins in their rooms. They used kerosene lamps despite the availability of gas piping for households well below Andrew's means. He'd bought the house because of the short walk to his downtown banks and crowning achievement, the A. J. Borden building, and cared little for comforts.

The Borden house was peculiar in another respect: most of the rooms, including the closets, were kept locked. Everyone in the house locked their bedroom when they left it, even if only going down to the kitchen. Andrew locked his and Abby's room each morning, but oddly always left the key on the sitting room mantle.

The Bordens had lived in the house on Second Street for twenty years, but they had never belonged, a rich man's family in a working man's house and neighborhood.

CHAPTER 2

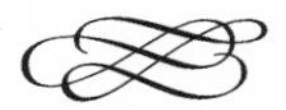

At 11:12 a.m. a haggard Bridget hurried up the front walk of Borden family friend Alice Russell's small cottage a block from the Borden house.

Alice was not married but lived on her own. She worked as a bookkeeper and managed to support herself despite earning half what a man would for the same work.

She knew Bridget's arrival meant trouble, and not only because of Bridget's agitated state. The previous evening, on Wednesday, Lizzie had visited Alice and shared fears about the family's safety.

"I feel depressed," Lizzie said that evening. "I feel as if something is hanging over me that I cannot throw off, and it comes over me at times, no matter where I am."

Alice had previously lived next door to the Bordens and knew the family well, especially the daughters.

"Father and Mrs. Borden were awfully sick last night. We were all sick. All but Maggie," Lizzie went on. Lizzie and Emma always called Bridget "Maggie," the name of the Bordens' previous girl and a nickname for Irish maids. Bridget appeared to take no offense, though. The long line of Borden family maids all seemed to like Miss Lizzie best.

"Something you have eaten?" asked Alice. The Bordens ate poorly, often keeping the same unrefrigerated mutton stew or leftovers for days.

"We don't know. We think our milk might be poisoned."

Alice, confused, said, "It is light when your milk is brought from your farm. I shouldn't think anyone would dare to tamper with the cans for fear somebody would see them."

"I shouldn't think anyone could," said Lizzie. "But Father and Mrs. Borden were awfully sick and in the morning Mrs. Borden thought they were poisoned and went over to Dr. Bowen's." She raised her hand to her mouth, perhaps remembering the sickness.

"Who would poison your parents, Lizzie?" Alice asked.

"I don't know but Father is so discourteous to people. A man came to see Father, who I did not see. They quarreled about a property. Father ordered him out of the house. I feel as if I want to sleep with one eye open half the time, for fear they will burn the house down over us."

Alice reassured Lizzie as best she could, but stayed awake, wondering, long after Lizzie left. Only twelve hours later, Bridget also arrived at Alice's door. She gasped for breath, having apparently run from the Borden house.

"What is it, Bridget? Are they worse?"

"Yes." Bridget could hardly get the words out. "I don't know but what Mr. Borden is dead."

"Oh!" said Alice, and then, "I'll be over as quick as I can."

Bridget turned back toward Second Street and Alice went to put on a better dress and a hat for going out.

At the paint store, the newspaper seller said, "I've got to use your telephone. There's a stabbing, I think, up at the Borden place." First he called his friends at the *Fall River Daily Globe,* the *Fall River Herald,* and the *Fall River News*. Then he called the Fall River Police, at 11:15.

"Trouble at the Borden house, Dr. Bowen," Mrs. Churchill's man hollered when the doctor's carriage turned onto Second Street. "Best get over there." Bowen nodded and his driver flicked the reins. Bowen knew the Bordens well, as their neighbor for twenty years and family physician for twelve. Dr. Bowen's wife, Phebe, also waved him down. "They want you quick over to Mr. Borden's!"

He grabbed his medical bag and raced over, rushing in the side door just before Bridget, who'd run back. They both stopped short; Adelaide and Lizzie were in the entryway. Adelaide rubbed her own arms, as if it was cold instead of hot in the house. Everyone attended to Lizzie, still on the stairs. She seemed stunned.

Bowen said, "Lizzie, what is the matter?"

"Father has been stabbed or hurt, I do not know."

"Has there been anybody here?"

"No, not as I know of."

"Where is he?"

She pointed. "In the sitting room."

Dr. Bowen had been in the sitting room just the day before, after Abby came to see him. She'd arrived at his door before eight that morning, bone white and unsteady. "We've been poisoned!" she said. Bowen had needed to help her into his office. "Andrew and I vomited for hours last night," she said. "I've never been so sick, nor heard of anyone else so." Even as she spoke she struggled to keep her stomach down.

Having eaten only baker's white bread and cake for supper herself, Abby said one or the other must have been poisoned; bakeries sometimes used chemicals and other substances to make bread whiter or thicker.

Bowen had not liked the look of her, but assured her, "It's most likely summer sickness." Summer sickness was the common name for food poisoning borne of poor or no refrigeration. Whole households took ill repeatedly in the hotter months.

Bowen sent her home with instructions to take castor oil with a little port wine for the taste. Later that morning he paid a visit. Bridget let him in. Tall, thin Andrew rested on the sofa in the sitting room, even paler than Abby had been. He worked to sit up.

"Are you all right, Mr. Borden?" Bowen had said.

Andrew didn't answer but asked, "Did someone send for you?"

"No. Mrs. Borden was over. She said the family had been ill and I thought I would come and see."

“I feel a little heavy,” said Andrew, breathing hard. “I don’t feel right. But I don’t need any medicine.”

Bowen generally liked everyone, but liking Andrew Borden wasn’t easy. Andrew took pride in a casual cruelty explained as a Puritanical ethic of austerity. That ethic affected many people, including the Borden women who were dependent on him. He controlled their choices and they lived with less, despite Andrew’s wealth.

No doubt that morning Andrew was most concerned about a doctor’s bill. Andrew was so penny-pinching that he sold eggs from the farm out of a basket while walking to the bank where he was president.

Neither Abby nor Lizzie came down that morning.

Now, a day later, Bowen went to the sitting room door and listened. He heard nothing except the women behind him, and steeling himself, eased the door open.

It was sunny and bright inside. One figure, motionless, rested on the horsehair sofa. The same sofa where, just yesterday, Andrew had rested while speaking with Bowen.

The figure looked almost to be napping, with booted feet resting on the floor. The hands were relaxed, at ease. But the head told the story. The left side was cut, crushed in, and demolished. Bone chips scattered around the body and the sofa. A long, deep line cut through the nose, the lips, and into the chin through a white beard. The left eyeball, split, hung out of its socket by the optic nerve, resting against the nose.

Bowen’s breath escaped in a grunt. The man was so freshly dead that blood still oozed from the wounds, worked down through the sofa, and dripped to the floor.

Bowen would not have recognized him had he not known the wool suit Andrew wore every day. Despite knowing it could not help, Bowen lifted Andrew’s wrist. There was no pulse but the flesh was still warm.

It struck Bowen that the sitting room looked otherwise undisturbed. The key to Andrew’s bedroom waited in its usual place on the mantle.

Bowen returned, in a stunned haze, to the kitchen and the waiting women.

CHAPTER 3

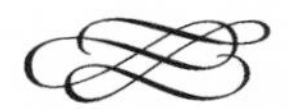

Family friend Alice had arrived and joined Bridget and Adelaide around Lizzie, who rocked herself in a kitchen chair. The room, closed in with the stove, was especially hot.

Though Dr. Bowen had been a family doctor for many years, he'd never seen or imagined anything like Andrew's cruelly crushed face and skull. Standing in the kitchen, Bowen still saw the split eyeball hanging loose. "This is awful. Mr. Borden is killed," he said.

Lizzie gasped. Alice and Adelaide both reached out to steady her, afraid she might slide to the floor. Bridget stood by, watching, her eyes darting to every sound.

Bowen, dazed and airy, for a moment needed someone, anyone, to also see the decimation of Andrew Borden so that he would not be the only one. "Addie," he said to Adelaide, whom he'd known for decades, "come in and see Mr. Borden."

"Oh, no, doctor," she replied, shocked. "I don't want to see him. I saw him out in the yard this morning. He looked so nice. I don't want to see him now."

"Perhaps you should not," Bowen replied, gazing somewhere near her chin. His ears rang.

Adelaide fanned Lizzie with newspapers while Alice cooled Lizzie's head and neck with a wet dishcloth and rubbed her hands for circulation.

Bowen leaned on the table until he recovered himself. Turning to Bridget, he said, "Get me a sheet, and I will cover Mr. Borden over."

"I'll not go by myself!" Bridget cried. She sounded so scared that Adelaide agreed to go, too, even though she didn't want to.

Bowen got the key to the Borden parents' bedroom from the sitting room mantle and Bridget and Adelaide slowly, quietly, inched their way up the dimly lit back stairs. They listened and peered around corners but that part of the house appeared empty. The bedroom door was locked as it should have been. The bedroom and inside dressing room, with the sheets and Mr. Borden's desk, were also apparently undisturbed.

It took two sheets to cover tall Andrew.

An officer sprinted the three blocks from City Hall to the Borden house. City Marshal Rufus Hilliard had sent him to find out the goings on.

Already loiterers gathered at the Borden front gate. The officer summoned neighbor Charles Sawyer from the group and deputized him. Charles was to guard the side door and let no one enter or leave except officers.

Inside the house, Dr. Bowen was saying, "I must be off to get officers."

"Doctor, will you also send a telegram to Emma for me?" Lizzie said. "She is visiting Miss Helen Brownell in Fairhaven." Fairhaven was fifteen miles from Fall River.

"I will do anything for you," replied Bowen, prompting a grimace from Adelaide. She wished he would not speak to Lizzie that way, even if he meant it only to be supportive and fatherly. Some in the neighborhood said he was too close to Lizzie and even that they'd had an affair.

"Please do not tell her the worst," said Lizzie, "if you can help it. The old lady where Emma is visiting is feeble. She had better not have the shock."

On his way out Bowen met the officer at the side door and led him through to the sitting room to see Andrew's body, pulling back the sheet from the crushed head. "You go down and tell the marshal all about it. Get the police as fast as you can."

The officer quickly checked the ground floor. He found all three locks on the front door, including the bolt which was only set from inside, firmly in place. He sprinted back to City Hall.

"Is he dead?" Hilliard asked.

"Yes, sir. Killed."

Everyone in the neighborhood soon knew about the stabbing at the Borden house.

Fall River was not a small or quiet town. Founded in 1803 to mill textiles, using the river for power, the city had grown so successfully that by 1892 the population was nearly eighty thousand.

For rare events like murders, though, Fall River felt very small. Word of mouth spread so fast that ordinary citizens quickly knew more than the police. Whether what they knew was true or not was another matter.

A crowd began to gather in the street in front of the Borden house. Many were from the working class: factory workers, domestics, and laborers. Resentment simmered between those who earned just enough or not enough to survive from their labors, and those whose vast wealth had been built on that labor. Some in Fall River had acquired Gilded Age wealth while factory work required six twelve-hour days per week, and had few protections against quick death from faulty equipment or fire.

News of a rich man's murder drew a crowd that came to see who would be taken away for the crime. It would, they hoped, be another of the exalted few who lived lives of leisure at the expense of workers. They watched the house, and were oddly quiet as they waited.

A few men and boys ventured onto the Borden property. They looked into the old barn, disused outhouse and well, pear trees, grape arbor, and wood pile. They saw the wooden back fence, with barbed wire on the top, bottom, and along the runners.

They looked into what they could, talked, and waited to see what would happen next. The Borden place was likely to get busy and exciting, and they wanted to be the first to know.

Alice Russell was always surprised at the spare kitchen in the house of such a rich man, with its old stove and worn table and chairs. Magazines perched in disarray on shelves near the stove.

Lizzie sat rocking, surrounded by her helpers.

Neighbor Charles Sawyer, deputized and stationed just inside the side door near the kitchen, eyed both exits from the back stairs warily. One led down from above and one up from the cellar. He also peered into the small sink room, which hosted the icebox. The ice man would have brought fresh ice that morning, but an icebox was no good in August.

Bridget stood in the entryway near Charles and the exit.

"Is he dead?" Charles asked.

"Oh yes, he's dead," said Adelaide from the table.

"Would you like to go in and see?" offered Dr. Bowen.

Charles hesitated and then nodded. Bowen ushered him into the sitting room and Charles had his look though he hadn't really wanted to see.

Someone, no one could quite remember later who, asked Lizzie where she was when her father was killed. "I went out to the barn to get a piece of tin or iron to fix my window," she said. "I heard a groan, came in and found the door open and found my father."

Bowen left to see his wife and send the telegram. Alice slid into the chair with Lizzie, who rested her head on Alice's shoulder.

"I wish somebody would go find Mrs. Borden," said Lizzie. "I thought I heard her come in."

"We'd better look," agreed Adelaide, though she did not want to. "We'd better go. She might be upstairs dying from the shock."

Adelaide and Bridget crept through, together again, this time to the front of the house. They already knew Abby was not in her bedroom. By going through the dining room they only needed to step through a corner of the sitting room to get by Andrew's body.

Halfway up the front stairs, eye level with the second floor landing and the floor of the guest bedroom, Adelaide saw a form on the floor in the dim light on the far side of the bed. "That must be her," she said softly.

Bridget looked and saw, too. Nothing moved or made a sound in the room. Bridget hurried the rest of the way up and into the guest bedroom. Adelaide ran back down.

In the kitchen, Alice saw the look on Adelaide's face. "Is there another?"

Adelaide stooped and gasped, tears welling in her eyes. "Yes, she is there."

Lizzie moaned, and increased her rocking, her chin trembling. Alice gripped her shoulder and soothed, "It'll be all right."

There was no door to bolt from the upstairs but Charles closed and bolted the cellar door and then stood just inside the side door, to make a quick escape if needed.

Adelaide's heart raced. She lived just steps away, with a son, mother, sister, niece, and tenants. "I'm sorry, Lizzie. I cannot stay here and I will go home for a little while. If there is anything I can do for you, I will do it."

"Perhaps there will be something later," Lizzie said with a distant look.

Bridget came back, shivering, and went through to the entryway.

"Is she killed, too?" asked Adelaide.

Bridget nodded.

Just then Dr. Bowen returned from his errands.

"Dr. Bowen, you must go up to the guest bedroom," Adelaide said. "We have found Mrs. Borden."

Bowen hurried through and Adelaide stayed a bit longer.

"Maggie," Lizzie said, "go across and get Mrs. Bowen to help."

Bridget did not ask why but went to get the doctor's wife.

Thinking that perhaps Abby had only fainted after seeing Andrew's body, Dr. Bowen walked around to the foot of the guest bed. She was face down, the back of her head crushed and bloody. Her body trapped her hands as if she'd turned away from her attacker and tried to catch herself, falling forward. A yardstick she might have used to smooth the bedspread waited nearby.

He returned to the kitchen. "Mrs. Borden is dead. Killed the same as Mr. Borden," he said.

A gasp again passed through the room.

Only then did he notice his wife. The news of Abby's death had affected her, too. "Phebe, you go right back home. I don't want you here."

She paused to touch his arm reassuringly, and left.

Alice guided Lizzie to the dining room, where it was cooler. The room looked as it always did, though an ironing board with handkerchiefs sat on the table. Alice tried to help Lizzie cool down by loosening her shirt but Lizzie stopped her, saying, "I am not faint."

Adelaide stayed in the kitchen, catching her breath and calming herself. She'd had quite enough and wanted to run right out of the house, but there was nowhere to go except home and she feared frightening her own family.

It was Abby's killing that bothered Adelaide most. Abby had never belonged with the Bordens. The Borden daughters were young, five and fourteen, when Abby became their stepmother, but they appeared only ever to tolerate her. Even Andrew had not seemed to especially like Abby, though it was harder to tell with him.

For twenty-seven years, Abby's life as a Borden consisted of light housekeeping, supervising the Borden girl, marketing, church on Sundays, and a few social visits with friends and family.

And someone had killed her.

Adelaide cried softly into her hands. She let out despair at seeing two murdered bodies, of people she'd known.

CHAPTER 4

"Clear off!" shouted an officer at the bystanders on the Borden property, though a *Fall River Daily Globe* reporter who panted from his sprint to the house was allowed to stay.

Many of the Fall River Police officers who arrived at the Borden house that day had, like Bridget, immigrated to the United States from Ireland after the Potato Famine. Starting in the 1840s, millions of desperate Irish immigrants made their way to the United States. Those who survived the journey sometimes disembarked in New England without the money to buy a meal and no connections in America except those made on the trip. They lived in crowded rooms and ghettos and sometimes alleyways, even in deepest winter.

Some in their host states called them lazy, criminal, and disease spreaders. By the 1890s, many still looked on the Irish with distrust and distaste, but the Irish had gained some measures of acceptance. The first Irish mayor of Fall River took office in 1885. Mayor John Coughlin, also Irish, was elected in 1891. By 1892 most of the Fall River Police department was Irish. New England and the officers turned their own distrust to the next wave of immigrants — the Portuguese.

When they began their searches at the Borden house one officer climbed the wood pile to see into neighboring yards, cutting his hands on the barbed wire as he went over the fence. A workman in that yard startled; he'd been focused on cutting stone. None of the men there had seen or heard anything awry that morning, they said.

Officers Doherty and Mullaly made their way into the Borden house, the reporter on their heels, and Mullaly noted the dining room occupants: Lizzie Borden, daughter and resident; Bridget Sullivan, the Borden girl; Adelaide Churchill, neighbor; Alice Russell, family friend. Dr. Bowen and the reporter listened from the sitting room.

"City Marshal Hilliard sent me to get a report of all that happened to your father. What can you tell me?" Mullaly said to Lizzie.

"Nothing," said Lizzie. "I was out in the barn and came in and found Father hurt or stabbed, I did not know."

"You saw him?"

"Yes."

"Did you see anyone else around the house?"

"No. I came in, saw, and called Maggie." She gestured to Bridget.

"And you, Miss?" asked Mullaly.

"I was in my room upstairs," said Bridget. "I did not see or hear anything until Miss Lizzie called."

"Do you know if your father had any property on him when he left this morning?" Mullaly asked Lizzie.

"Yes, he had a silver watch and chain. Also, pocket money and a gold ring on his little finger."

Mullaly wrote while Doherty searched Andrew and found the items still on his body, including eighty-one dollars and sixty-five cents. He had not been robbed.

"Do you know if there are any axes on the property?" Doherty asked Lizzie after seeing Andrew's body.

"In the cellar," said Lizzie. "Maggie will show you."

Mullaly continued. "You know nothing else of what happened?"

"Nothing," said Lizzie.

Mullaly could not think of anything else to ask. "Hmmph," he said. He and Doherty joined Bowen and the reporter in the sitting room.

Bowen spoke in low tones. "There is something more wrong here. The whole household was sick yesterday, and Mrs. Borden is lying dead upstairs." He took them up to see Abby's body.

"My God, her head is all smashed in," Doherty said.

The reporter, almost forgotten, wrote many notes.

Doherty went back to the dining room and Lizzie. "Do you know of anyone who would harm your father?"

"No."

"Do any laborers work for your father?"

"Father has a farm over the river, in Swansea," she said.

"Was there a Portuguese working for your father over the river?"

Lizzie bristled. "That man isn't a Portuguese, he is a Swede."

"Was this man on good terms with your father, or could he have been responsible?"

"Certainly not," she said, glowering at Doherty. "I do not believe he could have."

Doherty hurried back to the station while other officers searched the house and property. They found no blood anywhere except near the bodies and they found no one hiding in the house.

It was pure coincidence that County Medical Examiner Dolan happened by the Borden house in his carriage at 11:40.

Dr. William Dolan, only thirty-four years old, had been the medical examiner for less than a year. In his training as a general practice physician he had performed autopsies, but he was not a forensic expert.

The onlookers outside told him of murder in the house and he hurried in. Dr. Bowen showed him, "This is Andrew Borden."

"Mr. Andrew J. Borden?" Dolan had heard of the man, but had not known him personally.

"Yes."

Dolan stared at the body.

"Would you want to make an inspection?" prompted Bowen.

"Yes, I guess I'd better." Dolan steeled himself for a closer look.

Many distinct wounds were visible on the left side of Mr. Borden's bloodied head and face. All appeared to have been made by a sharp, heavy, bladed weapon like an axe. There were no other wounds on Mr. Borden's body. The entire attack focused on the left side of his face and head, and had continued long past death.

Blood soaked through the pillow under the head, to a folded Prince Albert coat underneath the pillow, and dripped to the rug.

"Two killed?" said City Marshal Hilliard with surprise and dismay.

"Yes sir, two, and with an axe, looks like," said Doherty.

Hilliard's officers responded to only a few murders per year, generally the result of domestic disputes or drunken brawls gone too far. This was different. His men were determined but had limits. They were beat cops who dealt with petty crimes and broke up mobs.

Worse, Thursday was the annual policeman's picnic. Many officers were out of town at the event.

Fall River had been founded, in part, by the Borden family. The Borden name demanded attention and Hilliard knew to respond to a Borden murder with full police resources and a speedy arrest.

First, he sent a man to Assistant Marshal John Fleet, who was home with his sick wife and the doctor. Fleet had a keen mind and was the best man Hilliard had to investigate a crime like this.

Next, Hilliard sent wires to the picnic, calling officers back, and to the state police for help. Then he sent every officer he could to the Borden house or fanning out across town looking for anyone suspicious, especially any Portuguese.

A horse-drawn trolley car stopped at the corner of Second and Pleasant Streets. A man of perhaps fifty years got off and walked the two blocks uphill to the Borden house. The tall, trim man, wearing a suit, passed through the crowd in front of the house, walked up the Bordens' drive, and passed the side door.

Charles watched the man, who appeared not to notice anyone else as he went to the backyard. From his station at the side door, Charles watched as the man picked up a pear from the ground and ate it. Then the man walked back to the side door steps, seemingly surprised to find Charles there.

An impressive stink wafted from the man. Outer clothes were not generally washable in the 1890s; most everyone smelled. This man, though, especially so.

Adelaide knew he was Lizzie and Emma's uncle, John Morse, and let him in. "Mr. Morse, something terrible has happened. Somebody has killed both Mr. and Mrs. Borden."

"What? In God's name!" He called into the house, "Lizzie!" and rushed to the dining room where Lizzie reclined on the lounge, attended by Alice. "They were murdered?"

Lizzie said nothing but Alice gasped and reached up to protect her own throat. Somehow it had not registered with her until that moment that they were in a house with murder. She began to shake.

After a moment, John went in and saw Andrew's body in the sitting room. An officer told John about the other body in the guest bedroom. John went far enough up the stairs to see Abby's body on the floor on the other side of the bed. He went back down to fall into a chair in the kitchen, next to Adelaide.

Only then did any officer ask his identity.

"Miss Russell," Dr. Bowen said to Alice in the dining room. "You'd best take Miss Lizzie up to her room."

Alice mustered her strength to help Lizzie up from the lounge. Lizzie leaned on Alice as they stepped through the sitting room and up the front stairs. They did not look into the guest bedroom.

Lizzie unlocked her bedroom door. "Alice, will you tell Dr. Bowen that when it is necessary for an undertaker, I want Winward?" she said.

"Of course," said Alice, and went back down.

When Alice returned, Lizzie had changed her dress and walked out of Emma's room in a pink-and-white-striped wrapper with a red ribbon and bow tying the waist. It must have been only the dress that Lizzie changed, and not her undergarments or corset — those would have taken much longer than the few minutes Alice had been gone for a Victorian lady to change.

. . .

Marshall Hilliard's best man for the job, Assistant City Marshal John Fleet, arrived at the Borden house at 11:45, thirty minutes after the alarm reached the station.

He hadn't changed into his police blues and wore a civilian suit instead but he was, as always, precisely groomed. Like many New England men, he had a thick mustache grown long and parted in the middle, with no beard.

Officer Medley met Fleet outside. "Both Mr. and Mrs. Borden in residence are killed. Mr. Andrew J. Borden," Medley said with emphasis.

Fleet's eyebrows went up, both in recognition of the important man's name and at the rich man's modest house.

Medley continued. "It looks, sir, as though someone killed Mr. Borden in the sitting room and then Mrs. Borden came in and was chased upstairs and killed."

"Anyone else in the house?" Fleet asked.

"Yes, sir," said Medley. "Quite a few. The Borden girl and an uncle are in the kitchen. The daughter, Miss Lizzie, is upstairs."

Fleet saw other officers on the scene investigating. Although they could not easily coordinate, each officer knew to pursue what clues and ideas he had for himself and report back.

Fleet decided to view the bodies first and question the household after. By the time the other officers reported to him and Marshal Hilliard, Fleet would have his grounding in the crimes.

When they went in, a man and young woman sat at the kitchen table. They were strangers to Fleet, though he knew from Medley's report that they must be the uncle and the Borden girl.

Adelaide was also there and known to Fleet and Medley—she was Adelaide Buffinton Churchill, daughter of former Fall River Mayor Buffinton. People in town still called her home the Mayor Buffinton House even though Edward P. Buffinton had died years before.

Fleet and Medley passed through to the sitting room to see Mr. Borden, and then upstairs. Fleet went into the guest bedroom. Medley questioned Lizzie in her room. She told him she'd been up in the barn looking for a piece of iron when her father was killed.

Medley found the barn door latched, not locked, and went inside.

CHAPTER 5

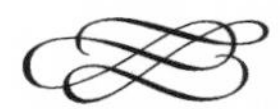

Reverend Edwin Buck arrived at noon. He'd hurried over as soon as he heard that Andrew and Abby were stabbed to death.

Known as "Father Buck" in town, he was sixty-eight and city missionary at Lizzie's church, the Central Congregational. Buck had known Lizzie since 1885, when they met and he invited her to his church. He'd looked out for her since.

Lizzie was active in church charities and social groups. She'd taught Sunday School and helped care for the sick and hungry in town. The rest of the family attended church but participated perfunctorily.

Buck braced himself for what he would find in the Borden house. His great strength as a spiritual leader was his deep and full heart, which was also so intense that his feelings were ever close to the surface.

Adelaide, John, and Bridget, in the kitchen, dully pointed him toward Lizzie's room. "Mr. Borden is in there," Adelaide warned as Buck started into the sitting room.

An officer stepped forward, too late, to block Buck from a view of the dark, clotted blood collecting in the hollows of Andrew's eye socket and half-gone face. Nothing could have prepared Buck, who choked, doubled over, and tried not to vomit. The officer helped him keep his feet.

"My God," said Buck, panting. "How did this happen?"

"Wish we knew," said the officer gently. Another officer pulled the bloody sheet back up over Andrew's head and gestured to one of the chairs. "Do you want to sit?"

"No. I'll be all right." Before he left, Buck prayed over Andrew, the officers joining in solemn observance as Buck bowed his head.

Upstairs, Lizzie let him into her room and then sat on the lounge under the south windows, appearing as calm as Buck had expected her to.

In the years Buck had known her, he'd come to see that Lizzie was in a way backward from expected behavior for a Victorian lady. In ordinary moments, Lizzie was prone to exaggeration and emotional language. In more distressing situations, however, she could be guardedly stoic and calm. Or at least seemed so. She had a coolness under pressure that Buck envied.

Buck also knew that in that moment she needed all the support he could give, in spite of her outward calm.

Alice Russell also needed his help that day. She shook as she sat on the edge of Lizzie's bed, holding onto the bed post.

Adelaide went home and told her mother and sister what she'd seen at the Borden house. The three of them, along with hostler Mr. Bowles, searched their house and property to be sure no one was hiding there.

Medical Examiner Dolan knelt next to Abby's body in the guest bedroom, sweating from exertion and the heat. Dr. Bowen and Fleet watched Dolan examine the wounds.

At least seven times a sharp, heavy blade had driven into Abby's head, crushing the bone. Dolan felt brain matter where he pressed with his fingers. One deep strike in her upper back cut into her spine, almost severing her head.

Dolan gently rolled her head and shoulders up so that he could see the front and side of her head. He counted more than a dozen total gashes, but there was less blood spatter than he would have expected.

Like her husband, most of her wounds were fatal and could have come from the same weapon that killed Andrew. Abby might have been dead before she hit the floor.

Bowen paced and said, "I can't imagine who could have done this. It's a miracle neither Miss Lizzie nor Bridget was harmed."

Dolan looked up to make sure no suspects were in the room. "Unless they did it," he said.

Bowen was aghast. "I have known both for years, and been Lizzie's doctor for more than ten. You will never convince me that they had any part of this."

"I surely hope they didn't," said Dolan, and turned back to Abby's crushed skull.

Fleet noticed the thickly congealed blood in the rug around Abby's head. He'd served in the Civil War and knew by the look of it that Abby had died some time before Andrew, not after. Fleet also knew from experience that medical examiners were not inclined to take notes from officers.

Instead, Fleet knocked on Lizzie's bedroom door and Reverend Buck let him in, greeting him with a nod. They were acquainted. He also found a woman Fleet would learn was Alice Russell.

"You are Miss Borden, Miss Lizzie Borden?" Fleet said to Lizzie.

"Yes." She sat on the chaise near the windows. Buck and Alice listened but did not interrupt.

"Can you tell me what happened here today?" Fleet said.

"I do not say that I know what happened," she said, "All I know is that Father came home about half-past ten or quarter to eleven. He went into the sitting room, sat down, took out some papers, and looked at them."

Fleet noted the times but did not take them to be precise. Most people did not have clocks nearby or pocket watches, and the timepieces they did have were not accurate. Only the City Clock down street was dependable.

"I was ironing some handkerchiefs in the dining room," Lizzie continued, "and was about to go back to it, but saw that Father was feeble and pale. I told him he should lay down, and I helped him to lay down."

Fleet found her demeanor most peculiar. She spoke as if she were a disinterested party rather than the daughter of the murdered couple. Nor did she behave in a way he would expect from someone who'd just committed or been involved in axe murders.

"Where were you at the time your father was attacked?"

"As I told the *other* officers," she said, "I went up in the barn."

"What did you go to the barn for?"

"For a piece of iron to fasten the screen. When I came downstairs from the barn, I saw Father on the sofa. I went to the stairs and called to Maggie."

"And who is Maggie?"

"Our girl, who cooks for us."

"And she was upstairs when you called?"

"Yes. I told her Father had been hurt or stabbed, I can't remember, and to run to Dr. Bowen's. He was not at home, so I sent Maggie to get Miss Russell." Lizzie indicated Alice.

"And what do you mean by 'up in the barn'?"

"I mean up in the barn, upstairs. I had been there about half an hour and I came down again into the house, and found Father where I had left him, but killed or dead."

"Who was in the house this morning or last night?"

"No one but Father, Mrs. Borden, Maggie, Mr. Morse, and myself."

"Mr. Morse?"

"He is my uncle. He came here yesterday and slept in the room where Mrs. Borden was found dead."

Fleet watched her carefully as he asked, "Do you think that Mr. Morse had anything to do with the killings?" A guilty party might be eager for other suspects.

There was no pause or hesitation. "No, I don't think so, because Mr. Morse left this morning before nine o'clock and did not return until after the killings."

"Do you think Maggie had anything to do with the killings?"

"No, Maggie had gone upstairs before Father lay down on the lounge. When I came in from the barn I called her downstairs."

"Do you have any idea who could have killed your father and mother?"

"She is not my mother, sir. She is my stepmother; my mother died when I was a child." Even with the heat in the house, she did not perspire much. She seemed quite casual.

"Do you know who might have killed her?" Fleet asked.

"I do not know. I believe I saw Mrs. Borden receive a note or letter this morning. I thought she had gone out of the house."

"Has there been anyone around this morning whom you would suspect of having done the killings?"

"I did not see anyone, but about nine o'clock this morning a man came to the door and was talking with Father. I thought they were talking about a store. He spoke like an Englishman. That is all I know."

Fleet made to leave and Alice said, "Tell him all, Lizzie. Tell him what you was telling me."

Lizzie continued. "About two weeks ago a man came to the house, to the front door, and he had some talk with Father, and talked as though he was angry."

"What was he talking about?"

"He was talking about a store, and father said to him, 'I cannot let you have the store for that purpose.'"

Fleet thanked her, and also scanned her room, including the bed, lounge, cabinet, and writing desk, but saw nothing that seemed related to axe murders. He went back to the kitchen. The uncle and Borden girl still sat at the table.

"You are the Borden girl, Maggie?" Fleet asked.

"They call me Maggie here, sir."

"What is your proper name?"

"Bridget Sullivan."

"You were here at the house this morning?"

"Yes, sir, all morning."

"Tell me what you saw."

"I saw nothing to tell, sir. I made breakfast as always. Mrs. Borden told me to clean the windows inside and out. I did and later went up to my room to rest; I was not feeling well. Miss Lizzie called me down after Mr. Borden was killed."

"Mr. Borden came in about what time?"

"About 10:40, I saw him come in and into the dining room and look at some papers which he had in his hands. Miss Lizzie was ironing some handkerchiefs in the dining room. I went upstairs at 10:55. After I had been in the room about ten minutes, Lizzie called me downstairs, saying that her father was dead, someone had killed him, go and get Dr. Bowen."

"Did you see anyone that you think would or could have done the killing?"

"No, I did not. I was washing the windows outside, and did not see anyone but Mr. Morse that morning; and he went away before nine o'clock." She nodded at John Morse.

"Are you sure you were upstairs no more than ten minutes?"

"I am very sure I was not upstairs more than ten to fifteen minutes."

"Noises carry in this house. Did you hear anything?"

"I heard the city clock strike eleven o'clock. That's all."

It was hard for Fleet to imagine that someone had hit Andrew Borden so many times with an axe and Bridget heard nothing, but he excused her to assist officers in the cellar.

Fleet turned to the man, who had an impressive stench to him. Perhaps he'd been especially active earlier. "You are?" Fleet said.

"John Morse. Mr. Borden was my brother-in-law."

"You're married to his sister?"

"No, he married my sister."

"The murdered woman was your sister?"

"No. My sister was Mr. Borden's first wife. My sister died some years ago."

"I see," said Fleet. "You were here this morning?"

"Yes, I got here yesterday. I spent the night in the room where Mrs. Borden's body is."

"What did you do this morning?"

"I got up about six. I had breakfast with Mr. and Mrs. Borden and then we talked in the sitting room."

"Did you see or hear anything that might be related to these killings?" said Fleet.

"No."

"When did you leave?"

"Shortly before nine, I would think. I am not sure."

"Did you take your things with you?"

"My things?"

"Overnight things. You spent the night."

"I brought nothing."

"What did you sleep in?"

"Underclothes," said John.

"You had planned to stay the night?"

"Yes, and for several days."

"And brought no clothes?"

"I wear this every day." He gestured to his suit.

Fleet made notes. "Where did you go when you left this morning?"

"First to the post office, then cross town. I visited with my niece."

"With Miss Lizzie?"

"No, another niece who is in town."

This man Morse did not seem to realize that his answers were not clear. Or, he was nervous.

Fleet waited for details but John did not continue. "Where did you go?" asked Fleet.

"Number four Weybosset Street."

Weybosset Street, a good distance across town, took time to get to. "And you came back here for noon meal?"

"Yes, Andrew, Mr. Borden, had invited me back. I said I would."

"When you spoke to Mr. and Mrs. Borden this morning was there anything unusual?"

"No," said John, and then added, "Only that they had been ill on Tuesday. Mrs. Borden thought they were poisoned."

"Poisoned?" Morse hadn't thought to mention a poisoning when asked earlier about anything relevant to the murders? Fleet asked, "How?"

"It was in the bread or the milk, she thought."

Fleet made more notes. "You did not see anyone or anything odd when you left?"

"No."

"Have you any idea who did this?"

"I can't see who could do this. I do not know that he has an enemy in the world." John assumed, perhaps, that Abby did not have enemies, either.

Fleet left up the back stairs to look around the second and third floors, then down to the cellar.

Officer Phillip Harrington arrived at the Borden house after noon. He heard the details from other officers, went up to Lizzie's room, and got much the same answers as the previous four officers. Harrington, though, made notes about Alice Russell, as "very pale, and much agitated, which she showed by short sharp breathing and wringing her hands. She spoke not a word."

Lizzie, by contrast, "stood by the foot of the bed, and talked in the most calm and collected manner. There was not the least indication of agitation, no sign of sorrow or grief, no lamentation of the heart, no comment on the horror of the crime, and no expression of a wish that the criminal be caught. All this gave birth to a thought that was most revolting. I thought, at least, she knew more than she wished to tell."

On his return to the kitchen, Harrington saw Dr. Bowen dropping bits of paper into the stove.

"What are those?" asked Harrington.

"Oh, nothing. Just some scraps," replied Bowen.

Harrington looked into the fire. The scraps had already burned but he saw another paper, rolled up in the back. It, too, was blackened beyond salvage.

In the cellar, Officer Mullaly crouched over two axes and two hatchets laid out on the floor. One had a red spot on the handle and was otherwise clean, as if it had been wiped or washed. Two others had red spots and one had a gray hair stuck to it.

Fleet nodded to him and continued through the cellar rooms. Coal bins, a wood cellar, and two keep cellars contained many shelves of household things, including baking soda, vinegar, and boxes of neglected tools.

There was a laundry area on the east side of the house, near the cellar stairs leading up into the backyard. The bolt on that door was firmly in place.

Fleet noticed a small pail of bloody napkins in the wash cellar, something he knew about because he was married. It was not surprising, in a household with multiple women, to find such a pail. He sent Dr. Bowen to find out which woman in the house those napkins belonged to. Bowen returned to say that they were Lizzie's, that she'd had fleas that week. "Having fleas" was the more socially acceptable way for a lady to refer to her menstrual cycle.

Fleet went out into the yard, where several officers mulled around. "You, men. Go out and cover the highways and depots. The murderer must be covered in blood and would stand out. Ask and see if anyone has seen anything." The men hurried off.

"Medley," Fleet said, waving Medley over. "Have you found any evidence of blood outside the house?"

"No, sir," said Medley. "Not a drop."

"There are hatchets and axes in the cellar. At least one could have blood on it. It may be that the killer is one or more of the household."

Medley nodded. That consensus had already been reached amongst the officers.

Fleet said, "We need to search the house again, and more thoroughly."

At one o'clock, Mrs. Marianna Holmes, mother of two of Lizzie's childhood friends, arrived at the house. It was not yet two hours since the alarm was first raised. A matronly woman, Mrs. Holmes immediately joined the group in Lizzie's bedroom and began mothering Lizzie.

. . .

The *Fall River Herald* made it to press first, within hours of the murders. "SHOCKING CRIME," read the headline. "A Venerable Citizen and His Aged Wife... HACKED TO PIECES AT THEIR HOME...AT THE HANDS OF A DRUNKEN FARM HAND. Police Searching Actively for the Fiendish Murderer."

The edition sold out. Other editions followed with scoops and speculation. Outside the Borden house, the crowd grew.

CHAPTER 6

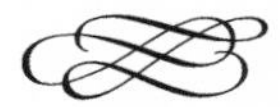

Lizzie stayed in her room all Thursday afternoon with her friends Alice, Reverend Buck, and Mrs. Holmes. Dr. Bowen often joined them. The dozens of officers and others in and around the Borden house were easily heard from Lizzie's room.

"This is all so much," Lizzie told Bowen. "I do not know how to manage."

Bowen pulled a pill bottle from his bag. "This is Bromo Caffeine. Take two now, two before bed, and we'll see how you do." He patted her hand as he placed the pills in it, and gestured for Alice to get a nearby glass of water.

"Bromo Caffeine is for headaches," said Lizzie. "I've never much benefited from it."

"We'll start with this, and try something else if it doesn't help," Bowen said.

Lizzie swallowed two and, settling back into the chaise, gazed out the window at the officers below and the crowd in the street.

More than two dozen officers searched the neighborhood and spoke with everyone they could.

The Kelly girl, the live-in maid at Dr. Kelly's house next door, said she'd chatted with Bridget for about fifteen minutes that morning at the Borden south fence. She saw nothing unusual.

Mrs. Mary Chase had seen a man in the Borden backyard at 10:45 that morning, eating pears. When he saw her, he jumped the fence.

No one else the officers spoke to had seen or heard anything unusual until after the alarm went out, but they still talked.

Elle Gifford of neighboring Franklin Street said, "I know nothing personally of the domestic relations of the Borden family, but I have heard much rumor to the effect that they did not get along very pleasantly."

Neighbor Mrs. Jane Grey said, "Dr. Bowen's character is at least suspicious. Four years ago, while the Borden family were summering over the river on the farm, Lizzie remained at home. One Sunday evening, she and Dr. Bowen came to church together, and sat in the Borden pew. I myself saw them that evening. At the time, and since, there was much comment on this act. Some remarked how courageous she was to remain in the house alone; but others replied in a knowing way, perhaps she has very acceptable company."

"I don't like that girl," said Officer Harrington as he and City Marshal Hilliard stood in the yard outside the barn.

"What's that?" asked Hilliard.

"I don't like that girl, the Borden daughter. Under the circumstances she does not act in a manner to suit me; it is strange, to say the least."

In the barn they found another sink and not a drop of blood. Upstairs, officers were already looking into the workbench and hay pile.

"I want you men to give this place a complete going over; every nook and corner must be looked into, and this hay turned over," said Hilliard.

Harrington said, "If any girl can show you or me, or anybody else, what could interest her up here for thirty minutes, I would like to have her do it."

District Attorney Hosea Knowlton also arrived at the house to speak to Hilliard and see the bodies.

. . .

Fleet found the door to Lizzie's room locked the second time he went to speak with her.

Dr. Bowen answered from inside without opening it. "Who is it?"

"Assistant Marshal Fleet. I'm here with two officers. We have questions for Miss Lizzie and need to search the rooms."

"She has been bothered considerable by these visits," Bowen said through the door. "I will see Miss Lizzie about it. Just wait a moment."

The officers waited.

Bowen returned and opened the door a crack. "Is it absolutely necessary that you should search this room, Lizzie wants to know?"

"Yes, I have got to do my duty as an officer, and I cannot leave the premises until I have searched the whole of this house," replied Fleet.

The door closed. If Fleet hadn't wanted to search the rooms before, he did now.

The door opened. Alice and Reverend Buck were still there, along with another woman who introduced herself as Mrs. Holmes.

"I've got to search the house," Fleet apologized.

"How long will it take?" asked Lizzie.

"Not long."

"It is no use in searching here," said Lizzie. "Nobody can get in here, or put anything in. I always lock my door when I leave it. There is no possible way for anybody to get anything in there."

"We need to search anyway," replied Fleet.

"Then I do hope you will get through soon," said Lizzie. "It will make me sick."

"I also wish to ask you some more questions," said Fleet.

"Please be brief. I am very weary. I have answered a great many questions," said Lizzie.

He nodded. "You say, Miss Borden, that you went out in the barn this morning, and remained half an hour."

"No, sir, I do not," she replied.

"Oh? What do you say, then?"

"I say I went out in the barn, and was out there from twenty minutes to half an hour."

"You told me before that you was in there for half an hour."

"Well, I do not say so now. I was there from twenty minutes to half an hour."

"What do you make it now, twenty minutes?"

"No. From twenty minutes to half an hour."

Buck noticed with a new nervousness the way Fleet watched and pressed her. Buck wondered for the first time if the police could possibly suspect Lizzie.

Fleet and the officers searched the room, looking into drawers even though it was not proper for police to go through a woman's bedroom things. They also search Emma's room off of Lizzie's, and in and under the beds.

Most of the books in the house, other than household manuals, were in Lizzie's room. She favored fiction and romantic poetry, though not exclusively.

In Emma's room there were two trunks. One they opened and glanced through. The other, wide, heavy, and locked, they did not attempt to open.

Another door, somewhat blocked by Lizzie's bed, was locked.

"Where is the key to this door?" asked Fleet.

"That is Father's room, he has the key," replied Lizzie. "It is always locked. The only way is by going around the back stairs."

When Fleet tried to open the dress closet on the second floor landing he also found it locked. "I want to look in there," he said.

"Well, there is nothing in there but clothing," said Lizzie.

"I want to see, I want to look in there," repeated Fleet.

Lizzie produced the key from a drawer in her writing desk.

The closet was five feet by eight feet, with a window to the front of the house. The shutters, partially closed, let in some light. The closet contained dresses, hung along one side. A cloth, wedged a the gap around the window, prevented dust from coming in from the street.

Fleet and another officer moved the dresses aside and patted them down. Nothing in the closet looked like blood or a weapon.

The officers then went back downstairs and Bridget went with them up the back stairs to the second floor, where the men opened the parents' tidy room with the key. Other officers searching in the parents' room broke open the door between there and Lizzie's room, much to their own surprise and that of the group in Lizzie's room. The officers hadn't realized what was on the other side of the door.

Bridget provided keys for the attic rooms. Officers turned over mattresses and opened boxes, but found nothing.

Down in the cellar, in a box of rubbish, Fleet found a hatchet with the handle recently broken off. He left it in the box.

Medley asked Dr. Bowen about the pail of bloody napkins. "It has been explained to me, and is all right," Bowen said.

The police took the pail to the station anyway, with other evidence.

A group of more than a half dozen doctors in the guest bedroom, led by Medical Examiner Dolan, stood around Abby's body. A local physician who came to the house on hearing of the murders said, "She must have been killed much earlier than him, by at least an hour. See how the blood clotted."

They measured her at average height, five feet three inches. Dolan visually estimated her weight to be over two-hundred pounds.

Standing near Abby's feet, a crime scene photographer took several pictures. It took six men to slide the heavy bed away, to make room for pictures from the side.

Then the doctors rolled her onto a coroner's cot, revealing her stomach, arms, and fronts of her legs for the first time. Most of the blood surrounded her head and shoulders, and the soaked carpet captured it before it reached below, leaving her white day dress mostly undisturbed.

Four officers lifted the cot and slowly walked Abby down the front stairs.

New York papers, and further, reported the murders the same afternoon:

> "THEIR MURDERER STOLE IN. A RICH MAN AND HIS WIFE KILLED STEALTHILY AT HOME.
>
> Millionaire Andrew J. Borden of Fall River Had Just Returned

> from the Bank and Was Lying on a Lounge in His Sitting Room When an Assassin Slipped in and Struck Him with an Axe or Cleaver — Mrs. Borden Was Upstairs and Was Murdered by the Same Instrument — The Bodies Discovered by a Daughter Who Had Been Out of the House Only a Few Minutes — The Servant Upstairs Heard No Noise — All Avenues of Escape Covered but No Trace of the Murderer Secured."
>
> — *The Sun*, New York

Many doctors, including Fall River Mayor Coughlin, a medical doctor, assisted with the preliminary autopsies. These were performed in the sitting room.

Dr. Dolan did the work, guided by the others. By the force applied, they decided that the weapon must have had leverage—a long handle, so a small axe or a hatchet.

He removed the stomachs and sealed them with wax in glass jars to preserve them for the forensic expert, Professor Wood of Harvard.

When Dolan finished the autopsies, both bodies were placed in the dining room. The deceased's heads were to the east, so that their faces would greet the rising sun. The city did not have a morgue; the Borden parents would stay in their home until the memorial service.

CHAPTER 7

People in the street made way for Emma Borden's carriage at just after five o'clock. Emma, glancing nervously around at the hundreds of people, hurried up the drive.

Charles met her at the side door. "Sorry, Miss. No one's to come in or out." In fact, Charles had let everyone except children in that day, including neighbors and reporters.

"I live here. I was summoned home. My father is ill." Small and trim Emma eyed the officers in the backyard and in the barn.

"Let her in," called Dr. Bowen from inside, and then, "You'd better sit."

He guided her to the kitchen table with Bridget and John. Bridget rose to leave but Bowen stopped her. "Please stay, Bridget. We may need you."

John met Emma's eyes but did not speak. Emma sat very straight.

"It is bad, then," Emma said. "Your telegram did not tell, save that father is taken ill."

An officer started into the kitchen from the sitting room and Bowen waved him back.

Bowen sat down. "My telegram was not clear." He nodded in agreement. "Lizzie thought it best not to risk alarming your host."

"Is Lizzie here?"

"Yes, she's upstairs in her room, resting."

Emma paused for a moment, looking between John and Bowen. "Father has passed away."

"Yes," Bowen said. "And there is more." There seemed no way to convey what had happened without causing shock and distress. "Both your father and Mrs. Borden are dead," he said. "Someone got into the house and killed them both."

"Killed?" Emma started. "But Lizzie is all right?"

"Yes, we'll go up and see her."

"How did someone get in? When?"

"Perhaps during the night, and hid in the house. They were both killed this morning," said Bowen. "The police have checked and made sure all is safe now."

Bridget brought a small glass of cooking sherry, which Emma did not drink. "How were they killed?" asked Emma.

"Looks to have been an axe," Bowen answered.

Emma's eyes widened. After a moment she said, "Was it...a crazed man?" She looked to John.

"They do not know," he said.

"Perhaps a disgruntled farm worker, or unhappy tenant...?" Bowen left the statement open, but no one answered him. "Do you want to go see Lizzie now? I'm afraid we will need to go through the sitting room, where your father was killed. But I will go with you all through," said Bowen.

Bowen and John both reached out to help Emma to her feet, but she'd kept her composure and did not need help.

Conversations between the officers and doctors stopped as Emma passed through. She paused to look at the bloody sofa and rug underneath. Medical Examiner Dolan cleaned sharp metal tools. If she was shocked, she did not show it.

She and Bowen continued through to the front hallway and up the stairs to Lizzie's room, where Lizzie flew up to embrace Emma. "Oh, Emma. Thank God you're here. I did not know what to do."

"It's all right, Lizzie," said Emma. "I'll take care of things."

"The police have asked me so many questions but I know nothing. I didn't know what to say." Lizzie's voice broke for the first time.

Reverend Buck said, "They've asked six times."

"Six?" said Emma. She and Buck exchanged a look. "Then we must have a lawyer. Reverend, can you go to Mr. Jennings and send him here tomorrow?"

"Of course," said Buck. "I'll go as soon as I leave."

"Thank you," said Emma. She sat on Lizzie's bed. "I do not believe what has happened. As Dr. Bowen told me, both Father and Mrs. Borden are killed by an axe. It is impossible."

"Agreed," said Bowen, "but it is so. I examined the bodies myself."

"It is the work of a madman," said Mrs. Holmes. "The police will catch him soon, if they have not done so already. A terrible tragedy, but over now. Should we go downstairs? Poor Lizzie needs better than the stifling air in this shut up room."

"Best to wait," said Bowen. "The coroner and other doctors are cleaning up. We should not want to walk her past them."

The group fell silent.

"I'll lead us in prayer," offered Buck.

"Yes, please," said Lizzie.

Officer Harrington and another officer spotted two men on William Street who just didn't look quite right and took them to the station. The marshal ordered them locked up. The officers detained another man at the New Bedford Savings Bank. Harrington explained in his notes: "We found a Portuguese who was drawing out his full deposit of sixty-odd dollars. He could speak English but poorly, so we brought him to the station. After we went for an interpreter, and the suspect giving a satisfactory account of himself, he was allowed to go."

At 4 Weybosset Street, an officer checked John Morse's alibi. John's niece confirmed that he had been there from about 9:40 until 11:20 that morning. She also said that John had not been expected that morning, though they were happy to have him.

The alibi, including time for the horse-car rides in each direction, was exactly the time John needed to be away to be gone when the Borden parents were murdered.

At six Charles decided he wanted a hot supper and abandoned his post at the Borden house side door to go home. No one noticed.

Dr. Bowen had tended to Miss Lizzie all day. Now he gently took her wrist as she reclined again on the chaise. Emma, Reverend Buck, Alice, and Mrs. Holmes were all still with her.

Bowen checked her pulse. "You're just fine," he said. "I'll be back tomorrow morning to see about you, my dear."

Mrs. Holmes patted Lizzie's other hand. "You're handling all of this very well, Lizzie."

"You're so kind to come and tend to me, all of you," Lizzie said. "I could not have been here by myself."

"Uncle John and I will be here tonight, Lizzie," said Emma. "And perhaps Alice will stay with us for a few days?" She looked to Alice.

Alice did not hesitate. "Of course."

"Lizzie should have something to eat before retiring," said Bowen. "And I imagine the rest of you could do with something as well. We should be able to go down to the kitchen now."

After the last one left her room, Lizzie locked it.

The bright evening exposed the blood soaked into the horsehair sofa, the spattered doors and walls, and pooled stains on the carpet as they passed through the sitting room.

Alice stepped outside, relieved to see several uniformed officers in the yard. People crowded the street and stared at her unabashedly.

An old friend approached and offered to escort her home.

"Yes, please," Alice said. "I'm just getting a bag to stay."

"Stay here?"

"Yes."

Alice, accustomed to being on her own, was not new to taking risks and doing hard things. But tonight she feared for her own safety and that of her friends. The murderer had not been caught, the officers had said. A murderer who managed to get into and out of the Borden house undetected.

Before leaving for the night, Dr. Bowen stopped in the dining room. The bodies did not smell too badly yet. But he did not envy the living occupants, staying in the house over the next few days as the bodies aged in the August heat and humidity.

He left by the side door and made his way through the crowd across the street to his home, nodding in what he hoped was a companionable manner to those who scrutinized him.

Once inside, he bolted the door and checked all the windows and locks before sitting down with Phebe in the kitchen.

"I am so sorry for poor Abby, especially," said Phebe. "Who would have imagined, all those years ago when Mr. Borden made his offer of marriage, that her promised life of much more comfort and ease would end this way?" Phebe wiped her nose with a handkerchief. "She had so few friends."

Dr. Bowen said, "It's all over now." He'd managed all day but now he felt he could not do another thing.

"Is it?" Phebe asked. "I'll not sleep a wink until they find the madman who did this."

Lizzie, John, Mrs. Holmes, and Reverend Buck were still in the kitchen when Emma came down the back stairs. "I've spoken to Maggie. For tonight she will stay at the Miller's across the street, and return tomorrow."

"I'll take her through the crowd when she leaves," said John, "and go to get her in the morning."

"Thank you, Uncle John," said Emma. "I also asked her about the note Mrs. Borden received today. She did not see it herself." She turned to Lizzie. "We need to find it."

"It was a simple page inside an envelope," said Lizzie. "It could not have been more ordinary. Perhaps she burned it in the stove." Their house did not have refuse pickup, so they burned discarded items.

"Well, then it is lost forever. Still, we must do everything possible," said Emma. She looked inside Abby's sewing bag in the sitting room. She also went up and searched a small bag that Abby carried when she left home. There was no note.

"It must be that she burned it," said Lizzie when Emma returned.

"There is nowhere else to look, I think," said Emma.

Mrs. Holmes said, "Surely it is of little consequence now."

"I cannot imagine why anyone is concerned with it at all," agreed Reverend Buck.

Officers Harrington and Doherty got to D. R. Smith's Drug Store, two blocks from the Borden house, late in the evening.

"You sent for us, Eli?" Harrington said to Eli Bence, druggist. "You know something about these killings?" Bence had called the station.

"Maybe," replied Bence.

"You heard about it," said Doherty.

"Couldn't fail to," said Bence. "Lots of business for incidentals today, as people stopped in and, 'Oh by the way did you hear?' A lady came in the shop and said to me, 'Why, I understand they are suspecting Miss Lizzie Borden, the daughter.'"

News had spread impressively fast, even for Fall River.

Bence said, "She was here, yesterday, trying to buy prussic acid. I think it was her."

"Lizzie Borden? What for?" said Harrington.

"She said to clean a sealskin cape."

"Did you sell it to her?"

"No. I told her we need a doctor's order. She said she'd bought it here before without a prescription, but I doubt it."

"Is it used for cleaning a sealskin cape?"

Bence shrugged. "Not that I've heard."

"What else could she need it for?"

"It's prescribed in small amounts as a sedative. Also, it was used for killing pests, rodents or stray cats. It's not sold for that these days, though."

"Why not?"

"Because it was also used for killing people."

Deputy Marshal Fleet and the last officers in the house left before eight thirty. A full patrol remained outside, though, watching both outside and inside the house. Reverend Buck and Mrs. Holmes left soon after.

Harrington and Doherty returned to the Borden house with Bence, who waited in the darkened kitchen entryway. Harrington sent for Lizzie and met her in the kitchen.

"Thank you for coming down, Miss Borden," said Harrington. "I won't take much of your time."

"What is it?" said Lizzie.

"I'm asking about a man possibly seen in the area around your home in recent days. Have you seen any such man?"

"A man not of the neighborhood?"

"Yes, a stranger who was around multiple times but had no business in the neighborhood."

"I did not see anyone like that, or notice if I did."

"Has anyone else reported a stranger to you?"

"No, no one."

"All right. Thank you."

Lizzie left and Harrington escorted Bence outside to where Doherty waited.

Doherty asked, "Was that the woman who tried to buy poison yesterday?"

"Yes."

Before bed, Alice and Lizzie took a kerosene lamp down the front stairs, through the sitting room and kitchen, and into the cellar. An officer outside tracked them by the lamp light. He saw them do something in the cellar. Perhaps they dumped a slop pail. They returned the way they had come.

Shortly after, Lizzie repeated the journey alone. The officer could not see what she did, except that she went near the laundry sink.

John slept in the spare bedroom on the third floor, next to Bridget's room, instead of in the guest bedroom.

Alice slept in Andrew and Abby's room, and they kept the door between that and Lizzie's room open so that the women were in connecting rooms that night.

The Boston Advertiser released a late edition.

> "MURDER MOST FOUL. ANDREW BORDEN AND HIS WIFE KILLED...Fall River Excited by a Crime Which Has No Equal in its History—By an Assassin who Leaves no Clew to the Awful Deed — Police Baffled by the Lack of a Definite Clew, Though Members of the Family Are Suspected—The House Now Guarded by Officers.
>
> "So far as known, the dead couple had no enemies. There were several stories got up and sent out during the day of discharged workmen, one, a Portuguese, being seen at Mr. Borden's house early in the morning. There was nothing in them. He had not been employing Portuguese, and had not discharged anyone. So on the whole, the police believe that the deed was done in the interests of someone who would benefit by the death of the old couple.
>
> "At this hour police suspicions rest on persons who were in the family circle, particularly on Morse and on the daughter Lizzie, who first discovered the body of her father. At one time the police threatened to place Morse in custody, but it has been decided to keep him under close surveillance until further developments.
>
> "Several arrests have been made during the day, none of them of any account, but merely of suspicious persons. Two were Russian Jews traveling through town and the third a Portuguese, and they were locked up simply by way of precaution. No one believes they had anything to do with the crime. More arrests, and more important ones, are promised for tomorrow."

"Lock your doors," the Fall River Police told people that night. Women and children were herded inside early. "Lock your doors," people repeated to their family and friends. "Keep watch."

Many sat awake that night with weapons at easy reach. They'd checked and triple-checked their locks and windows. They'd closed their curtains and blinds and waited.

Adelaide, next door to the Bordens, sat awake listening to every sound. The officers outside the Borden house were some comfort, but whoever killed the Bordens might still be nearby, perhaps in the crowd that had gathered and watched all day.

Most had dispersed by nightfall, but not all.

CHAPTER 8

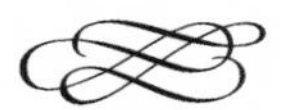

FRIDAY, AUGUST 5

The *Fall River Globe* headline pondered, "What did Lizzie want of poison?" They had all the details of Bence's account, apparently from police sources. Fall River began to sense a much safer and juicier explanation for the Borden murders than an at-large lunatic.

The crowd outside the Borden house grew still larger.

Officers and a safecracker arrived to break into Andrew's safe, which was so secure it took hours. When they did manage it, they found cash and business contracts, but no will.

Andrew Borden's legal advisor, Andrew Jennings, arrived in the morning.

Reverend Buck's urgent, desperate, visit the previous night had set off alarms for Jennings, who knew some of the Fall River officers. He trusted their intentions but not their investigative skills. They were, Jennings thought, liable to make many mistakes.

Though not primarily a criminal defense attorney, Jennings was a well qualified and respected attorney. He'd been known to the daughters all their lives. Andrew Borden had mentored and assisted Jennings since Jennings' boyhood, and was a driving force behind Jennings' career successes. Jennings' loyalty to Andrew was absolute.

Inside the Borden house the curtains were drawn and the clocks stopped. The mirrors were covered to prevent the departed souls from getting trapped inside.

Jennings directed Emma to sit in the parlor. They could not use the dining room, where the bodies remained, or the sitting room with the bloodied sofa, rug, and wall. "I understand that the police suspect Miss Lizzie," Jennings said.

Emma's lips went flat. "I will not believe for a moment that my sister had any part in this."

Jennings nodded. "I agree the idea is preposterous. Given that, I will advocate for you both, as best I can, as my final act of service to your father."

"Thank you," said Emma with relief. "We are in desperate need of it. My sister is greatly upset and unable to rest or eat."

"Unimaginable, what has happened," said Jennings, shaking his head as he brought some papers out of his bag. "But there are immediate matters, regarding your father's estate. Do you know of him having a will?"

"If he did, he did not mention it to me or my sister, I am certain. I heard in the past that he had one, but I do not believe he did now."

Jennings nodded. "I believe he would have mentioned it to me if he had, so we'll proceed on the understanding that there is no will. In that case I need to prepare some papers for you and Miss Lizzie. May I work here in the parlor?"

"Of course."

Jerome Borden, first cousin to Andrew and a prominent Fall River citizen in his own right, was not the wealthiest of the Fall River Bordens. He was, however, among the most connected and in those ways, powerful. The crowd parted for him, with his confidence and fine attire, as he approached the Borden house. When his knock at the front door went unanswered, he tried the knob and the door opened. Calling out as he walked through the entry to the parlor, both Emma and Jennings jumped.

"Goodness, how did you get in, Mr. Borden?" said Emma.

"The door was closed but not sealed," Jerome replied with an apologetic gesture.

Emma regained herself. "Do come in please, Mr. Borden."

Jerome, hat in hand, said. "My condolences on your loss, Miss Emma."

"Thank you."

Jerome turned to Jennings. "I heard you would be here, Andrew. I've come to discuss the matter at hand."

"Oh?" said Jennings.

Emma offered Jerome a seat next to Jennings and sat down herself.

"Of course the reports and rumors are false," said Jerome. "that a Borden could be the murderer."

"Lizzie is innocent," said Emma.

"Decidedly," said Jennings.

"Whatever the circumstance," said Jerome, "the Borden name cannot be associated with a conviction. What steps have you taken to prevent any further accusations or, God forbid, an arrest?"

Jennings frowned. "I'll defend Miss Lizzie as I can and according to the law."

Jerome had known that Jennings would follow the letter of the law as he saw it. However, that might not be enough. "You should offer a large reward," said Jerome. "Five thousand, I would say."

"Five thousand?!" Emma said, shocked.

"Yes, at least," said Jerome. "to show your commitment to finding the murderer."

Jennings considered and then agreed. "It might be helpful."

"All right, Mr. Borden," Emma said. She and Lizzie would have plenty of money, from their father's estate.

"And consider," said Jerome, "inviting editors and owners of the local papers to be pallbearers."

"Pallbearers?" said Emma.

"Yes. They'll not want to decline the honor and will later not want to print negative stories about a family they are associated with."

"Oh, my," said Emma.

Jennings gave a cross look to Jerome. "You do not need to," he said to Emma.

"My sister and I will consider it," she said.

Jennings had not meant to eavesdrop when he walked into the sitting room toward the kitchen later to speak to Emma.

"Mr. Jennings does not have to help us, Lizzie," he heard Emma say in the kitchen. "Please do be kind to him. This could all go very wrongly."

"How could it go wrongly? I've done nothing."

"According to Mr. Jennings, the police suspect you."

"Ridiculous. The police blame me only because they cannot yet name anyone else. They are incompetents."

"Even if so, we must act to protect you."

"Then you should speak most with Mr. Jennings. I do not know how you can be so civil to him, Father's favorite, when we had so little from Father ourselves."

"We cannot change the world we live in," Emma said.

Lizzie, Emma, John, Bridget, and Alice spent a quiet day in the house. The sisters wore black, as they began their year of mourning the loss of parents.

The mourning period also required greatly reducing social activities. The sisters, already too old and too awkward for many parties and balls hosted and frequented by their peers, had few invitations to cancel. Lizzie bowed out of a fishing trip to Marion with friends. She had been expected to depart on Monday.

The notice appeared later that day in local and other papers, including *The New York Times*:

"$5,000 REWARD

The above reward will be paid to anyone who may secure the arrest and conviction of the person or persons who occasioned the death of Andrew J. Borden and his wife.
- Emma L. Borden
- Lizzie A. Borden"

In the evening, when John Morse left the house toward downtown, some broke off from the crowd in front of the house and followed. Not all in that crowd were casual loiterers anymore. Some had heard that the killer was in the house and they'd come to get him, if they could. John seemed not to notice as they shadowed him.

Halfway down the block one of the followers yelled, "That's the murderer. Lynch him!"

Rope appeared as John turned in surprise, weaponless.

The mob moved to encircle John as he looked on, wide-eyed, unto another voice shouted, "We've had enough of that!"

Two plain-clothes officers had been assigned to follow John, secretly, any time he left the house. They'd casually joined the followers.

"We're policemen. Move along," said the officers to the group, which deflated and dispersed.

After that, the officers escorted John on his errands.

John went to the post office. He said he'd mailed a letter marked "In Haste," for urgent delivery to a Mr. William A. Davis of South Dartmouth, Massachusetts. John declined to disclose the contents of the letter.

He also tried to enter the offices of the *Daily News* but found the doors locked.

The police escorted him back to the Borden house.

Dr. Bowen checked on Lizzie at her home several times on Friday. She told him she could not rest and he gave her a prescription of one eighth of a grain of sulfate of morphine, to be taken before bed.

Morphine could affect perception and memory, and also cause hallucinations. But this was a low dose.

CHAPTER 9

SATURDAY, AUGUST 6

James Winward, undertaker for the best families in town, arrived at the Borden house early on Saturday and arranged the caskets in the sitting room.

Winward had himself a task preparing the bodies. According to custom, it was to be an open casket service, but not only had both parents been killed by axe strikes to the head, their bodies had reposed in the dining room for two hot days. Both were bloated and exuded rot and the distinct smell of sewage.

Winward positioned each in their casket to hide the damage as much as he could against the interior lining. Andrew's face he carefully turned so that only the right, mostly undamaged side, showed. There was no disguising or hiding the split through Andrew's nose, lips, and chin, though. Winward also squeezed the split left eyeball back into the remains of its socket.

Lizzie came down, supported by Mrs. Holmes, not wearing "proper mourning." Lizzie's dress, though black, was not the proper fabric, cut, and style for mourning. The sisters were expected to wear clothing as instructed by the household manuals, *The Queen* or *Cassell's*, which prescribed black wool with crepe trim. If the sisters did not own proper attire, they should buy or borrow it. They did neither.

Mrs. Holmes and Winward waited to the side as Lizzie spent a few quiet moments in front of her father's body. She cried openly and then, leaning forward, kissed him on the lips.

The *Fall River Herald* printed an interview with Hiram Harrington, brother-in-law of Andrew Borden.

Hiram said Andrew was, "an exceedingly hard man regarding money matters, determined and stubborn" and that, "nothing could change him" once Andrew set his mind to something.

On questioning by Officer Doherty, Hiram said, "When the perpetrator of this foul deed is found, it will be one of the household."

Jennings had also given an interview, this one to the *Fall River Daily Globe*. In it, Jennings said, "I know the elder one, Emma, better than Lizzie. Emma is about my age, and I have known her almost all my life. They are quiet and modest ladies."

He had no theory or explanation for the crimes at all, he said. "I have never heard of a case as remarkable as this. A most outrageous, brutal crime, perpetuated in midday in an open house on a prominent thoroughfare — and absolutely motiveless."

When prompted to agree that for a man to commit the murders and escape undetected would be a miracle, Jennings looked out for his client when he replied, "It would be a remarkable combination of circumstances, but not a miracle."

As to whether the killer could be a member of the household, Jennings said, "It is almost impossible that this frightful work could have been done without the clothes of the person who did it being bespattered with blood. This, together with the improbability that any woman could do such a piece of work, makes the suspicion seem altogether irrational."

. . .

More than two thousand onlookers and reporters gathered outside the Borden home and along Second Street to watch the funeral attendees arrive. Officers escorted carriages through, pushing back the masses.

At least the August heat had abated some, though that would not spare those who packed inside the house. Seventy-five mourners crowded on the first floor, along with Reverends Buck and Adams.

The mourners included relatives, neighbors (including the Bowens and Adelaide Churchill), friends of the sisters, and friends and business associates of Andrew. Many important men were there. In hushed voices they shared greetings and condolences and delicate mentions of the crimes. The mourners did not share affectionate stories or interesting anecdotes about Andrew or Abby. They had none.

Mrs. Sarah B. Whitehead, Abby's much younger half-sister, had always been more of a daughter to Abby. Abby's loss was as painful to Sarah as losing a mother.

Sarah found herself out of her element among the well-dressed and well-connected. Sarah's husband, George, was not successful, and Sarah wore a faded, poorly fitting mourning dress belonging to a friend. And Sarah had only rarely been in the Borden house before. Abby went to Sarah's home instead, two streets over, for visits.

Sarah had, like everyone else, read in the papers that more than one person in the Borden household was suspected of the murders.

Abby's sudden death also made Sarah afraid for herself and her family. Through an unusual circumstance, five years ago Andrew bought half of the house where Sarah lived with her husband and children. He'd deeded it to Abby and Sarah did not know if the deed passed to herself or Emma and Lizzie.

Sarah went to Abby's casket for a quiet moment with her sister, though the state of Abby's mashed head shook her.

"My condolences, Mrs. Whitehead," said Reverend Buck.

"Thank you, Reverend," she replied. When she turned, both Emma and Lizzie rose from their seats. Lizzie's eyes were red.

"We're so sorry. How are you?" said Emma, leaning in to speak privately.

Sarah hardly knew the Borden sisters. They'd never been friendly, though they'd been related for twenty-seven of Sarah's twenty-eight years and she and Lizzie were close in age. "We are all shocked," Sarah said. "No one in our family can understand why someone would harm Abby."

"Or our father," said Lizzie.

"Yes," said Sarah, though she thought it harder to understand a reason to hurt Abby, whose death seemed to have benefited no one. "I've explained to my children that Abby will not be back." Sarah's three children were all under ten years old.

"She must have been like a grandmother to them," said Lizzie. "She was sixty-nine, like Father, wasn't she?"

"She was sixty-four," said Sarah.

"Oh, I didn't realize there was that much difference. I thought they were the same age," said Lizzie.

Sarah said nothing.

Reverend Buck took up the conversation. "It must have been such a shock for you, Sarah, to learn of these terrible events."

"Yes," said Sarah. "My family and I were away during the day on Thursday. We did not know what had happened until a neighbor told us when we returned. I do not know what to do." She began to cry.

Buck said, "I will call on you next week, if that suits you, Mrs. Whitehead."

She nodded through tears.

Lizzie said, "Mrs. Borden had planned to be at your house on Thursday, hadn't she?"

"Yes, she was to watch our youngest, little Abbie, while our family was at the annual policeman's picnic. She did not come because she was not feeling well."

"It is unfortunate she was not there Thursday," said Lizzie. "She'd have been away from here when the murderer struck."

Sarah gasped. Emma frowned. No one replied. Sarah took her seat and the others followed.

Promptly at eleven, the service began. Reverends Adams and Buck led the assembled through scripture readings and then prayers, but no eulogy. To the relief of all in the stifling and fetid house, the service lasted less than thirty minutes.

The twelve pallbearers, six for each casket, were Andrew's associates and prominent Fall River men. They included Jerome Borden and the owners of two local papers. They carried the closed caskets out the front door.

The crowd pushed and shoved as Lizzie made her way to her carriage, supported on the arm of Undertaker Winward. Officers held the crowd back.

Some observers later described Lizzie as frail, shaking, and faint, and others as stoically strong and unemotional. They noted her improper dress, as well as the fact that she was not wearing a veil.

The crowd jostled Emma as well when she followed, but Lizzie was the main attraction.

At 12:20 p.m. the funeral cortege left the Borden house and made its way north to Fall River's Oak Grove Cemetery.

Thousands lined the streets. Some knew Mr. Borden personally. Some had come for the spectacle, and to say they'd been.

Men held their hats high for the passing.

No sooner had the mourners left than Marshal Hilliard and a state police officer entered the Borden house again, this time for a search of the bedrooms. They were determined to find anything hidden in or under beds or in bedrooms.

They dismantled each bed, pulled off the sheets and each mattress to search underneath for hidden objects or blood stains. Hilliard also searched behind the lounge in Lizzie's room. They found nothing, remade the beds, and left.

This secret search would not remain secret for long. Alice and Bridget were still in the house.

The mourners stayed in their carriages at the cemetery, as was customary. The Reverends and the pallbearers made slow progress to the gravesites with the caskets. John Morse alone joined.

Less than five minutes of prayers later, the service was over. A few friends and family cried for Abby. Those who knew and liked Andrew were not of sentimental natures.

After a respectful delay, the carriages set off back to homes and businesses. But the bodies were not interred. Winward had received new instructions that morning from Medical Examiner Dolan.

Shortly after the mourners disappeared from view, the caskets were moved to a storage vault on the cemetery grounds, where they waited.

> "NO MOTIVE YET FOUND FOR THE BORDEN MURDER.
>
> Lizzie and Emma, the Daughters, and Morse, the Brother-in-Law, Are Suspected and Kept Under Close Surveillance. While the People Are at the Cemetery the Police Push Their Investigations, but Decline to Say with What Results"
>
> — *New York Herald*, August 6

At three o'clock, long after the family had returned from the cemetery, the police arrived again. This time they were in full force for the most thorough search yet. Marshal Hilliard, Deputy Marshal Fleet, and other officers were there, along with Medical Examiner Dolan.

The men's movements and voices could be heard throughout the house. They began in Bridget's attic room.

The search, in a house so peculiarly full of locked doors, closets, and trunks, repeatedly needed keys. Emma and Lizzie went to the attic to help open a trunk in a storage room for which the key could not be found. It turned out to contain clothes.

Deputy Marshal Fleet climbed out an attic window to the roof, looking for a weapon or evidence hidden there, and found nothing.

The officers searched the sisters' rooms again, including opening the trunk in Emma's room that had been locked on Thursday afternoon. They opened drawers and searched behind furniture, and found nothing of interest.

In the dress closet at the front of the house, above the front entryway, there were nineteen dresses. Fleet and a state officer examined each. They held them in the light of the window, looking for spots or stains. They inspected all but three of the dresses; those three were of heavier and fancier fabrics, and the officers did not believe a woman would wear her nicest or heaviest dress to commit murder.

Marshal Hilliard requested, by way of Attorney Jennings, Lizzie's clothes from the morning of the murders.

Jennings spoke to Lizzie in the parlor. "Miss Lizzie, the officers need the dress you wore Thursday morning. Also, the underskirt."

"Why should they want those?"

"It is for testing. They will check them for blood."

"They can look and see there is not blood on them."

"They will test for traces, small spots that are not visible to the eye."

Lizzie sighed and went upstairs. She returned with a dark blue shirt-waist, skirt, and an underskirt, which Jennings gave to Marshall Hilliard.

The search continued in the rest of the house, including the cellar, and outside in the barn. Officers raked the yard for items hidden in the grass. They searched every drawer, box, and bag that day, and even the old outhouse vault.

On his return to City Hall, Marshal Hilliard found Mayor Coughlin in his office, sitting at Hilliard's desk, examining the four axes and hatchets found at the house.

"Can we tell whether any of these are the murder weapon?" Coughlin asked. At thirty-one years old, Coughlin was younger than many of the officers and more than a decade younger than Hilliard.

"Not yet." Hilliard remained in the doorway.

"So it's possible the assailant fled with the weapon."

Hilliard shrugged. "Possible. Though he should have been seen. There might need be blood outside the house."

Coughlin had only been Mayor for a year. Prior to that he had a private medical practice. He knew little about police work.

Coughlin continued, "I cannot make heads or tails of it. If the assassin meant to kill Andrew Borden, he must have known Borden would be home early. The household would have been gathered for the noon meal with no opportunity to kill him and escape unseen. Yet from those who spoke to him that day, it doesn't appear that Borden himself knew he would be home early. If the assassin meant to kill Mrs. Borden, why wait, or return, to kill Mr. Borden?"

Hilliard had been with the Fall River police for fourteen years. In that time there were many mayors who thought they knew enough to direct the police.

Coughlin said, "Who do you suspect?"

Hilliard had considered little else for two days. "All of them. First, Morse. It's too much coincidence that he arrived the day before. He has a perfect account for his time away from the house, as if he knew when to be gone. And he behaves oddly. Then, Lizzie, whose story of going to the barn is unbelievable. She has deceived from the start. Neither could Bridget have been in and around that house and know nothing. The other daughter, Emma, also inherits. For all we can say the four conspired together."

Coughlin pondered the weapons, with the red spots and the hair. "It certainly points to Lizzie and the maid at least, though I don't like that. Why would either kill, and in such a fashion? Also, with no bath in the house, how could they have cleaned up after Mr. Borden's killing. There wasn't time." Coughlin sighed. "I hate to believe it was either of those girls, regardless. What a problem we'll have in this town if it was, a Christian lady and her Irish maid. We'll never hear the end."

"People call for Bridget's arrest and hanging," said Hilliard. "Irish and immigrant is reason enough, but we must guard all in the house. If my men hadn't been handy yesterday, the mob would have had Morse. That does not make any of them innocent. Especially Lizzie. She may have helped as a lookout, if not as a killer."

Mayor Coughlin nodded. "I want to talk to her myself."

Hilliard mentally prepared himself for another fruitless trip to the Borden house.

"Last Monday, a young woman tried to buy arsenic from a druggist on Pleasant Street and was reportedly willing to give any price for it," proclaimed the *Fall River Daily Herald*.

This was three days before the Bordens were killed and two days before Lizzie allegedly approached druggist Eli Bence about prussic acid.

"A woman also called at *Corneau & Letourneau's Drug Store* on Pleasant Street on the same date, but it was found out afterwards that it was the wife of Inspector McCaffrey, who was on a crusade against drug stores," and she was part of an attempt to catch druggists selling poisons illegally.

That woman, it said, "resembled Miss Borden."

Mayor Coughlin and City Marshal Hilliard drove a police carriage to Second Street at 7:45 that evening. In the gathering dark, several hundred people still crowded the street. The carriage could not drive in.

"Good Lord," Coughlin said. "Take us to a Police box and have officers clear these people out."

On their return Bridget let them in the side door and to the sitting room to wait, with the blood still there.

"We'd like to speak to the household, please," said Coughlin.

A few minutes later Emma, Lizzie, John, Coughlin, and Hilliard were in the parlor. Alice eavesdropped from the second floor landing and Bridget from the sitting room.

"First," said Coughlin, "I have a request to make of the family, and that is that you remain in the house for a few days longer. I believe it would be better for all concerned if you did so."

John gave a little start. "How will we get the mail?"

Coughlin turned to John in surprise. What mail did John expect at the Borden house, where he did not live? "Best to send someone to retrieve it," said Coughlin. "There is much excitement around the house."

"Why, is there anybody in this house suspected?" said Lizzie.

"Perhaps Mr. Morse can answer that question better than I, as his experience last night, perhaps, would justify him in the inference that somebody in this house was suspected," said Coughlin.

"I want to know the truth," said Lizzie and again, "Is anyone in the house suspected?"

"Well," replied Mayor Couglin, "Miss Borden, I regret to answer, but I must answer yes, you are suspected."

Hilliard cleared his throat. He had not expected Coughlin to inform

Lizzie that she was a suspect. An official declaration on the matter could affect whether they could legally question her without her lawyer. Coughlin seemed not to notice the cough.

Lizzie's chin went up. "I am ready to go now."

Coughlin also ignored her declaration. "Your accounts of your time when your father was killed, Miss Lizzie, are not clear. It would help us to understand all you did that morning. Where did you go after leaving your father as he napped in the sitting room?"

"I went to the barn for some lead for sinkers," said Lizzie.

"How long did you remain in the barn?"

"About twenty minutes."

It did not seem they would hear anything new.

Coughlin and Hilliard got up to leave and Coughlin addressed the group. "If you are disturbed in any way, or if you are annoyed by the crowds upon the street, I would like to have you notify an officer in the yard. I shall see that you receive all the protection that the police department can afford from the annoyance and the disturbance of the people congregating about the streets."

After the men left and the officers finished clearing the crowd, Bridget retrieved her bag from her room and left, back to the Miller house.

Alice continued to stay in the Borden house, but she no longer slept in the parents' bed. From that night on she slept in Emma's room instead. Emma and Lizzie both slept in Lizzie's room.

The day had taken its toll on Lizzie.

Dr. Bowen doubled Friday night's morphine dose, and future doses, to one-quarter of a grain. It was now a high dosage.

CHAPTER 10

SUNDAY, AUGUST 7

Alice made breakfast for the Borden household. It seemed the least she could do for her friends in such difficult times. Though to be fair, no one seemed quite distraught.

They ate in the kitchen. The bodies were at the cemetery, but no one had much stomach for eating in the dining room.

After breakfast, Alice went upstairs to change her clothes. When she returned to the kitchen, Lizzie had a large cloth in her hands.

Emerging from the sink room, Emma said. "What are you going to do?"

"I am going to burn this old thing up," said Lizzie. "It is covered with paint."

"I think you'd better," said Emma.

Getting closer, Alice saw the fabric cotton Bedford cord dress, similar to corduroy. The print was light blue with dark figures, with at least one dark stain on the skirt.

Officers could wander past the kitchen windows at any moment as Lizzie tore the skirt into strips and burned it, piece by piece, in the stove.

Alice said. "If I were you I wouldn't let anybody see me do that, Lizzie."

Generally even old and worn cloth was salvaged for use in other garments, quilts, or rags. Even if stained in parts, there was usually something that could be reused.

Lizzie burned the entire garment. A dress with stains.

The murders consumed Fall River. Even members of the church gossiped and accused and spread the latest rumor. Lizzie did not attend service that day but Reverends Buck and Jubb took to the pulpit to defend her.

"It seems to me a terrible thing to insinuate guilt in a case like this without some apparently convincing proof," said Buck, imploring the police to catch the real killer and admonishing the press. "A charge so serious, however clearly it may be rebutted, throws a shadow over a life which time can never remove. Thus an additional murder is committed."

Jubb reminded the congregation that Lizzie had lived "a life which has always commanded respect, whose acts and motives have always been pure and holy." He closed with a prayer. "Save us from blasting a life, innocent and blameless; keep us from taking the sweetness from a future by our ill-advised words."

One of Lizzie's defenders had spoken to the *Boston Herald* and the account appeared that day. "As a child she was of a very sensitive nature, inclined to be non-communicative with new acquaintances. This characteristic has tenaciously clung to her all through life and has been erroneously interpreted. As a scholar she was not remarkable for brilliancy but she was conscientious in her studies. She was a girl with anything but an enthusiastic idea of her own personal attainments. She thought people were not favorable disposed toward her and that she made a poor impression."

Fall River had split. Those of the upper classes generally insisted on the obvious innocence of Miss Lizzie, a Victorian Christian lady. And, worst of all, there was no evidence against her. Laborers and mill workers, including many immigrants, were often on the side of her guilt.

The crowd on Second Street was mixed between advocates for guilt and innocence.

A few blocks away in Marshal Hilliard's office, Dr. Dolan examined the two hatchets under a glass. In particular, he scrutinized the hair on the claw hammer head.

Marshal Hilliard, watching from nearby, suspected that Dolan had no idea what he was doing.

Officers again searched the house, cellar, and barn that Sunday. The household ignored them.

Detective Hanscom, superintendent of the Pinkerton private law enforcement agency, arrived at the Borden house with Jennings. A former Boston police officer, Hanscom had been hired by Jennings, on behalf of the Borden sisters, to evaluate the case.

Hanscom did not interfere or comment on the goings-on in the house. Instead, he spoke briefly to the household and observed the police searches and discussions. He had a more experienced eye than perhaps anyone else involved. He watched closely but said little.

Hanscom left in the evening and gave an interview to a reporter from the *Fall River Daily Globe*.

"I have been in town too short a time to form any definitive opinions in the case," he said. "In Mr. Jennings' company I went to the Borden residence and talked with Miss Lizzie, who impressed me favorably. She was very earnest in her manner, and was anxious that no stone be left unturned to find the guilty parties. There is yet no motive that can be suggested for the killings. I shall try to find one, however, as it is the key to the situation."

Alice returned from errands to discover that, after the police left that afternoon, Emma cleaned the blood spatter off the parlor door, the wall, and as much as possible out of the carpet.

The police had not told the household not to clean, Emma said, though Alice felt sure the police and the medical examiner had not wanted the evidence removed.

John had seen Emma cleaning and not stopped her.

MONDAY, AUGUST 8

Alice spent the night in Emma's room again. She rose early and crept through Lizzie's room, downstairs to make breakfast for herself and John, who was already up.

Bridget was back from the Miller house across the street and said she was no longer allowed to stay with the Millers. The police wanted her in the Borden house where they could watch her and the Millers said their maid's quarters, where Bridget slept, were not large enough for two.

She sat in the Borden kitchen and watched but did not help.

Detective Hanscom of the Pinkerton agency returned midmorning and settled himself in the parlor. He began his job that day by interviewing the household.

First he spoke to Lizzie, who answered as she had to the police officers.

Emma said she'd been out of town and could add nothing herself.

Hanscom also interviewed Alice who, he hoped, had observed something on the day of the murders or in the neighborhood which could lead to the murderer.

"I saw or heard nothing strange that day, before Bridget came," said Alice. "I saw no one strange on my way to this house that morning."

"Have you heard of anything from those in the neighborhood?"

"No, nothing," said Alice.

"You've stayed in the house since the day of the murders?"

"Yes, four days now."

"Are all of the dresses that were in the house on the day of the tragedy still here, as far as you know?" Hansom asked.

Alice hesitated a moment. "Yes."

As Hansom watched her closely, Alice considered. She felt certain Lizzie did not kill her parents. But in that case, it should not be necessary to lie.

The word was out, though, and Alice did not take it back.

Alice rejoined Lizzie and Emma in the dining room after she spoke to Hanscom. "I've told Mr. Hanscom a falsehood."

Lizzie said nothing but watched Alice and waited.

Emma looked confused. "What was there to tell him a falsehood about?"

"He asked me if all the dresses were in the house that were here the day of the tragedy. 'Yes', I told him," said Alice. "I am afraid, Lizzie, the worst thing you could have done was to burn that dress."

"Oh, what made you let me do it? Why didn't you tell me?" Lizzie said.

"It makes you look as if you're hiding things, Lizzie," said Alice.

"I certainly am not, and my business is no one's but my own. You should not be speaking of me to others, Alice," said Lizzie.

"Alice is only speaking to Mr. Hanscom because we asked her to," Emma said.

Lizzie softened her response. "Yes, you've looked out for me. Thank you." Then she added, "Isn't that your carriage waiting?"

A horse and carriage could be heard at the front of the house. Alice had scheduled the carriage for her morning errands.

"Yes," said Alice. "I'd best go."

First she went home. She'd planned to get fresh clothes. Instead, she only dropped off her laundry. Then she went to her employer and told him she'd return to work the next day.

Jennings met with the sisters in the dining room, where they could have privacy. "There is to be an inquest. Both of you will be called to testify."

"Good," said Lizzie. "Let us answer their questions and be done. All of these officers in our home, outside the house at all hours, with their never-ending searches. They cause the crowds outside."

"I understand your desire to see an end to this, Miss Lizzie," said Jennings. "However, since they have been unable to find the killer, they progress to a new stage in their hunt. They have named you as a suspect, and we must proceed carefully. They will be looking for any evidence, anything at all that makes you appear guilty."

Her gray eyes burned. "I have done nothing to hide."

"That is so," he replied, "but the court of law and court of the public look upon you with suspicion. We must be careful not to give them anything that could be misunderstood. And because it is an inquest rather than a trial, I am not allowed to represent you in person, in the room. You will appear alone to answer questions."

Lizzie looked less certain. "I am forced to testify?"

"Yes, surely she cannot be made to go, and alone," said Emma.

"She is not forced," said Jennings. "She can decline to testify—"

"Then I shall decline," said Lizzie.

"—but only if she states she is declining in order to avoid making statements that would criminate herself," Jennings finished.

"Criminate myself?"

"Make yourself appear guilty."

"But I am not guilty."

"Those are your choices. Testify, and risk what they will use against you, or decline, saying that you are doing so in order to avoid criminating yourself."

"Why can you not represent her?" asked Emma.

"I can represent her, as I am doing now, but I cannot be present for the questioning. The inquest is for the state to determine facts. I believe the prosecutor and judge are in the wrong to require it of her, after she was named by the mayor as a suspect. I am pressing the matter and will know later today if I am allowed to attend. However, I suggest, regardless of whether I can be present, that you appear when required to do so but do not answer any questions. I will inform the court that you will decline to respond, so that there is no problem."

"Just stand there?" said Lizzie.

"There will be a chair, but yes, decline to answer all questions."

"Will that not make me appear guilty? If I am the only one who does not answer?"

"Those are the choices."

"I am blocked at every turn," she said with huff.

Jennings rose. "I will return this evening with Judge Blaisdell's decision. Please decide what you would like to do, but remember my caution."

"Yes, you must decline to testify, as he says," said Emma.

"I will consider it," said Lizzie, turning away.

Jennings met with Hanscom in the parlor, and informed him of the developments. "There is not one piece of direct evidence against this girl, but they will have her one way or another. Have you found anything to help?"

"Not so far," said Hanscom. "The officers bumbled the start but are quite intent now on finding everything of evidence in this house, and outside as well. They are not all fools."

Hanscom went to the cellar and watched the officers, who had arrived again that morning. A mason opened the cellar chimney. He dismantled some of the brickwork and found no hiding places or loose bricks. He showed the officers and rebricked the fireplace. He did not open the fireplace in the sitting room, but inspected it for hiding places and found none.

Officer Medley pulled a handleless hatchet, the one Fleet had seen on Thursday, from a box of tools. The hatchet had the fresh break and the appearance of dust on it, but the dust differed from the dust on the other items in the box. It looked more like ash. Picking up the hatchet head, Medley saw it was coated on both sides, not just on top.

Preserving the dusty coating as well as he could, he showed it to other officers. One of the officers produced papers from elsewhere in the cellar, to wrap it.

"I am going down street," said Medley, and left with the hatchet head.

Hanscom left the cellar and returned to the parlor, where he sat quietly, pondering.

On return from her errands, Alice found Lizzie and Emma still in the dining room.

Emma said that she and Lizzie had discussed the matter. "Go and tell all about it," she said to Alice. "Tell him that we told you to correct your statement."

"Mr. Hanscom," Alice said to him in the parlor. "I need to make you aware of something that happened yesterday morning. Something I failed to mention earlier."

"Yes?"

"Yesterday morning I saw Miss Lizzie burn a dress in the kitchen stove. I saw stains on it."

Mr. Hanscom's eyebrows went up. "Tell more, please."

"Lizzie said she was burning the dress because it had paint on it. Emma said she thought Lizzie had better do that. Lizzie tore the dress and waist into strips and I believe burned the whole of it."

"I see," said Mr. Hanscom.

"Emma and Lizzie insisted that I tell you all, so I have done so."

"Thank you." Mr. Hanscom watched her leave. Shortly after, he left the Borden house and did not return. He made no further investigations nor statements to the press.

Alice also took her leave of Emma and Lizzie. "I'm sorry I can't stay longer."

"We're so grateful for your help," Emma said.

"You were so helpful, Alice," said Lizzie. "I can never thank you enough."

"You are welcome. I'm so sorry for your tragedy."

Alice left for the short walk home. Gawkers watched her down the street as she went, but Alice did not mind. It was such a relief to be out of the Borden house.

Officer Medley delivered the handleless hatchet to Marshal Hilliard in his office.

Hilliard inspected it closely. "Where's the handle?"

"Didn't find it, sir. No sign of it."

Hilliard examined the break. "Looks fresh."

"Yes. And the ash there, on both sides," Medley said, "the other tools in that box had dust, not ash."

"Someone put ash on it?"

"Maybe to make it look like the other tools. To look like it wasn't recently used and washed."

At midday Marshal Hilliard ordered a warrant sworn for Lizzie's arrest for the murder of both parents. He received the document but held it himself and did not have it served. Instead, he waited for the results of the inquest.

The *Fall River Daily Globe* followed up on the account of a woman attempting to buy poison the Monday before the murders. The woman at *Corneau & Letourneau's Drug Store* was not McCaffrey's wife as previously reported, they said, but was in fact a partner in the operation to catch druggists selling poisons illegally.

"An attempt was made on Saturday night," they said, "to float the theory that Eli Bence, the drug clerk, had mistaken Miss Lizzie Borden for the woman who works with State Inspector McCaffrey. Mr. Bence may be mistaken, of course, but State Inspector McCaffrey's partner looks about as much like Lizzie as she does the boxer John L. Sullivan."

Bridget tried multiple times to move out of the Borden house. She tried to leave in spite of being told she could not, and wept more and more hysterically when the officers prevented her from going. Finally the officers sent word to the station and Marshal Hilliard himself came to the house to reassure her that it would only be a few more days.

"Murders were done here," she pleaded. "Someone got in and out and isn't found yet." After checking that they were not within hearing of the household, she lowered her voice and said, "I'm afraid of the man, John Morse. He sleeps in the room next to mine in the attic, since he's not to sleep in the guest room. Please, I cannot stay."

Still Hilliard did not allow her to leave. He did resolve to speak to Prosecutor Knowlton and ask that questions for Bridget be resolved as soon as possible, so that she could leave if cleared.

In the evening, Jennings returned to the Borden house. "It is decided, by both the judge and District Attorney Knowlton, that Lizzie will be called to testify and I cannot be present. I counsel you again, Miss Lizzie, to appear as directed and decline to answer questions."

"But I will appear guilty if I do," she pleaded. "I'll not have people saying that I am guilty more than they do now."

"If you speak you will likely give them information to use against you, however innocently. They must have their killer, Miss Borden." He turned to Emma.

Emma had nothing but a resigned shrug. "I have tried to dissuade her, Mr. Jennings."

Lizzie set her shoulders. "And I have decided. I'll appear and answer their questions, because I am innocent. The law protects the innocent."

"Sadly not always, Miss Lizzie," said Jennings.

"It shall me. They will see that I have had no part in this."

Dr. Bowen stopped by later to check on Lizzie and left as she prepared to take the double dose of morphine, as prescribed.

CHAPTER 11

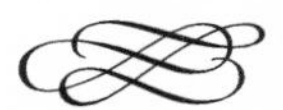

TUESDAY, AUGUST 9

Bridget answered the door that morning. This time it was Officer Doherty and he was there to get Bridget. She cried, "Am I arrested?"

"No, I'm to take you for questioning."

"I have done nothing," she pleaded.

"It's for the inquest," Doherty said. "Only questions."

Bridget went to get her bag, shawl, and hat. No one else in the household came to the door, or appeared.

Doherty escorted Bridget to his police carriage. Some in the crowd commented that Bridget was being arrested, and rightly so. Doherty and Bridget went to the station, Bridget sobbing all the way.

This inquest was not conducted to determine whether a crime had been committed. There was no doubt the Bordens had been murdered.

Often in the case of murder, an inquest was a formality. Not so this time.

This inquest was a quest to discover more evidence, to illuminate the events surrounding the murders, and point to the murderer or murderers who had so far defied detection.

It was presided over by seventy-two-year-old Judge Josiah Blaisdell, and was conducted in the Fall River Courthouse at City Hall, about a mile from the Borden house.

The courtroom was almost empty. The judge was on the bench and District Attorney Hosea Knowlton of the Southern District of Massachusetts prepared to question the witnesses. Mayor Coughlin, Medical Examiner Dolan, Fall River Marshal Hilliard, and a state detective were also present.

Knowlton had graduated second in his class from Tufts University and been district attorney for the Southern District of Massachusetts for more than ten years. He did most of his work in Fall River, the largest city in the county.

The son of a pastor, he was a lifelong adherent to the Universalist Church. His belief in the law was inextricably tied to his belief in the necessity of doing good works. Hosea Knowlton had established himself as a man of drive but also integrity and unwavering certainty in moral rightness.

He and Marshal Hilliard had agreed that the next and necessary step must be an inquest where Knowlton could engage the witnesses in more thorough and strategic questioning under oath.

Five days after the crimes the evidence was extensive and muddled. Knowlton meant to make it clear.

Bridget, shaking and crying, was sworn and sat in her place as the first witness. She was of average height and strong, and watched warily as Knowlton gathered his thoughts.

Bridget's testimony was important. She could provide accounts of the goings-on in the Borden house. Or, if guilty, she could misdirect.

Although there were others in the courtroom, once Knowlton began his questioning it might as well have been only the two.

"Your name is Bridget Sullivan?"

"Yes, sir."

"Did you go by the name of Maggie at the house?"

"Yes, sir."

"So if anybody says anything about Maggie, it means you?"

"Yes, sir."

Her frightened face did not change. It seemed she was not bothered by the nickname. Or, she was able to hide anger and resentment, and perhaps other things, if she chose.

"You were employed at Mr. Borden's house?"

"Yes, sir. For about two years and nine months. I done the washing and ironing and cooking."

"Anything else besides that?"

"A little sweeping and scrubbing."

"Which part of the house did you have the sweeping of?"

"I had the front hall to do, the front entry."

"What days did you sweep the front hall?"

"Every other week, Friday."

"Only once in two weeks?"

"Yes, sir."

"Did you have any other duties in the front part of the house, except sweeping the front hall?"

"No, sir."

"Did you have the care of any of the beds?"

"No, sir."

The Borden house was a strange house, employing a full time girl who did not attend to the front of the house or any bedrooms.

Next, he questioned Bridget about Emma's and John's whereabouts before the murders. Bridget said that Emma had been away from home for about two weeks before the murders. John had arrived at the Borden house on Wednesday, the day before the murders, and spent the night.

"Had there been any sickness in the family before that Thursday that you know of?"

"Yes, sir. They were sick Wednesday. In the morning, Mrs. Borden came down, and said her and Mr. Borden were sick all night, taken with vomiting."

"How did they appear to be Wednesday morning?"

"They looked pretty sick."

"Did you hear Miss Lizzie say anything about being sick too?"

"Yes, sir. I heard her say she was sick all night, too."

"Do you remember what they had for supper Tuesday night?"

"Yes, sir. Some toasted bread, and some swordfish, some tea, and cake and cookies."

"Fresh fish?"

"Yes, sir; fried for dinner, and warmed it over for supper."

'Dinner' referred to the noon meal. The swordfish would have sat on the stovetop, unrefrigerated, throughout the hot afternoon.

"Did you make that bread?"

"They had baker's bread, and some bread that I made."

"Did you eat any of the baker's bread?"

"No, sir."

Knowlton turned his attention to John's arrival on Wednesday. "When did you first see him?"

"I think it was, about, pretty near two o'clock, or half past one."

"In the afternoon?"

"Yes, sir."

"You got him some dinner?"

"Mrs. Borden waited on him, and got him some dinner."

Again, someone in the Borden family did work that should have been Bridget's responsibility.

"When did you see Mr. Morse again?"

"I saw him going out in the afternoon, going over the river, as I understood."

"You understood he was going over the river to Swansea?"

"Yes, sir."

"Did you see him when he came home that night?"

"No, sir."

"Who was at supper that night?"

"Miss Lizzie, and Mr. and Mrs. Borden."

"What time did you go to bed Wednesday?"

"After ten o'clock."

"Did you have anything to do with shutting up the doors when you went to bed, or any of them?"

"No, except the side door. I locked that, had a key for it, when I got in."

So Bridget had gone out after the Bordens' supper, and not returned until after ten. This, too, was unusual for a family's girl.

"When you came downstairs in the morning, how did you find the side door?"

"Just as I left it."

"What time did you get up Thursday morning?"

"Quarter past six I should judge I was downstairs." Bridget said that she'd gone down to the cellar twice, first to take the ashes down and return with coal. Then she got wood for the stove.

"When you came down that morning, did you open the side doors, the wood and screen doors?"

"Yes, sir, and took in my milk can."

"The milk can was outside?"

"Yes, sir."

"After you took in the milk can, did you do anything to the screen door?"

"Hooked the door."

"Did you shut the wooden door up again?"

"No, sir."

"Was that kept open all day?"

"Yes, sir."

"That was the habit at the time?"

"Yes, sir. About quarter of seven I opened the screen door for the ice man to come in."

"After the ice man came in, did you hook it again?"

"I can't say. I don't remember. I kept it hooked as far as I could know about it."

Bridget said that Mrs. Borden came down about half past six. Mr. Borden appeared ten minutes after and went out to the yard. "He took a slop pail out, and threw it all over the yard." Mr. Borden must have emptied the slop pail from his and Mrs. Borden's bedroom. In the Borden house, the slop pail contained only dirty wash water. The household generally used the toilet in the cellar rather than chamber pots.

"What did you have for breakfast that morning?"

"Some cold mutton and some soup, and johnny cakes."

Johnny cakes were a kind of cornbread fried in a pan like pancakes. The cold mutton would also have sat out on the stovetop all night, unrefrigerated.

"Who sat down to breakfast?"

"Mr. and Mrs. Borden and Mr. Morse."

"Could you tell what time it was?"

"I should judge it was quarter past seven."

"Where were you?"

"Out in the kitchen."

"After breakfast, what were they doing?"

"I don't know. They were in the sitting room."

"You saw Mr. Morse go out?"

"Yes, sir."

"Who let him out?"

"Mr. Borden."

"How long after breakfast was that?"

"I should judge quarter of nine. I can't tell the exact time."

"Which door did he let him out of?"

"The side door."

"At what time did Mr. Borden go out?"

"I did not see him go out."

"Did you go out of the kitchen anywhere?"

"I was out in the backyard. I was not feeling very well, and I was out there."

"How long did you stay out there?"

"I might be out there ten or fifteen minutes. I was sick to my stomach, and was out in the yard, and I was vomiting."

"Did Lizzie come downstairs before you went out in the yard to vomit?"

"Yes, sir."

"Where was Lizzie when you went out in the yard?"

"Eating on the kitchen table. I asked her what did she want for breakfast. She did not know, she did not want any. If she felt like eating something, she would have some coffee and cookies."

"About what time was that?"

"I don't know. I could not tell."

"Did you see Mrs. Borden afterwards?"

"I did, about nine o'clock."

"When you saw Mrs. Borden, where did you see her?"

"In the dining room, dusting. She wanted to know if I had anything particular to do that day. I told her no. Did she want anything? Yes, she said she wanted the windows washed. She said on both sides, inside and outside; they were very dirty."

"You had nothing to do with the work in the spare room?"

"No, sir."

"Do you know who did the work in the spare room?"

"I did not know as Mrs. Borden ever done it before, except her own friends were there."

"When did you next see her after that?"

"Not until I saw her dead."

Next, Knowlton asked about the work of cleaning the windows and what Bridget saw. "What preparations did you make about washing the windows?"

"I went down cellar and got a pail, and got a brush head out of the closet, and went out to the barn and got a stick that's the brush handle. Miss Lizzie came through the kitchen then, as I started to go out. She wanted to know if I was to wash windows. I said yes. I told her she need not hook the door, for I would be around there; but I told her she could if she wanted to."

"When you started to go out, to go through the screen door, was it hooked then?"

"Yes, sir."

"When you came out of the barn, did you see her?"

"No, sir."

"How many windows outside did you wash?"

"Six."

"Which?"

"The sitting room, two, and the parlor and the dining room."

There were in fact ten windows to wash on the ground floor: three in the kitchen, two in the sitting room, three in the parlor, and two in the dining room.

"You were on both sides of the house then, and on the front side of the house, too?" said Knowlton.

"Yes, sir."

"During the time you were washing windows outside, did you go in the house?"

"Yes, sir. I went in after a dipper, in the sink."

"Have you any particular idea how long it took you to wash the windows outside?"

"No. I should think it was twenty minutes past ten when I got in the house."

If correct, that meant Bridget had taken more than an hour to wash six outside windows, during the time when someone killed Mrs. Borden.

"Did you see any person around the house when you were washing the windows outside?"

"No, sir."

"Then what did you do?"

"I came in and got the hand basin and started to wash the sitting room windows inside."

"When you came in at that time, did you see Miss Lizzie?"

"No, sir, I did not."

"Did Mr. Borden come in any time during that time?"

"Yes, sir. I heard a person at the front door trying to get in, and I let him in. It might be later than half past ten; I could not tell."

"Up to the time you let Mr. Borden in, had you seen Miss Lizzie?"

"She was upstairs at the time I let him in, for I heard her laugh."

"Up the back or front stairs?"

"The front stairs."

"Was that the first you had heard or seen of her since you spoke to her at the side door."

"Yes, sir."

"What was the occasion of her laugh?"

"I got puzzled on the door, and I said something, and she laughed at it; I supposed that must make her laugh, I don't know."

"She laughed when you said something?"

"Yes, sir. I went to open the door as usual, and it was locked and stuck. I said, 'Oh pshaw,' and Miss Lizzie laughed, upstairs."

"Did you see her then?"

"No, sir."

"Where did Mr. Borden go when he came in?"

"Into the dining room. He sat at the head of the lounge in a chair when I saw him, reading."

"You were still at work in the sitting room, washing the windows?"

"Yes, sir."

"How soon did you see her?"

"It might be five or ten minutes after, she came downstairs; she came through the front hall to the sitting room, then she went into the dining room. I heard her ask him if he had any mail for her. I heard her telling her father that Mrs. Borden had a note that morning, and had gone out."

"What happened then, did she stay there?"

"I do not know where she went then, I cannot tell."

"What did you do then?"

"I stayed washing the windows, right along until I got through in the sitting room, then I came right into the dining room."

"Where was Mr. Borden when you came into the dining room?"

"Coming downstairs from his room."

"When you went into the dining room, did you see Miss Lizzie then?"

"No, sir."

"Did you see her in the kitchen?"

"No, sir."

"What did he do then when he came back?"

"He took a chair and sat down near the window in the sitting room with a book or paper in his hand."

"How soon did you see Miss Lizzie?"

"I was washing the last window in the dining room. She came out from the kitchen, brought an ironing board, put it on the dining room table and started to iron."

"What was this that she was ironing?"

"Handkerchiefs. She always done them herself."

"What did you do then when you finished washing the windows?"

"I went out in the kitchen, and Miss Lizzie asked was I going out that afternoon. I told her I didn't know, I might, or I might not. I was not feeling very well. She said Mrs. Borden was going out, or gone out, I could not catch the two words she said; that somebody was sick. I asked who was sick. She said she did not know, but Mrs. Borden had a note that morning."

"What did you do then?"

"I went out in the kitchen. Hung up my cloth I had to wash with, and threw away the water, and went upstairs in my room."

"Where was Miss Lizzie?"

"She came out in the kitchen, as I was starting to go upstairs. She told me there was a sale in Sargeants that afternoon of dress goods for eight cents a yard. I told her I would have one."

"When you went upstairs, what time was it?"

"It might be four or five minutes to eleven."

"How do you know that?"

"By the length of time I was upstairs when the city clock struck eleven o'clock."

"When did you next see anything, or hear anything?"

"Not until Miss Lizzie called me."

"What time was that, as near as you can fix it?"

"I might be upstairs ten or fifteen minutes, as near as I can think."

"When she called to you, what did she say?"

"She holloed to me. Of course I knew something was the matter, she holloed so loud. She said 'come down quick', that her father was dead. I came down, and asked what was the matter."

"Where was she when you went down?"

"Standing in the side door, leaning against it, right by the screen door."

"Did you ask her where she was when it happened?"

"Yes. She said she was out in the yard and heard a groan. She came in and found her father."

"What did you do then?"

"She told me to go for Dr. Bowen. I went right over."

"Who was at the Borden house when you came back?"

"Nobody but Miss Lizzie. I told her he was not in. Miss Lizzie told me to go after Miss Russell."

"Do you remember what dress she had on that morning?"

"No, sir."

That ended Bridget's testimony. Knowlton thought she seemed forthright and non-evasive. Also, he could not imagine how she'd been so near to both murders but saw and heard nothing. An officer took Bridget back to the Borden house.

Before they got there Marshal Hilliard and Officer Harrington fetched Lizzie and escorted her to the courthouse, so that the two women could not talk. The Second Street crowd followed on foot.

Inside the courthouse, Knowlton had his first opportunity to observe Lizzie directly. Her face was flushed and her pale eyes active, with wide pupils and a glazed look. She held her arms tightly to her sides. She was not so much overweight as solidly built, with a softer chin and lacking the trim waist ladies sought.

Knowlton was determined to get direct and complete answers about her whereabouts on the morning of the murders, this time under oath.

She was sworn and sat in the witness chair.

CHAPTER 12

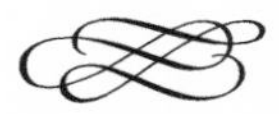

Knowlton stood. "Miss Borden, I am Hosea Knowlton, District Attorney for Bristol County. You may have seen me around your father's property in the last week."

"I don't think so." She stared back at him.

"Regardless, it is my responsibility to conduct this inquiry into the deaths of your parents. You are here to answer questions in that inquiry. Do you understand?"

"Yes," said Lizzie.

"Give me your full name," he said.

"Lizzie Andrew Borden."

"Is it Lizzie or Elizabeth?"

"Lizzie."

"You were so christened?"

"I was so christened."

"What is your age, please?"

"Thirty-two."

"Your mother is not living?"

"No, sir."

"When did she die?"

"She died when I was two and a half years old."

"You do not remember her, then?"

"No, sir."

"How long had your father been married to your stepmother?"

"I think about twenty-seven years."

"Have you any idea how much your father was worth?"

"No, sir."

"Do you know something about his real estate?"

"I know what real estate he owned, part of it; I don't know whether I know it all or not."

"Tell me what you know of."

"He owns two farms in Swansea, the place on Second Street, and the A. J. Borden building and corner, and the land on South Main Street where McMannus is, and then a short time ago he bought some real estate up further south that formerly, he said, belonged to a Mr. Birch."

"Did you ever know of your father making a will?"

"No, sir, except I heard somebody say once that there was one several years ago; that is all I ever heard."

"Who did you hear say so?"

"I think it was Mr. Morse."

"What Morse?"

"Uncle John V. Morse."

"Did you ask your father?"

"I did not."

"Have you heard anything of his proposing to make a will?"

"No, sir."

"Do you know of anybody that your father was on bad terms with?"

"There was a man that came there that he had trouble with. I don't know who the man was."

"When?"

"I cannot locate the time exactly. It was within two weeks."

"Tell all you saw and heard."

"I did not see anything. I heard the bell ring, and Father went to the door and let him in. I did not hear anything for some time, except just the voices; then I heard the man say, 'I would like to have that store.' Father says, 'I am not willing to let your business go in there.' And the man said, 'I thought with your reputation for liking money, you would let your store for anything.' Father said, 'You are mistaken.' Then they talked a while, and then their voices were louder, and I heard Father order him out, and went to the front door with him."

"Have you any idea who that was?"

"No, sir. I think it was a man from out of town, because he said he was going home to see his partner."

"Have you had any efforts made to find him?"

"We have had a detective; that is all I know."

"You have not found him?"

"Not that I know of."

"Beside that do you know of anybody that your father had bad feelings toward, or who had bad feelings toward your father?"

"I know of one man that has not been friendly with him; they have not been friendly for years."

"Who?"

"Mr. Hiram C. Harrington."

"What relation is he to him?"

"He is my father's brother-in-law. My father's only sister is married to Mr. Harrington."

"Anybody else that was on bad terms with your father?"

"Not that I know of."

"Do you know of anybody that was on bad terms with your stepmother?"

"No, sir."

"Had your stepmother any property?"

"I don't know, only that she had half the house that belonged to her father."

"Where was that?"

"On Fourth Street."

"Who lives in it?"

"Her half sister, Sarah."

"Did you ever have any trouble with your stepmother?"

"No, sir."

"Have you, within six months, had any words with her?"

"No, sir."

"Within a year?"

"No, sir."

"Within two years?"

"I think not."

"When last that you know of?"

"About five years ago."

"What about?"

"Her stepsister, half sister."

"What name?"

"Her name now is Mrs. George W. Whitehead."

"Nothing more than hard words?"

"No, sir, they were not hard words; it was simply a difference of opinion."

"You have been on pleasant terms with your stepmother since then?"

"Yes, sir."

"Cordial?"

"It depends upon one's idea of cordiality, perhaps."

"According to your idea of cordiality?"

"We were friendly, very friendly."

"Cordial, according to your idea of cordiality?"

"Quite so."

"What do you mean by 'quite so'?"

"Quite cordial. I do not mean the dearest of friends in the world, but very kindly feelings, and pleasant. I do not know how to answer you any better than that."

"You did not regard her as your mother?"

"Not exactly, no, although she came there when I was very young."

"Were your relations towards her that of daughter and mother?"

"In some ways it was, and in some it was not."

"In what ways was it?"

"I decline to answer."

Knowlton regarded her curiously. "Why?"

"Because I don't know how to answer it."

"In what ways was it not?"

"I did not call her mother."

"What name did she go by?"

"Mrs. Borden."

"When did you begin to call her Mrs. Borden?"

"I should think five or six years ago."

"Before that time you had called her mother?"

"Yes, sir."

"What led to the change?"

"The affair with her stepsister."

"So that the affair was serious enough to have you change from calling her mother, do you mean?"

"I did not choose to call her mother."

"Have you ever called her mother since?"

"Yes, occasionally."

"To her face, I mean?"

"Yes."

"Often?"

"No, sir."

"Seldom?"

"Seldom."

"Did your sister Emma call her mother?"

"She always called her Abby from the time she came into the family."

"What is Emma's age?"

"She is ten years older than I am. She was somewhere about fourteen when she came there."

"Why did you leave off calling her mother?"

"Because I wanted to."

"Is that all the reason you have to give me?"

"I have not any other answer."

"Can't you give me any better reason than that?"

"I have not any reason to give, except that I did not want to."

"In what other respect were the relations between you and her not that of mother and daughter, besides not calling her mother?"

"I had never been to her as a mother in many things. I always went to my sister, because she was older and had the care of me after my mother died."

"In what respects were the relations between you and her that of mother and daughter?"

"That is the same question you asked before; I can't answer you any better now than I did before."

"You did not say before you could not answer, but that you declined to answer."

"I decline to answer because I do not know what to say."

"That is the only reason?"

"Yes, sir."

Knowlton paused but after a moment he left that topic. "What dress did you wear the day they were killed?"

"I had on a navy blue, sort of a bengaline or India silk skirt, with a navy blue blouse." The term "silk" included any more expensive fabric, even if it wasn't true silk. "In the afternoon they thought I had better change it. I put on a pink wrapper."

"When did you first see Mr. Morse there, before your father and mother were killed?"

"I did not see him at all."

"How did you know he was there?"

"I heard his voice."

"You did not see him Wednesday evening?"

"I did not; I was out Wednesday evening."

"You did not see him Thursday morning?"

"I did not; he was out when I came downstairs."

"Where were you Wednesday evening?"

"I spent the evening with Miss Russell."

"As near as you can remember, when did you return?"

"About nine o'clock at night."

"The family had then retired?"

"I don't know whether they had or not. I went right to my room."

"Which door did you come in at?"

"The front door."

"Did you lock it?"

"Yes, sir."

"Did you eat supper at home Wednesday night?"

"I was at home; I did not eat any supper, because I did not feel able to eat supper; I had been sick."

"You did not come down to supper?"

"No, sir."

"You felt better in the evening?"

"Not very much better. I thought I would go out, and see if the air would make me feel any better."

"When you came back at nine o'clock, how did you know it was right to lock the front door?"

"That was always my business."

"How many locks did you fasten?"

"The spring locks itself, and there is a key to turn, and you manipulate the bolt. I used them all."

"Then you went to bed?"

"Yes, directly."

"When you got up the next morning, what time did you come downstairs?"

"As near as I can remember, it was a few minutes before nine."

"Who did you find downstairs when you came down?"

"Maggie and Mrs. Borden."

"Did you inquire for Mr. Morse?"

"No, sir."

"Your father was there?"

"Yes, sir."

"Had there been anybody else around the house that week, or premises?"

"No one that I know of, except the man that called to see him on this business about the store."

"Was that that week?"

"Yes, sir."

"I misunderstood you probably, I thought you said a week or two before."

"No, I said that week. There was a man came the week before and gave up some keys, and I took them."

"I see. Do you remember of anybody else being then around the premises that week?"

"Nobody that I know of or saw."

"Where was your father when you came down Thursday morning?"

"In the sitting room in his large chair, reading the *Providence Journal*."

"Where was your mother? Do you prefer me to call her Mrs. Borden?"

"I had as soon you called her mother. She was in the dining room with a feather duster, dusting."

"Where was Maggie?"

"Just come in the side door with the long pole and brush; she was going to wash the windows around the house. She said Mrs. Borden wanted her to."

"Did you get your breakfast that morning?"

"I did not eat any breakfast; I did not feel as though I wanted any. I don't know whether I ate half a banana; I don't think I did."

"What was the next thing that happened after you got down?"

"Maggie went out of doors to wash the windows and Father came out into the kitchen and said he did not know whether he would go out or not, he was not feeling well. And then I sprinkled some handkerchiefs to iron."

"Did your father go downtown?"

"He went down later."

"What time did he start away?"

"I don't know."

"Did you let your father out?"

"No, sir; he went out himself."

"Did you fasten the door after him?"

"No, sir."

"Did Maggie?"

"I don't know. She had charge of the side door."

"Did you say anything to Maggie?"

"I think I told her I did not want any breakfast."

"How long a job was ironing your handkerchiefs?"

"I did not finish them; my flats were not hot enough. If they had been hot, not more than twenty minutes, perhaps."

"How long did you work on the job?"

"I don't know, sir."

"When did you last see your mother?"

"I did not see her after when I went down in the morning and she was dusting the dining room."

"Did you or she leave the dining room first?"

"I think I did. I left her in the dining room."

"You never saw her or heard her afterwards?"

"No, sir."

"Did she say anything about making the bed?"

"She said she had been up and made the bed up fresh, and had dusted the room and left it all in order. She was going to put some fresh pillow slips on the small pillows at the foot of the bed, and was going to close the room, because she was going to have company Monday and she wanted everything in order."

"How long would it take to put on the pillow slips?"

"About two minutes."

"Can you give me any suggestion as to what else occupied her when she was up there, when she was struck dead?"

"I don't know of anything except she had some cotton cloth pillow-cases up there, and she said she was going to commence to work on them. That is all I know. And the sewing machine was up there."

"Did you hear the sewing machine going?"

"I did not."

"What explanation can you suggest as to the whereabouts of your mother from the time you saw her in the dining room, and she said her work in the spare room was all done, until eleven o'clock?"

"I don't know. I think she went back into the spare room, and whether she came back again or not I don't know; that has always been a mystery."

"Had you any knowledge of her going out of the house?"

"No, sir."

This answer also puzzled Knowlton. The police notes mentioned a message for Abby from a sick friend.

He asked again. "Had you any knowledge of her going out of the house?"

This time Lizzie said, "She told me she had had a note, somebody was sick, and said, 'I am going to get the dinner on the way,' and asked me what I wanted for dinner."

"Did you tell her?"

"Yes, I told her I did not want anything."

"Then why did you not suppose she had gone?"

"I supposed she had gone."

"Did you hear her come back?"

"I did not hear her go or come back, but I supposed she went."

"Did she tell you where she was going?"

"No, sir."

"Did she tell you who the note was from?"

"No, sir."

"Did you ever see the note?"

Lizzie's eyes lost focus for a moment. She said, "No, sir," but teetered in her seat.

Knowlton checked the clock. They were nearing the day's end. He pushed on, determined to get answers. "Miss Lizzie, where were you when your father returned?"

"I was down in the kitchen."

"What doing?"

"Reading an old magazine that had been left in the cupboard, an old Harper's Magazine."

"Had you got through ironing?"

"No, sir. Stopped for the flats."

"Were you waiting for them to be hot?"

"Yes, sir."

"Was there a fire in the stove?"

"Yes, sir."

"How long was your father gone?"

"I don't know, sir; not very long."

"An hour?"

"I should not think so."

"Will you give me the best story you can, so far as your recollection serves you, of your time while he was gone?"

She sighed and adjusted herself in her seat. "I sprinkled my handkerchiefs, and got my ironing board and took them in the dining room. I left the handkerchiefs in the kitchen on the table and whether I ate any cookies or not I don't remember. Then I sat down looking at the magazine, waiting for the flats to heat. Then I went in the sitting room and got the *Providence Journal*, and took that into the kitchen. I don't recollect of doing anything else."

"Are you sure you were in the kitchen when your father returned?"

"I am not sure whether I was there or in the dining room."

"Did you go back to your room before your father returned?"

"I think I did carry up some clean clothes."

"Did you spend any time up the front stairs before your father returned?"

"No, sir."

"Or after he returned?"

"No, sir. I did stay in my room long enough when I went up to sew a little piece of tape on a garment."

"You were not upstairs when he came home?"

"I was not upstairs when he came home; no, sir."

"Who let your father in?"

"I think he came to the front door and I think Maggie let him in."

"Where were you when he came in?"

"I think in my room upstairs."

"Then you were upstairs when your father came home?"

"I don't know sure, but I think I was."

"What were you doing?"

"As I say, I took up these clean clothes, and stopped and basted a little piece of tape on a garment."

"Then you were upstairs when your father came to the house on his return?"

"I think I was."

That put Lizzie right next to the guest room, and Abby's body. "How long had you been there?" Knowlton asked.

"I had only been upstairs just long enough to take the clothes up and baste the little loop on the sleeve. I don't think I had been up there over five minutes."

"You remember, Miss Borden, I will call your attention to it so as to see if I have any misunderstanding, not for the purpose of confusing you; you remember that you told me several times that you were downstairs, and not upstairs when your father came home?" An edge of mocking sliced through the words. "You have forgotten, perhaps?"

Lizzie snapped back. "I don't know what I have said. I have answered so many questions and I am so confused I don't know one thing from another. I am telling you just as nearly as I know."

He pressed on. "Calling your attention to what you said about that a few minutes ago, and now again to the circumstance you have said you were upstairs when the bell rang, and were on the stairs when Maggie let your father in; which now is your recollection of the true statement of the matter?"

"I think I was downstairs in the kitchen."

"And then you were not upstairs?"

"I think I was not; because I went up almost immediately, as soon as I went down, and then came down again and stayed down."

"What had you in your mind when you said you were on the stairs as Maggie let your father in?"

"The other day somebody came there and she let them in and I was on the stairs; I don't know whether the morning before or when it was."

Officers escorted Lizzie home. Jennings was waiting, with Emma. When Lizzie did not volunteer, Jennings asked. "What happened in your testimony, Miss Lizzie? It was many hours. Did you remain silent?"

"I answered all," said Lizzie.

Jennings sighed. "Then how did the questions go? Did anything seem to be a problem I should prepare for?"

"Certainly not," she said. "Everything was well."

"Were you dismissed? Is your testimony complete?" asked Jennings.

"I do not know," said Lizzie, seeming to realize for the first time that she might need to appear again the next day.

"If they did not say, you will most likely be called again tomorrow."

"Then I will answer more tomorrow," said Lizzie tiredly.

"Recall that, as your advocate, I've directed you not to answer questions."

"I have and will answer whatever questions," said Lizzie with a scowl, "even from that horrible man."

She went up to her room.

CHAPTER 13

WEDNESDAY, AUGUST 10

Lizzie sat straight as she waited for her second day of testimony to begin, but darkness shaded the skin below her eyes. Knowlton felt he'd made progress the day before. Lizzie had equivocated and restated. But it wasn't enough. With more pressure, he might get damning statements or even a confession.

He stood closer that second day, not wandering more than five or six feet from Lizzie as he questioned her. "I call your attention, Miss Borden, to the fact that yesterday you told me, with some explicitness, that when your father came in, you were just coming downstairs?"

"No, I did not, I beg your pardon."

"That you were on the stairs at the time your father was let in, you said with some explicitness. Do you now say you did not say so?"

"I said I thought first I was on the stairs; then I remembered I was in the kitchen when he came in."

"First you thought you were in the kitchen; afterwards you remembered you were on the stairs?"

"I said I thought I was on the stairs; then I said I knew I was in the kitchen. I still say that now. I was in the kitchen."

"You were always in the kitchen or dining room, excepting when you went upstairs?"

"I went upstairs before he went out."

"After your father went out, you did not go upstairs at all?"

"No, sir, I did not."

"So, then," said Knowlton, "it would have been extremely difficult for anybody to have gone through without your seeing them?"

"They could have gone from the kitchen into the sitting room while I was in the dining room, if there was anybody to go."

"A large portion of that time, the girl Maggie was out of doors?"

"I don't know where she was, I did not see her."

"So far as you know you were alone in the lower part of the house, a large portion of the time, after your father went away, and before he came back?"

"My father did not go away I think until somewhere about ten, as near as I can remember; he was with me downstairs."

"What were you doing in the kitchen when your father came home?"

"I think I was eating a pear when he came in."

"What had you been doing before that?"

"Been reading a magazine."

"How soon after your father came in, before Maggie went upstairs?"

"I don't know. I did not see her."

"Did you see her after your father came in?"

"Not after she let him in."

"Did you see Bridget washing the windows inside?"

"I don't know."

"You don't know whether she washed the dining room and sitting room windows inside?"

"I did not see her."

"Do you think she might have washed the windows in the dining room and sitting room and you not know it?"

"I don't know, I am sure, whether I should or not. I might have seen her, and not know it."

He stepped toward her. "Miss Borden, I am trying in good faith to get all the doings that morning of yourself and Miss Sullivan, and I have not succeeded. Do you desire to give me any information or not?"

"I don't know it, Mr.—," she started to address him directly but finished with, "I don't know what your name is."

He leaned down and raised his voice to anger. "It is certain beyond any reasonable doubt she was engaged in washing the windows in the dining room or sitting room when your father came home," he spat, though it was not certain. "Do you mean to say you know nothing of either of those operations?"

Lizzie pulled back but seemed to gain, not lose, composure as he pressed her. "I knew she washed the windows outside; that is, she told me so. She did not wash the windows in the kitchen, because I was in the kitchen most of the time." She blinked back at him.

He continued more sternly, as a scolding father might. "The dining room and sitting room, I said."

Lizzie considered and tilted her head as she answered almost thoughtfully. "I don't know, whether she washed the windows in the sitting room and dining room or not."

Knowlton thought he saw, perhaps, the touch of a smirk. "How long was your father in the house before you found him killed?"

"I don't know exactly, because I went out to the barn."

"When you went out to the barn, where did you leave your father?"

"He had laid down on the sitting room lounge, taken off his shoes, and put on his slippers. I asked him if he wanted the window left that way. Then I went into the kitchen, and from there to the barn."

"Whereabouts in the barn did you go?"

"Upstairs."

"How long did you remain there?"

"I don't know, fifteen or twenty minutes."

"What doing?"

"Trying to find lead for a sinker."

"What made you think there would be lead for a sinker up there?"

"Because there was some there."

"Did you bring any sinker back from the barn?"

"I found no sinker."

"When you went out did you unfasten the screen door?"

"I unhooked it."

"You went straight to the upper story of the barn?"

"No, I went under the pear tree and got some pears first."

"Did you look for anything else beside lead?"

"No, sir."

"When you got through looking for lead did you come down?"

"No, sir, I went to the west window over the hay, to the west window, and the curtain was slanted a little. I pulled it down."

"What else? Tell me all that you did."

"Nothing."

"That is the second story of the barn?"

"Yes, sir."

"Was the window open?"

"I think not."

"Hot?"

"Very hot."

"How long do you think you were up there?"

"Not more than fifteen or twenty minutes, I should not think."

"Do you think all you have told me would take you four minutes?"

"I ate some pears up there."

"I asked you to tell me all you did."

"I told you all I did."

"I don't suppose you stayed there any longer than necessary?"

"No, sir, because it was close."

"I suppose that was the hottest place there was on the premises?"

"I should think so."

"Can you give me any explanation why all you have told me would occupy more than three minutes?"

"Yes, it would take me more than three minutes."

"To look in that box and put down the curtain and then get out as soon as you conveniently could; would you say you were occupied in that business twenty minutes?"

"I think so, because I did not look at the box when I first went up."

"What did you do?"

"I ate my pears."

"Stood there eating the pears, doing nothing?"

"I was looking out of the window."

"How many did you eat?"

"Three, I think."

"You were feeling better than you did in the morning?"

"Better than I did the night before."

"You were feeling better than you were in the morning?"

"I felt better in the morning than I did the night before."

"That is not what I asked you. You were then, when you were in that hot loft, looking out of the window and eating three pears, feeling better, were you not, than you were in the morning when you could not eat any breakfast?"

"I never eat any breakfast."

"You did not answer my question, and you will, if I have to put it all day! Were you then when you were eating those three pears in that hot loft, looking out of that closed window, feeling better than you were in the morning when you ate no breakfast?"

"I was feeling well enough to eat the pears."

"Were you feeling better than you were in the morning?"

"I don't think I felt very sick in the morning, only— Yes, I don't know but I did feel better. As I say, I don't know whether I ate any breakfast or not, or whether I ate a cookie."

"Were you then feeling better than you did in the morning?"

"I don't know how to answer you, because I told you I felt better in the morning anyway."

"Do you understand my question? My question is whether, when you were in the loft of that barn, you were feeling better than you were in the morning when you got up?"

Lizzie gazed back at him. "No, I felt about the same."

Knowlton let out a sigh. "When you came down from the barn, what did you do then?"

"Came into the kitchen. I went into the sitting room."

"What did you do then?"

"I found my father, and rushed to the foot of the stairs."

"When you saw your father where was he?"

"On the sofa."

"Did you notice that he had been cut?"

"Yes. That is what made me afraid."

"Did you notice that he was dead?"

"I did not know whether he was or not."

"You saw his face covered with blood?"

"Yes, sir."

"Did you see his eyeball hanging out?"

"No, sir."

"See the gashes where his face was laid open?"

"No, sir."

"Nothing of that kind?"

"No, sir." Lizzie dropped her head into her hands and shook.

Knowlton waited for her to collect herself.

Before he excused her for the day Knowlton needed to get something else on the record. "Did you give to the officer the same dress you wore the day of the tragedy?"

"Yes, sir."

"Do you know whether there was any blood on the skirt?"

"No, sir."

Dr. Dolan had, in fact, found one tiny spot of blood on the outside of the underskirt.

"Assume that there was, do you know how it came there?"

"No, sir."

"Have you any explanation of how it might come there?"

"No, sir."

"Have you said it came from flea bites?"

"I told those men that were at the house that I had had fleas; that is all."

"Assuming that the blood came from the outside, can you give any explanation of how it came there?"

"No, sir."

"You cannot now?"

"No, sir."

Only then did he realize they'd missed something. "What shoes did you have on that day?" he asked.

"A pair of ties." 'Ties' were house shoes with thin soles.

"What color?"

"Black."

"Do you remember where you took them off?"

"I wore the shoes ever after that, all around the house Thursday, and all day Friday and Saturday."

"Where are they?"

"At home."

"What stockings did you have on that day?"

"Black."

"Where are they?"

"At home."

"Have they been washed?"

"I don't know."

"Will you give them to the officer?"

"Yes, sir."

Knowlton sent an officer back home with Lizzie to collect her shoes and stockings. Jennings supervised the transfer.

After the officers left he again asked about Lizzie's testimony.

She refused to speak with him and instead went to her room and locked the door.

Professor Wood, the Harvard forensic expert, met Marshal Hilliard at the police station and retrieved the claw hammer hatchets and two axes for testing. One claw hammer had stains that appeared to Wood to be blood.

Wood also took possession of Lizzie's blue skirt, blouse, and white underskirt. The shoes and stockings had not yet arrived.

THURSDAY, AUGUST 11

By Thursday morning Knowlton decided he would not get much more from Lizzie. Perhaps what he had already, of evasions and corrections, was enough. He had only a few final questions for her. He began by giving her an opportunity. "Is there anything you would like to correct in your previous testimony?"

She did not pause or hesitate. "No, sir."

He waited, in case she should reconsider. She did not waver.

"Your attention has already been called to the circumstance of going into the drug store of Smith's, on the corner of Columbia and Main streets, has it not, on the day before the tragedy?"

"Somebody has spoken of it to me; I don't know who it was."

"Did that take place?"

"It did not."

"Do you know where the drug store is?"

"I don't."

"Did you go into any drug store and inquire for prussic acid?"

"I did not."

"Where were you on that Wednesday morning?"

"At home."

"All the time?"

"All day, until Wednesday night."

When Prosecutor Knowlton finished his questions, Lizzie was not released to return home. Instead they took her to the matron's quarters inside the station to wait.

The Borden bodies had been in the vault at Oak Grove Cemetery since August 6, the day of the funeral. For a week following the deaths the bodies were stored in the summer heat until Dr. Dolan, guided by several other doctors, finally performed full autopsies.

He made measurements of the bodies and notes of the wounds, and took tissue and organ samples. Then he took something else from each body. He'd been instructed to by the Attorney General.

The doctors placed the bodies back in their caskets and called undertaker Winward, who buried them in their final resting places.

John Morse, the next inquest witness, testified that he'd been living in nearby South Dartmouth but actually lived in Iowa, where he had a farm. He'd rented out his farm while back east to sell horses. All had been sold some time ago but John had stayed on for a few years, living with and helping run the meat business of a Mr. Davis, an elderly friend who had cancer.

John said that he'd never married and had sufficient assets to live without working, if he chose.

John had long maintained regular correspondence with Emma and had occasional letters from Andrew.

"How often did you come to see the Bordens since returning East?" Knowlton asked.

"Sometimes once a week; sometimes once in three or four weeks; sometimes once in three months, just as it happened."

"Did you often stay overnight?"

"Yes, sir, quite often."

"Were you on good terms with all the family?"

"Yes, sir."

John swore that, as far as he knew, there was no trouble in the family. When asked specifically if Lizzie was on good terms with her stepmother, he replied, "I should think they were pleasant."

Before the murders he'd last been at the Borden house on July 10. At that time Mr. Borden asked him to find a man to take charge of one of the family farms, and John arrived the day before the murders mainly in respect to that business, he said.

Andrew had mentioned making some bequests for charitable purposes, and possibly creating a will.

The day before the murders John arrived by train around one thirty, had dinner, visited, then rented a carriage to go to the Borden Swansea farm to discuss business with the men there and get the eggs. He returned before nine, visited with the Borden parents in the sitting room, and went to bed at ten in the guest room, he said.

On the morning of the murders, John left at about nine to go to the post office and then to take the trolley car to his niece's house. Andrew had latched the side door behind John.

After John's testimony, Marshal Hilliard and an officer went to the Borden farm in Swansea to interview the two farm hands.

Frederick Eddy said he had worked for Mr. Borden for sixteen years. "John V. Morse came over to this house Wednesday evening August third, between seven and eight o'clock," the officer wrote in his notes on their conversation with Mr. Eddy. "He said Mr. Borden sent him over to see how I was, and get the eggs. He said Mr. Borden was coming with him, but then he, his wife, and Lizzie were taken sick and Mr. Borden couldn't come."

John had stayed perhaps ten or fifteen minutes.

Mr. Alfred Johnson, a Swede, sometimes went to Mr. Borden's house to cut wood and clean up the yard. Alfred said, "I have worked for Mr. Borden nine years, doing work at the house when not busy at the farm. The two last times I cut wood was early in the spring, and again just before planting. The hatchet and axes were always kept in one place, in a box in the wood room at the left of the furnace."

"Since hearing of the murder," said Frederick as the officers were leaving, "it has seemed to me a singular coincidence that Morse should have come over that night for the eggs, for, had he not, I should have been at Mr. Borden's Thursday morning."

Emma testified next. She had always lived in her fathers' home, she said, except for a year and a half during which she'd attended, but not completed, finishing school.

Prior to the murders of her parents she'd spent two weeks in Fairhaven with a Miss Helen Brownell and Helen's mother.

Emma had never heard her father speak of having a will and had never asked.

She and Lizzie, Emma said, were responsible for keeping the parlor tidy and also the guest bedroom. "Did your mother never have charge of the guest chamber?" asked Knowlton.

"I did not know that she ever did. When I was home I don't think she ever did."

"You don't know how it happened that she was having the work of the guest chamber on the morning that she died?"

"No, sir."

Knowlton asked about the habits of the household, and whether Lizzie in particular ate with their parents. He got no more satisfaction from Emma than Lizzie.

"Did she usually eat with the family?"

"Just as it happened. If she was there, sometimes she did, and a good many times she did not."

"Did she usually have breakfast with the family?"

"Hardly ever."

"Did not get up soon enough?"

"No, sir."

"Did you?"

"Not always."

"But oftener than she did?"

"Yes, sir."

Emma said she knew nothing about axes or hatchets found in the cellar, or even that they were in the cellar, except that a farmer would come over and cut up wood and that she'd once seen an axe or hatchet in the cellar. She could not tell which.

As for Andrews's enemies, Emma knew only of Mr. Hiram Harrington, his sister Lurana's husband, to whom he did not speak. Emma did not know of anyone on bad terms with Abby.

When asked whether her own relations with Abby were cordial, Emma answered similarly to her sister: "I don't know how to answer that. We always spoke."

"That might be, and not be at all cordial."

"Well, perhaps I should say no then."

"Were the relations between your sister Lizzie and your mother what you would call cordial?"

"I think more than they were with me."

"Do you mean they were entirely cordial between your step mother and your sister Lizzie?"

"No."

"Can you tell me the cause of the lack of cordiality between you and your mother, or was it not any specific thing?"

"Well, we felt that she was not interested in us, and at one time Father gave her some property, the half house where her sister lives, and we felt that we ought to have some too, and he afterwards gave us some."

"That, however, did not heal the breach, whatever breach there was? The giving the property to you did not entirely heal the feeling?"

"No, sir."

"That was some time ago?"

"Yes, sir. Some time ago."

When asked about John, Emma confirmed that he came to the house sometimes often and sometimes not. He commonly stayed the night. She described John as "a very dear uncle of ours, of mine."

Knowlton finished his questioning by asking about how the doors on the house were locked. She confirmed that all of the exterior doors were always kept locked. Sometimes, though, the spring lock on the front door failed to lock that door, but not very often. The family bolted that door overnight.

Dr. Bowen told of Abby's visit to his house the morning before the murders. "Mrs. Borden came to the door and said she was frightened, said that she was afraid she was poisoned."

"What morning was this?"

"Wednesday morning. She had heard of baker's cream cakes being poisonous, and was afraid there was something poisonous in the bread that made her vomit. I went over after breakfast."

Knowlton did not know to ask Dr. Bowen if he'd given Lizzie medication for her nerves and whether she might have been considered to be drugged at the time of her testimony. Dr. Bowen did not think to mention it.

Knowlton asked neighbor Adelaide Churchill, "Did you know anything about the relations between the girls and their father and mother?"

"I don't," she replied, but followed with, "I never thought they were as cordial as they might be, but I don't know nothing about it."

"What was it you observed that led you to think they were not?"

"Because I never saw them together."

When asked about Lizzie's dress that morning, Mrs. Churchill said, "She had on a blue and white calico with a deeper navy blue diamond on it; of a deeper shade of blue, this diamond was, as near as I can tell it; I am not observing of clothes."

"Are you sure it was calico?"

"No, it might be gingham; it was cotton goods I think."

"It could not have been India silk?"

"No, I don't think it was; it was calico or gingham I think. I do not think she would wear India silk in the morning, unless she was going out."

"Do you think you would know the dress if you saw it again?"

"I think I should."

Adelaide had not seen any blood on Lizzie that morning, nor anything apparently in disarray in the Borden house other than the murdered parents. Lizzie, she said, looked "perfectly clean."

Hiram C. Harrington had been characterized by both Borden daughters as a known enemy of their father.

"Were you related or connected with Andrew J. Borden?" asked Knowlton.

"I am not connected with him any more than I married his sister," said Hiram.

"Is your wife living?"

"She is."

"You and he were not on good terms?"

"We never had no words, or anything of that kind. Some years ago I thought he was hard, and I cut his acquaintance. That is, when he came to my house, I would leave the room, and he very soon saw I cut his acquaintance; and he did mine."

"But you continued on good terms with the rest of the family?"

"Yes, friendly to them."

"You don't know of anybody that was hostile to Mr. Borden?"

"Not a person."

"Nor Mrs. Borden?"

"Nor Mrs. Borden."

Alice Russell answered questions about the morning of the murders and how Lizzie had changed her dress. "I came into the room, and found her fastening a pink wrapper on," said Alice.

"Did she change her shoes or stockings?" Knowlton asked.

"No, sir. She could not have done that. I was not out of the room long enough."

"What sort of dress was it Miss Lizzie had on before she changed it?"

"I haven't any idea. I can't recollect."

He did not know to ask about a burned dress and Alice did not volunteer.

Knowlton took advantage, though, of having someone who'd known the family closely, for many years, for questioning. "I do not like to ask this question, but I feel obliged to," he said. "Did you see enough to notice what the relations were between Miss Lizzie and her mother or father?"

"In all my acquaintance, which is ten years sure, and most of that time quite intimate, I never heard any wrangling in the family." She paused, considered, and continued. "However, I have got to answer the question, and I will say I don't think they were congenial. Their tastes and natures differed in every way. Mr. Borden was a plain living man with rigid ideas, and very set. They were young girls. He had earned his money, and he did not care for the things that young women in their position naturally would. He looked upon those things—I don't know just how to put it."

"He did not appreciate girls?"

"No, I don't think he did."

"How did you get this, from the girls' talk, or what you observed?"

"From what I observed. Everybody knew what Andrew Borden's ideas were. It always seemed to me as if he did not see why his daughters should care for anything different."

"Did they complain about it?"

"Yes, they used to think it ought to be different. They would have liked to have been cultured girls, and would have liked to have had different advantages. It was natural for girls to express themselves that way. I would think it would have been very unnatural if they had not."

"Lizzie or Emma, or both?"

"Both."

"He did not give them the advantages of education that they thought they ought to have had?"

"I don't know as it is just that, but people cannot go and do and have, unless they have means to."

"Did you ever hear Lizzie speak of any trouble she'd had with her mother?"

"Yes, I suppose I have. I have heard her say that Mrs. Borden thought so and so; the same as any family. The whole thing was, as far as I could see, that an own mother might have had more influence over the father. It was the father more than the mother."

"What do you mean?"

"The father was the head of the house. They had to do as he thought. Mrs. Borden did not control the house. The whole summing up of it was that."

Hannah Gifford, cloak maker, said that she'd heard Lizzie speak ill of Abby.

"What have you heard Lizzie say?"

"Well, she called her mother 'a mean old thing.'"

"When was that?"

"That was this spring when I was doing work for them."

"How came she to say that?"

"It was some remark I made about her mother's garment, what would be becoming for her. You know Mrs. Borden was very fleshy; I spoke to Lizzie of what I thought would be becoming to Mrs. Borden. She says, 'Well she is a mean, good for nothing old thing.' I says, 'Oh, you don't say that Lizzie?' She says, 'Yes, and we don't have anything to do with her, only what we are obliged to,' she says."

"Anything more?"

"Well, she says, 'We stay upstairs most of the time; we stay in our room most of the time.' I says, 'You do, don't you go to your meals?' 'Yes, we go to our meals, but we don't always eat with the family. Sometimes we wait until they are through,' she says."

"Did she tell you why?"

"No. That is all she said. I did not say anything more. I was awfully surprised to hear her."

Last to appear were the druggist, Eli Bence, clerk Frederick Hart, and a witness in the drug store, Frank Kilroy.

Bence said that he had worked at D. R. Smith drug store for more than three years. Lizzie, he said, had asked him the day before the murders if his shop kept prussic acid. When he confirmed that they did, "she asked me if she could buy ten cents worth of me. I informed her we did not sell prussic acid unless by a physician's prescription. She then said that she had bought this several times. I says, 'well my good lady, it is something we don't sell unless by a prescription from the doctor, as it is a very dangerous thing to handle.' She then walked around, and went out, turned right around."

"Did she say what she wanted it for?"

"I understood her to say she wanted it to put on the edge of a seal skin cape."

"Did you then know who it was?"

"I knew her as a Miss Borden; I have known her for some time as a Miss Borden, but not as Andrew J. Borden's daughter until that morning. One of the gentlemen who was sitting there, when she turned around and went out, he says, 'That is Andrew J. Borden's daughter.'"

"What time of day was this?"

"I should say between ten and half past eleven, somewhere."

"On the night of the murders, did you go to the house?"

"I did, yes, sir."

"Did you there see Lizzie Borden?"

"I did, yes, sir."

"Where was she when you saw her?"

"In the kitchen, talking with Officer Harrington."

"Did you recognize her as the one that you had had the talk with the day before?"

"I did, Yes, sir."

"Positively?"

"I don't think I could be mistaken."

Frank Kilroy, a medical student, happened to be in D. R. Smith's drug store the day before the murders and had been talking with Eli Bence when Lizzie approached and asked for prussic acid. He did not know Lizzie personally but could recognize her, he said, and confirmed that it was Lizzie who tried to buy prussic acid.

"You feel sure that you know who she is?" asked Knowlton.

"Well, I think so," Frank replied.

Frederick Hart, clerk at D. R. Smith's drug store, testified that he also saw the woman attempting to buy prussic acid.

He did not know Lizzie Borden, he said, but the woman who tried to buy prussic acid looked like the one whose picture had since appeared in the papers.

After his testimony, it happened that when he walked out Miss Lizzie walked past him, escorted by the marshal. Knowlton recalled Frederick Hart.

"Did you see the lady that was in custody, in company with the Marshal, as you went out?"

"In black, yes, sir."

"Is that the woman?"

"That is the woman."

"You don't think you can be mistaken?"

"I don't think I can be mistaken."

The inquest closed and still the police did not allow Lizzie to leave. She waited, collapsed on the lounge in the matron's room. Emma consoled her and Jennings paced.

Judge Blaisdell, Prosecutor Knowlton, and Marshal Hilliard remained in the courtroom, discussing the evidence.

Hilliard wanted to arrest Lizzie. "She could not tell a clear story of where she was because she could not tell the truth. Because she's done the crimes."

Knowlton was more circumspect. "I cannot explain how she could commit these murders and not be marked with blood, but at minimum she has guilty knowledge and may have assisted the killer or killers. She should be arrested now. We can continue our investigations and may learn more after."

Marshal Hilliard finally appeared in the matron's room. "I have a warrant for your arrest—issued by the judge of the District Court," he said to Lizzie, and offered to read the warrant.

Jennings suggested Lizzie waive that right. She began to tremble. "You need not read it," she said, and collapsed into such a fit of sobbing and vomiting that they called Dr. Bowen.

Newsboys already shouted headlines of Lizzie's arrest outside the station windows as Bowen guided Lizzie to the bed.

The next day the police moved Lizzie to the women's section of the Bristol County Jail in Taunton, more than thirty minutes from Fall River, under the supervision of Sheriff Wright. By coincidence, the Sheriff's wife had lived near the Bordens decades before. Little Lizzie had played with Mrs. Wright's daughter.

Lizzie's dark, damp, and chilly cell was little more than seven feet square. Mrs. Wright prepared the cell with a few comforts not available to the other prisoners, including a softer pillow that belonged to Mrs. Wright herself and some "bright bits of color." Elderly Mrs. Wright cried and said, "Oh, Lizzie, Lizzie," when Lizzie arrived at the jail.

An account in the *Boston Post* of Lizzie as a child, around the time when she knew Mrs. Wright, described Lizzie as, "intelligent, but grave beyond her years."

The marshal and prosecutor allowed Bridget Sullivan to leave the Borden house and move into a friend's house in Fall River.

CHAPTER 14

In spite of Lizzie's arrest, the police continued inquiring into other suspects. Bridget was questioned again, repeatedly. John Morse was arrested but then released on bail. Neither the police nor prosecutor Knowlton believed either was innocent.

Reverend Buck gave an interview to the papers, addressing Lizzie's seeming unnatural calm in some moments that many said could only be explained as murderous indifference or insanity. Buck said, "She retains the same Christian spirit of resignation as at the onset, and her calmness is the calmness of innocence."

Jennings read the inquest transcripts and shared Lizzie's testimony with Emma. That testimony created a dire situation.

One morning when the matron let Jennings in he found Lizzie and Emma sitting silently, facing away from each other on the bed in Lizzie's cramped cell. They seemed to have been arguing.

The general coldness and sometimes contentiousness among the Borden women always surprised Jennings. Maybe they'd been discussing him again, as when he'd overheard them in the kitchen the day after the murders. He could not stop them from resenting him and the help he'd had from Andrew. Their father would have dedicated energy and influence to their successes as well, Jennings was certain, if the Borden girls had been boys.

They both turned as he said, "The preliminary hearing is in two weeks," he said. "It is not a jury trial. A single judge presides and considers evidence presented by Prosecutor Knowlton. The judge alone will decide whether there is sufficient evidence that Lizzie be bound over. We can put forward a defense case. The judge is a judge you already know from the inquest, Judge Blaisdell."

"Then it will never be fair," said Lizzie. "He will be against me from the start."

"I argued against it. In my view it is improper. He overruled my objection."

"Of course," said Lizzie.

Emma sighed. "Can you represent Lizzie in that hearing?"

"I will serve, but need help. Do I have your leave to hire the best legal counsel I can, regardless of cost?"

Lizzie started to speak but Emma interrupted. "Of course."

Lizzie gazed out the window. "How long will the trial take?"

"That depends on the evidence the prosecutor presents. Perhaps a week."

"If the judge decides I'm guilty?"

"The judge will only determine if you are probably guilty. The standard of 'innocent until proven guilty' is not the basis of his decision in a preliminary hearing. If he does find you probably guilty, he will refer your case to the grand jury. You might be formally indicted for one or both murders and go to criminal trial."

"And if I'm found guilty at criminal trial?"

"The penalty is death by hanging."

Two societies at Lizzie's church published statements supporting Lizzie in local papers, hoping the messages would reach the people of Fall River and also Lizzie in jail.

"We the members of the Young People's Society of Christian Endeavor, desire to express to our fellow member, Miss Lizzie A.

Borden, our sincere sympathy with her in her present hour of trial, and our confident belief that she will soon be restored to her former place of usefulness among us," said one.

The Women's Christian Temperance Union also declared their, "unshaken faith in her as a fellow worker and sister tenderly beloved, and would assure her of our constant earnest prayers that she may be supported under the unprecedented trials and sorrows now resting upon her."

Soon Knowlton was receiving correspondences from the public about the Borden case. Some were from self-proclaimed witnesses who hadn't yet been questioned. Others conveyed messages from the dead — mediumship and seances were popular at the time.

He sent officers, where possible and reasonable, to follow up, and saved every letter.

"Attorney Knowlton,

It appears to me that you are somewhat dazed in regard to the Borden murder but to me it is one of the plainest cases I have ever read of.

I get this from a dream I had Sunday night, why you found so little blood, it was wiped up with cloths which are hid on premises.

I am of the opinion of the Pastor which said the murders must be a fiend incarnate and from Lizzie's face I read that she is deep as the bottomless pit."

—Unsigned, from Providence, Rhode Island

"Dear Sir,

I don't know as what I am about to say will be of any use to you as I am a spiritualist and believe in the communications of the dead. I get it there is a closet at the end of the sofa upon which Mr. Borden lay and in that closet was a man secreted and committed the murderous act.

Yours most respectfully,
Delia Wilson"

"HOTEL KENMORE
Albany N.Y.

District Atty. Knowlton
Dear Sir -
Feeling quite safe from all possible arrest, I write you This information regarding the Fall River Mystery. The Killing of old man Bordon and his wife was not perpertrated by any immediate member of his family. But they were put out of the way by an illigitimate Son whom Bordon refused to recognize after the Mother of his off-spring died a number of years ago in a certain Insane Asylum of a Broken heart. That son is now twenty five years of age.

When he reached his age he went to Bordon and demanded recognition and some part of an understanding and mutually agreed to a certain contract. Through the influence of his Wife who disliked the said son, Bordon was persuaded to renounce his obligations & promises.

The son Brooded over his and his mothers past troubles and resolved upon Vengeance, with the result known to all. The girl is entirely innocent and it is only that justice may be done her that I write this otherwise I would not have written for I fairly hate the Bordon name.

And the illegitimate who took the revenge is the Writer of this confession. No use to track me for it will be an utter impossibility to do so.

- Yours Truly, Phillip Gordon Reed"

Some of Lizzie's friends spoke to the *Boston Daily Globe*.

"A great deal is said about her coolness now," said one, unnamed.

"That's exactly like her. Why, at the church sociable last winter, when a dumbwaiter fell on her wrists—it was a heavy dumbwaiter filled full of dishes, so heavy that it took a strong man to lift it off her arms where it had fallen and pinned them under it—instead of screaming or fainting or doing anything that any other woman but Lizzie Borden would have done, she merely said in a low voice, 'Will someone come here?'"

Another described Lizzie as "a monument of straightforwardness. I shall never believe, even were she convicted of the deed, that she committed it unless she were to confess herself, and then the marvel would be greater to me that she had concealed her act than that she did it. That is her character. If she had a reason sufficient for herself for murdering those people, it would be like her to say she did it and give her reason."

On August 18, Charles Peckham of South Westport confessed to the killing of Andrew Borden. The police quickly determined that Mr. Peckham had a history of "crazy spells" and his wife and neighbors confirmed that Mr. Peckham had been home on August 4. The authorities released him to his wife.

Jennings hired Melvin O. Adams, a former prosecutor and prominent Boston criminal defense attorney, for Lizzie's defense team.

Adams was of medium height and build and was known to be strategic in his questioning of witnesses but also genial and fair.

On the news that Adams had joined the defense team, *The Boston Globe* wrote, "Adams has brought into the Borden case talent and experience sufficient to do battle with even so distinguished an advocate as Attorney-General A. E. Pillsbury, who, in the event of retaining his present office, will probably prosecute Lizzie."

On August 19, Emma received a post letter and contacted Jennings.

"Waltham, Mass., Aug. 17, 1892.

Miss Emma Borden:

You must excuse that I take the liberty in sending you these few lines. My name is Samuel Robinsky. I am a Jewish pedler. When the fatal murder in Fall River occurred I was only a few miles from Fall River. While sitting on the roadside towards New Bedford, I met a man who was covered with blood. He told me that he worked on a farm and that he never could get his wages, so he had a fight with the farmer.

I helped him to fix up again and get cleaned, but by this time I did not know anything about the murder.

If I should see him in Boston, I am dead sure I know him again. He is of medium height, dark brown hair, reddish whiskers, weight about 135 pounds, a gray suit, brown derby hat.

If I come again to Fall River next week I shall call on you. If this man was the murderer I cannot say, but I shall find him out of fifteen thousand.

Hoping that my information may be of some use to you,

I remain very respectfully,

Samuel Robinsky"

Jennings sent a telegram to the mayor of Waltham, Massachusetts, asking him and the Waltham police to find Samuel Robinsky.

They replied the next day:

"Waltham, Mass., Aug., 20, 1892:

To Andrew J. Jennings, Fall River. Cannot find that he lives here. Am told that a peddler of that name is living in Boston, and sometimes comes out here. Signed, G. L. Mayberry."

This, Jennings believed, confirmed that peddler Robinsky existed.

Adams published the letter in the papers, both to increase the odds of finding Robinsky and to show the public that there were suspects other than Lizzie.

Knowlton dispatched Officer Medley to find Robinsky.

. . .

Bridget Sullivan received a subpoena to appear as a witness at the preliminary hearing in three weeks. She'd left town in the meantime and no longer had anywhere local to stay.

She told the prosecution she did not want to return, and, "I think it will be hard for me to get a place, for no one wants to hire a person for one month."

Knowlton and Hilliard made arrangements for her to stay, free of charge, at the women's jail in New Bedford.

CHAPTER 15

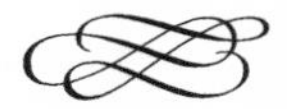

Lizzie was back at the Fall River jail for the preliminary hearing. She stayed in the matron's quarters rather than a cell.

Reverend Buck visited daily. He brought books for her to read and sat with her. They prayed.

Lizzie did not laugh so easily as usual in jail, but her spirits were high. "This will all be over soon," she assured him. "I look forward to exoneration. There is plenty of time for this hearing to resolve before I'm needed for holiday work with the church."

Emma cooked meals for Lizzie. Alice Russell did not visit, but other friends, including Mrs. Holmes and Lizzie's childhood friend Mary Brigham, came almost every afternoon.

One afternoon when all the ladies were there and Lizzie told how she could picture being free soon, Mrs. Reagan, the women's matron, said lightheartedly, "I can tell you one thing you can't do."

Lizzie said, "Tell me what it is, Mrs. Reagan."

"Break an egg, Miss Borden."

"Break an egg?"

"Yes."

"Well,“ said Lizzie. "I can certainly break an egg."

"Not the way I would tell you to break it."

Mrs. Reagan challenged Lizzie to a bet. For one dollar, Mrs. Reagan wagered that Lizzie could not crush the egg.

Lizzie agreed, but said, "I cannot afford a dollar. I must pay lawyers." Everyone laughed with her. "I'll wager twenty-five cents."

They agreed and someone fetched a fresh egg from the jailhouse kitchen.

Lizzie stood and Mrs. Reagan placed the egg, lengthwise, between Lizzie's facing palms. "You'd best get a little ways away, Miss Emma," said Mrs. Reagan, "because if she breaks it the wrong way it will destroy your dress."

Lizzie pressed her palms together first gently and then with as much force as she could. The egg did not break. The ladies remarked with amazement at Mrs. Reagan's trick.

"That is the first thing," said Lizzie, "that I undertook to do that I never could."

Everyone burst into laughter. No one seemed concerned about the hearing.

The hearing began on Thursday, August 25, exactly three weeks after the murders. It included witnesses from the inquest who appeared again and gave the same testimony.

This time, though, it was a public hearing. The public and press had their first chance to personally witness and report on testimony and evidence.

Some people who waited in line from the wee hours obtained gallery seats. Most who were not press had come to support Lizzie.

The court officers assembled while more than forty members of the press waited with eager pencils to capture newly revealed details. Most of what the police knew the public already knew from published reports, but this hearing promised more.

Silence fell as Lizzie walked in, wearing a dark blue dress with red trimmings. She appeared calm, as she would for most of the hearing. Emma and Reverend Buck sat near her, along with Mrs. Holmes, who had attended her on the day of the murders, and Mary Brigham.

. . .

"It was the most ghastly thing I have ever seen," Medical Examiner Dolan testified, about seeing Mr. Borden's body. He went on to describe sharp wounds, inches long.

Many members of the gallery grimaced but Lizzie did not react.

Dolan said that "a person, with a hatchet four or five pounds, an ordinary individual, could very easily cause the fractures."

Mr. Borden had eleven gashes. The murderer likely stood at the head of the sofa while Mr. Borden slept, and attacked from above and behind his head, perhaps standing some in the dining room.

Abby's eighteen wounds were mostly in the right and rear of her head, shoulders, and back. The killer stood astride Abby's hips as she lay face down on the floor.

There were two wounds from the front that would have been the first. One, shallow, had deflected from her skull and left a non-fatal skin flap above Abby's left ear. The second cut deeper. After these two, apparently, Abby had spun around and fallen forward. The murderer could not have avoided blood spatter from the feet up to their waist when killing Abby, he said.

"I should say that she died from an hour to an hour and a half before Mr. Borden, based upon the clotted, black condition of the blood around her head." That would place Abby's time of death at nine thirty or ten, compared to eleven for Andrew.

Buck grimaced and shifted in his seat while Lizzie listened with attention but also with what *The New York Times* described as a "strange calmness." She did not seem disturbed by the details of the crimes or autopsies.

Dolan said he had taken two samples of milk from the house, sealed them in jars, and sent them to Dr. Wood to determine whether they contained poison.

Adams asked about Lizzie's clothes. "Did you examine those?"

"Yes, sir."

"Did you find some blood on them?"

"One blood spot on the skirt."

"How big was it?"

"The size of a good pin head."

"That is on the white underskirt?"

"Yes, sir."

"Do you know whether it came from without or from inside?"

"From without. The meshes of the cloth on the outside were filled with blood, and it had hardly penetrated on the inside."

"How far up from the bottom of the skirt?"

"Probably a foot."

Other questioning of Dr. Dolan by the defense was more contentious, challenging Dolan's competence. They'd come prepared.

"Did you take minutes at that time, there at the house?" asked Adams.

"Yes, sir."

"In a book?"

"No, sir."

"What did you take them in?"

"On slips of paper."

"Where are those slips of paper?"

"I could not tell you where they are."

"The records of this important case," said Adams, "your original notes which the statute obliges you to take, what did you do with them?"

"That is putting a great big cover over it. The records of this great case are not lost, and have not been mislaid or misplaced."

"Does not the statute say you shall make minutes at the time of your view?"

"Yes, sir."

"Did you make minutes?"

"Yes, sir, I said I had."

"Where did you take them?"

"I took them in the house."

"Did you destroy them?"

"I could not tell you what I did with them."

"Can you tell me whether you destroyed them, or not?"

"I cannot. The last I saw of them they were in my pocket book, my case book."

"Have you your case book here?"

"Yes, sir."

"Are they in there?"

"No, sir."

"Do you also, understand," continued Adams, "that under the statue you are directed to file a report of your autopsy with the District Attorney and with the Justice of the District Court?"

"Yes, sir," replied Dolan.

"And that the public have access to it?"

"I do not know anything about that part of it."

"Have you filed a copy of the second autopsy record with the Justice?"

"No, sir."

Jennings took over, and showed the autopsy report that Dolan had created, from August 4, to Dolan.

"Now, Mr. Dolan is that your signature?"

"Yes, sir."

"And is that your report of the autopsy?"

"A partial autopsy."

"Does it say 'partial' anywhere?"

"No, sir."

"Where does the word 'partial' come in?"

"Because it was partial," replied Dolan.

"Does it say partial record or partial autopsy?"

"I say it is partial."

"Does this say so?"

"If it is there, I think you would see it."

Not only did Dolan squirm in his seat, but much of the gallery did as well. Only the press delighted in the exchange. Lizzie seemed bored.

Adams took over to address the second autopsies performed in the holding vault at Oak Grove Cemetery. Adams knew right where to lead Dolan.

"Have those bodies been interred?"

"Yes sir."

"You've removed samples from the bodies. Did you remove anything else from those bodies, either of them?" Adams waited, as if merely curious.

Dolan plunged forward, oblivious to the danger. "Yes sir, I removed the skulls, the heads."

The gallery spectators' heads popped up. Lizzie looked up in surprise.

"The skulls?" Adams appreciated the collective gasp in the courtroom.

"Yes sir."

"When?"

"The day of the autopsy."

"For what purpose?"

"Because I was instructed so to do."

"By whom?"

"By the Attorney General."

"He told you to remove the skulls?"

"Yes sir."

Adams paused. The pencil scratches of the reporters filled the otherwise silent courtroom.

"What do you do with them?"

"I cleaned them." Dolan had boiled the heads to remove the flesh.

"Do you mean to say these bodies are now buried without the heads?"

"Yes, sir."

"Where are these skulls?"

"At my office."

Dr. Dolan recoiled at the revolted faces directed at him from the gallery.

CHAPTER 16

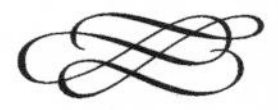

During the day an account appeared in the newspapers, attributed to matron Hannah Reagan at the police station. Mrs. Reagan was cleaning the toilet room, said the report, when she overheard Lizzie and Emma talking.

"You gave me away, Emma, didn't you?" said Lizzie.

"No, Lizzie, I only told Jennings what I thought he ought to know for your defense," Emma said.

"That is false and I know it," said Lizzie. "But remember I will never give in one inch. Never!"

The conversation had allegedly taken place on Wednesday, August 24, the previous day. Lizzie's detractors saw confirmation of her guilt and her supporters saw yet another defaming false report. Under pressure, Mrs. Reagan denied having spoken to the reporter.

Knowlton called witnesses to establish Andrew Borden's movements downtown on the morning of his death. Andrew had not looked well when he went to the post office after nine, then Union Savings Bank at half past, and National Union Bank shortly after that. After the banks, he was at Hats and Gents, Furnishing Goods, and then a retail space under construction in the A. J. Borden building.

Between ten thirty and ten forty-five he walked toward home.

The prosecution also called witnesses showing that there was someone in and around every house surrounding the Borden house on the morning of the murders.

John Morse repeated his accounts of the day before and morning of the murders.

Then he said, "I went particularly over there on Wednesday to see about some cattle I bought of him. I thought I would make arrangements to take them."

"How did you find Mr. Borden's health that day?"

"He was sick, indisposed, laying on the lounge."

"How did Mrs. Borden appear to you?"

"About the same."

"Did she say who was sick?"

"She said Mr. Borden, and Miss Lizzie, and herself."

"Did she say whether Lizzie had been up there in her room the morning or not?"

"Yes, sir."

"At any time had you had any talk with Mr. Borden about his farm, about giving that away?"

"Yes, sir. That was some time in May of this year. We were riding over by his place, we got to speaking about the Old Ladies' Home, you know. He says, 'I would give them some land here, if I thought they would accept it,' something to that effect."

The Fall River Herald summarized the day's testimony with their headlines:

"HEADLESS TRUNKS
Of the Victims of the Tragedy
PLACED IN THE GRAVES AT OAK GROVE.
Dr. Dolan Creates a Mild Sensation Today
BY TELLING THAT THE HEADS HAD BEEN REMOVED.

Unimportant Testimony Given by John V. Morse"

The next day Bridget gave substantially the same testimony she had at the inquest. Knowlton did not ask her whether she'd seen problems in the Borden family. Bridget could not have answered honestly if she had, because to tell private affairs of the family she served would mean never finding similar work again. She'd have denied problems either way.

Adams asked her about break-ins in the house and barn. "Since you have been there, that house has been broken into?"

"Yes, sir."

"And entered in broad daylight?"

"Yes, sir."

"Money and a gold watch, and things taken?"

"So they said."

"You were at home that day?"

"Yes, sir."

"Where were you?"

"Doing my work."

"You did not see anybody come in or go out?"

"No, sir."

"How long ago was that?"

"A year last July, I guess." That was thirteen months before.

"Since that time the barn has also been broken into?"

"Yes, sir."

The Boston Herald characterized Lizzie's lack of reactions in court.

> "There is nothing about this Fall River investigation to our minds more astonishing — not to say more abnormal — than the impassive coolness of the woman who is charged with the murder. No one has been calmer than this person who is more nearly affected by it than any other. It would be astonishing in a man of the strongest nerve and the most unlimited control of self; in a woman not very far past the age of

> girlhood it is so amazing as to seem incredible were not the facts before the public eye. There is nothing that tends more to induce the belief of insanity in the case than this most extraordinary exhibition."

The hearing resumed the next week with Alice Russell recounting the events at the Borden house on the morning of the murders.

Eli Bence, druggist, spoke next about prussic acid. Lizzie watched intently.

Knowlton asked, "Did you see Miss Lizzie Borden in your store at any time before the tragedy?"

"I did, yes, sir."

"When?"

"I saw her the day before." He told how she had requested, and been refused, prussic acid.

"Is this defendant the woman?"

"Yes, sir."

"Are you sure?"

"Positive."

Bence also told of going to the Borden house the evening of the murders.

Adams sought to shake Bence's account. "Where did you see her?"

"She was in the kitchen. I stood in the doorway. Officer Harrington spoke to her. I know it was the same voice I heard in the shop."

"Do you claim to have a particularly sensitive or educated ear for sounds?"

"Well, I do not know as I do."

"What was the peculiarity about this voice?"

"The peculiarity was in the way that she spoke; it was kind of—a little tremulous."

"It was tremulous when?"

"When she spoke to me for the acid."

"It trembled when she answered Harrington, did not it?"

"Yes, sir."

"The same tremor in it?"

"I should say it was."

"Before that morning, had you seen this lady, you said was Miss Borden?"

"I had seen the lady quite often before, and had her pointed out to me before as Miss Borden a good many times."

"How was she dressed the day she tried to buy prussic acid?"

"She had on a dark dress, that is all I could tell you."

"Dark blue or brown?"

"I could not tell you the color, only it was dark."

"Did she wear gloves?"

"I could not say."

"Did she have a purse in her hand?"

"I could not say."

"Did she have on a hat or a bonnet?"

"I do not know the distinction between a hat and bonnet, hardly."

Adams gestured to Lizzie. "Do you see what she has on now?"

"Yes, sir."

"Was it anything like that?"

"I could not say."

"Was it shaped like that?"

"I could not say."

"Did it have any feathers, or anything of that sort for trimming?"

"I could not say."

"Did she wear a veil?"

"I could not say."

Frank Kilroy, medical student, and Frederick Harte, drug clerk, testified in agreement with Bence's account of Lizzie attempting to buy prussic acid. They also identified Lizzie Borden as the woman they'd seen.

Officers who'd been at the Borden house the day of the murders appeared. Officer Mullaly's testimony did not start well.

Knowlton asked, "Where was Miss Borden when you saw her?"

Mullaly did not seem to know which room they were in, and hesitated. "Miss Borden was in the room north of where Mr. Borden laid on the sofa."

There was only one room to the north of the sitting room. Knowlton tried to help. "Was there a dining table in it?"

"I did not notice," said Mullaly.

Knowlton pushed on, for fear of letting that statement sink in. "Did you have any talk with her?"

"Yes, I did. She told me she had been out of doors, and when she came in she found her father dead on the sofa. Otherwise, she had not much to share."

Assistant Marshal Fleet described his actions and interviews at the house.

Knowlton asked him about Lizzie's demeanor. "At any of the time was she in tears?"

"Not any time."

Officer Harrington said that he asked Lizzie for help regarding the crime. "I asked her if she could tell me anything about this crime. She said, 'nothing.' She was cool and collected, and stood erect without any support at all."

Dr. Wood, Harvard physician and chemist, spoke to his analysis of the stomach contents and milk samples.

"To the best of my opinion," said Wood, "Mrs. Borden's death was in the neighborhood of an hour and a half or two hours before Mr. Borden's." He'd based his analysis on the state of digestion. That would place Abby's death between nine and nine thirty that morning.

Wood saw no evidence of prussic acid or other poison in the stomachs. "I found that both stomachs were perfectly natural in appearance," he said. He had not yet tested the milk samples.

The red spots on the four hatchets and axes he had tested turned out to be rust or other substances that were not blood. The gray hair on one came from a cow. He had not yet tested the handleless hatchet.

The small drop of blood, the size of a pin head on Lizzie's under skirt, was the only blood he found on her clothing.

Adams asked, "Would you not think it would be natural and probable that the assailant would receive more blood upon his person and clothes."

"I should say it was impossible for him not to."

"Standing as you imagine those blows must have been given, the blood would hit what portion of the assailant's body?"

"For Mr. Borden, anywhere from the knees up."

"Regarding Mrs. Borden, would it be possible for the assailant to deliver those blows without getting spattered with blood?"

"I should think not."

Judge Blaisdell added a question of his own. "Is it easy to efface blood stains from a hatchet, or the handle of a hatchet, with water, when they are fresh, so that there would be no indication of the stain left?"

"Oh, certainly," replied Dr. Wood. "It is possible to wash it off."

The Woodsocket Call published a recollection from one of Lizzie's former teachers:

"SAYS SHE IS INNOCENT

A Former Teacher of Lizzie Borden Speaks About Her Case.

> Mr. Horace Benson, at one time a successful teacher here, was in the city Saturday. Mr. Benson knew the family when Lizzie was one of his former pupils.
>
> As a pupil, he said, she was an average scholar, neither being exceptionally smart nor noticeably dull. She was subject to varying moods, and was never fond of her stepmother. She had no hesitation in talking about her stepmother.
>
> Mr. Benson became acquainted with Mrs. Borden, whom he grew to know as a kindly hearted, lovable woman, who tried, but ineffectually, to win the love of her stepdaughters. Still the household was far from being an unhappy one.
>
> When asked if he believed that Lizzie committed the murder, he replied quickly and emphatically, 'No, I do not. It is impossible. I

believe that she is innocent and her innocence will soon be established.'"

Now that she was the defendant, Knowlton could not compel Lizzie to take the stand. Instead, the clerk read Lizzie's inquest testimony into the record. The newspapers published it word-for-word.

Members of the public learned for the first time the testimony that had resulted in Lizzie's arrest. So did Lizzie's allies, including Reverend Buck. Lizzie's testimony did not help her case, Buck thought, but was hardly proof of any crimes.

Buck patted Lizzie's hand reassuringly. She turned and nodded at him, and did not seem much upset.

CHAPTER 17

Jennings and Adams presented eleven witnesses for the defense, with a primary strategy of showing that someone other than Lizzie could have committed the crimes.

John Donnelly, hack driver, went into the Borden barn that morning, after the murders, and saw a round impression in the hay pile, he said, as though somebody had slept there. Alfred Clarkson, a steam engineer, said the same. "It looked as though a man had laid there," he said.

Dr. Benjamin Handy, a Fall River physician and surgeon for more than twenty years, happened to drive past the Borden house twice on the morning of the murders and saw a strange man on the sidewalk south of Dr. Kelly's house next door. "He turned partially around several times while I was going by," said Handy. "He did not turn clear around. He seemed to be moving or turning or vacillating."

Jennings asked, "Did he appear to be drunk?"

"No, sir."

Handy did not know the man, but had seen him a few days previously, also on Second Street. None of the neighborhood men the police introduced Handy to were the man he'd seen.

Miss Delia Manley saw a man standing at the Borden's gate the morning of the murders.

Jennings asked, "What was this man doing?"

"He did not seem to be doing anything, only standing in the gateway."

"Stand up, please, Mr. Morse." John stood.

"Was that the man?" asked Jennings.

"No, sir."

"A younger man than he?"

"I should say it was."

"Did you leave him there when you went away?"

"I did."

"Did you ever see this man before to your knowledge?"

"No, sir, I did not."

"That you say was about what time?"

"Quarter or ten minutes of ten."

Mrs. Marienne Chagnon and her daughter, Martha, neighbors behind the Borden house, had heard a noise near the Borden fence the night before the murders. "It seemed to me it was like somebody jumping on the fence," Marienne said.

"It frightened you both?"

"Yes, sir."

Charles Sawyer, who'd been deputized to guard the Borden side door, testified to seeing Lizzie in the kitchen when he first arrived.

Jennings asked, "How near did you go to her?"

"I went within probably about three feet from her."

"Did you see any signs of blood on her?"

"No, sir."

"Was her hair disarranged at all?"

"No, sir."

"Did you see any blood on her dress, or any signs of anything of that kind?"

"No, sir, nothing."

Dr. Bowen's wife, Phebe, also told of seeing Lizzie that day. "She was sitting in the rocking chair in the kitchen," she said.

"How near did you go to her?" asked Jennings.

"I stood directly in front of her. Miss Russell was fanning her with a newspaper."

"Did she appear agitated?"

"She had her eyes closed, and her head on Miss Russell's shoulder. I thought perhaps she was faint. Miss Russell asked me to wet the end of the towel, as she was bathing Miss Lizzie's face."

"Did you see any signs of blood on the towel after Miss Russell had bathed her face?"

"No, sir."

"Did you see any blood on her hands?"

"No, sir."

"You saw her hair; was that disarranged, or not?"

"Not at all."

"How about her clothing, any spots of blood on it?"

"I saw none."

Lizzie did not testify in her own defense. Phebe Bowen was the last witness.

When Jennings addressed Judge Blaisdell for closing statements, he sought to convince the press and public, as well as the judge, of Lizzie's innocence. "May it please Your Honor, this complaint upon which you have to pass today, alleges that on the 4th of August last Andrew J. Borden was murdered by his daughter Lizzie."

Abby's murder was apparently not worth mentioning.

"Upon the decision of Your Honor will rest the liberty and good name of this young woman.

"There is no doubt that Andrew J. Borden was murdered in his house. We have had a description of the injuries." Jennings gestured at the prosecution. "I suggest that even the learned District Attorney himself cannot imagine that any person could have committed that crime unless his heart was as black with hatred as hell itself. Blow after blow was showered upon Mr. and Mrs. Borden both, cutting through blood, bone, and flesh into the very brain. Not one, not two, but in the case of the woman, eighteen. There is an unnecessary brutality about this that suggests nothing but insanity or brutal hatred."

The gallery and court, always attentive to Miss Lizzie, saw something they'd not seen before. Lizzie began, slowly at first, to cry. Her lip trembled and tears dropped from her eyes. That thing she'd lacked on the day of the murders, and which turned the police against her from the start, was there for all to see.

"The Commonwealth seems to have made up its mind," Jennings continued, "that the crime was committed by someone in that house.

"They say no one could get out on the south or east because neighbors are there. You have Mrs. Churchill on the north and others on the west.

"Now, what is the fact? They know that the house has been burglarized and the barn broken into. And Crowe's men, to the east, didn't see the officer climb the fence either.

"You know that Mrs. Manley saw a man standing at that gate. The police have had I don't know how many men in this case, but they never found this man. They never found the man Dr. Handy saw.

"Mr. John Morse appears to have satisfactorily accounted for his time, and that brings us to two parties, Bridget Sullivan and Lizzie Borden.

"In the natural course of things who would be the party to be suspected? Would it be the stranger, or would it be the one bound to the murdered man by ties of love?"

Lizzie bit her lip and covered her face with the handkerchief.

Jennings said, "I do not wish to be misunderstood. I do not believe that Bridget Sullivan committed that murder any more than I believe Lizzie Borden did.

"But why don't the District Attorney make Bridget Sullivan explain herself? Does it take her twenty minutes to wash the upper part of one window? Why isn't she questioned regarding every second as Lizzie Borden was?

"Mind you, I don't say Bridget Sullivan did it. I distinctly state she did not, but I call attention to these points.

"I consider the inquisition of the girl, Lizzie, at the inquest, an outrage. Here was a girl they had been suspecting for days. She was virtually under arrest, and yet for the purpose of extracting a confession from her to support their theory, they brought her here and put her upon the rack, a thing they knew they would have no right to do if they placed her under arrest."

Jennings had debated the risks, with Adams, of alienating Judge Blaisdell by including that point in the closing. Blaisdell himself, along with Knowlton, had required Lizzie to appear at the inquest without counsel. Jennings and Adams had decided it was better to get the concern on the record.

"As in the days of the rack and thumb screws, so she was racked mentally again and again. Day after day the same questions were repeated to her in the hope to elicit some information that would criminate her. Is it a wonder there are conflicting statements?

"About her whereabouts at the time her father came in, she first says she is upstairs. Then she says she is downstairs, and sticks to that. I submit that, if she was on the stairs when Bridget opened the door to let Mr. Borden in and laughed, as Bridget says she did, she must have been insane, and was insane at the time of the commission of the crime.

"She says she went out in the yard, and into the barn. She goes into the barn and looks for this lead. Is there anything improbable or unreasonable in this?

"Then she comes in and finds her father." He gestured to Lizzie, whose face was wet. "Is she the calm, collected being who hasn't been moved by this?

"Has there been a motive shown here? No, only that five years ago something happened. It was as a result of Mr. Borden's giving his wife's stepsister a residence, and the girls said they thought their father ought to have done as much as that for them. After that Lizzie called her Mrs. Borden.

"And yet to get the motive they've got to say that without hatred, bitterness or previous quarrel, she murders him to get possession of the money which, in the natural course of events would be hers within a few years.

"They say an attempted purchase of prussic acid by Lizzie Borden shows she was going to do some deadly deed. If there is one thing which is weakest in criminal cases it is the matter of mistaken identity.

"These three persons say it was Lizzie Borden who went into that store and attempted to buy prussic acid. None of them knows her, but all three assert it is she.

"Lizzie Borden declares that she never left her home Wednesday morning, and by a special providence, which seems to have watched over us in parts of this case, her words are corroborated by the dead woman who told John Morse that Lizzie had been sick in her room and had not left the house.

"I don't mean to say that these young men meant to tell anything untrue, but in the light of these facts was it Lizzie Borden who entered that drug store and attempted to purchase prussic acid, or was it some person who looked like her?

"Now let us look at other evidence in the case. This girl has got at most ten to fifteen minutes to commit the crime and conceal the weapon. If she had on an apron, where is the apron? The dress, the shoes she had on that morning. Are there any shoe buttons found in the fire? Is there any smell of burnt clothing? No!

"Day after day, hour after hour they have searched and examined, and the only thing they produced was those hatchets, which Professor Wood says contained no blood.

"They haven't proved that this girl had anything to do with the murder! They can't find any blood on her! They can't find any motive! They can't find the axe and so I say I demand the woman's release!

"Don't, Your Honor, when they don't show an incriminating circumstance, don't put the stigma of guilt upon this woman, reared as she has been and with a past character beyond reproach. Don't let it go out in the world as the decision of a just judge that she is probably guilty. God grant Your Honor wisdom to decide, and, while you do your duty, do it as God tells you to do it, giving to the accused the benefit of the doubt."

The courtroom applauded Jennings' closing. Mayor Coughlin and Medical Examiner Dolan shook his hand. Reverend Buck heaved heavy sighs, as if he might faint. Lizzie sniffled and seemed relieved. The court adjourned for the noon break.

CHAPTER 18

"I can fully appreciate Your Honor's feelings, now that the end of this hearing is about to be reached. The crime of murder touches the deepest sensibilities of feeling," Knowlton began as he summarized the case against Lizzie Borden for Judge Blaisdell.

"While it was not a pleasant summons that came to me, the almost despairing cry that came to me, I should not have been true to duty if I had not undertaken to ferret out the criminal. The murdered man's daughter was arrested. I perfectly understood the surprise and indignation that started up.

"That domestic and honorable lady, Abby Borden, was absolutely without harsh feelings on the part of the world, yet she was murdered, and there was a hand that dealt those blows, and a brain that directed them.

"The first obvious inquiry is, who is benefited by the removal?"

He gestured to Lizzie, who stared icily back at him, her face flushed. "I have discovered the fact that she has repudiated the relation of mother and daughter. We've got the terrible fact. I grant that that is not an adequate motive for killing. There is no adequate motive for killing.

"We have seen that he didn't provide the house with gas and that they quarreled about property. Do you suppose that was a sufficient motive?

"I listened to the eloquent remarks of my brother and failed to hear him tell how anybody could have got in there, remained an hour and a half, killed the two people and then have gone out without being observed.

"Here was a house with the front door locked, the windows closed, the cellar door locked and the screen door closed, with somebody on guard in the kitchen. Nay, you can't go from one part of the house to the other without keys.

"Of course, this is negative evidence. It is neither sufficient, reliable or conclusive, but all evidence is made up of circumstances of more or less weight. Yet from this house, on a main street, near the center of the city, passed by hundreds of people daily, no man could depart without being seen.

"Bridget Sullivan was brought here and was questioned as closely and minutely as any other member of the household.

"What took place? Mr. Morse went off that morning. Mrs. Borden told Bridget to wash windows and she goes out to do it. In the lower part of the house there was no person left and Lizzie and her mother were upstairs.

"Then the hatchet was driven into the brain of Abby Borden. Many a man has been convicted because he alone could have committed a crime.

"Bridget finishes her work, and then, until Mr. Borden comes in, Lizzie and Mrs. Borden are alone upstairs, and this is not all—Mr. Borden comes to the front door.

"I don't care to comment on Lizzie's laughter at Bridget's exclamation, but Lizzie was where, if Mrs. Borden fell to the floor, she could not have been twenty feet away from her.

"Then Lizzie comes downstairs and commences to iron. Bridget leaves her alone with her father. Less than fifteen minutes later the death of Mr. Borden takes place.

"I asked her where she was when her father came back, and we get this story: 'I was down in the kitchen.'

"That's the kind of thumbscrew I apply, and it was a most vital thing. Almost a moment after: 'Where were you when your father came home?' 'I think I was upstairs in my room.'

"'Were you upstairs when you heard?' Then, 'I think I was on the steps coming down.'

"Isn't it singular, isn't it a vital thing that upon this most important subject she should not tell the same story upon two pages of the testimony. Isn't it singular that I can't get a satisfactory explanation from her as to how she spent the hour and fifteen minutes while her father was out and her mother was being killed upstairs.

"Her bosom friend, Miss Russell, testifies that Lizzie told her she went out to get something to fix her window. Then Lizzie tells us in her inquest testimony it was to get a piece of iron for a sinker.

"I say to her, 'Where did you spend twenty minutes or half an hour on that hot morning?'

"She says she went to fix a curtain at the west end of the barn and ate pears there. Let me say I never saw an alibi labor as this one does; you can see by reading that testimony how she was going to that barn on the hottest of days to get something unnecessary.

"We also find here the suggestion of a motive which speaks volumes. The druggist told her plainly she couldn't have prussic acid. Then how could this thing be done? That is a dreadful thing. It makes one's heart bleed to think of it. But it is done.

"And while everybody is dazed there is but one person who, throughout the whole business, has not been seen to express emotion. When Fleet came there she was annoyed that anyone should want to search her room for the murderer of her father and stepmother.

"If Your Honor yielded to the applause which spontaneously greeted the close of the remarks of my earnest, passionate brother, if Your Honor could but yield to the loyalty of his feelings, we would all be proud of it, and would be pleased to hear him say: 'We will let this woman go.'

"But that would be but temporary satisfaction. We are constrained to find that she has been dealing in poisonous things, that her story is absurd, and that hers and hers alone has been the opportunity for the commission of the crime. Yielding to clamor is not to be compared to that only and greatest satisfaction, that of a duty well done."

Reverend Buck had, at some point, covered his ears with his hands.

Judge Blaisdell did not retire to consider his decision. "The long examination is now concluded," he said, "and there remains but for the magistrate to perform what he believes to be his duty.

"It would be a pleasure for him, and he would doubtless receive much sympathy, if he could say, 'Lizzie, I judge you probably not guilty. You may go home.' But upon the character of the evidence presented through the witnesses who have been so closely and thoroughly examined, there is but one thing to be done.

"Suppose for a single moment a man was standing there. He was found close by that guest chamber which, to Mrs. Borden, was a chamber of death.

"Suppose a man had been found in the vicinity of Mr. Borden, was the first to find the body, and the only account he could give of himself was an unreasonable one, would there be any question in the minds of men what should be done with such a man?

"So there is only one thing to do, painful as it may be. The judgment of the Court is that you are probably guilty, and you are ordered committed to await the action of the Superior Court."

Reverend Buck was right there, as always, to support Lizzie.

After a moment she turned to him and said, "It is for the best, I think. It is better that I should get my exoneration in a higher court, for then it will be complete."

Officers took Lizzie back to the matron's room. The tears she did not have on the day of the murders dropped freely as she went. The court, reporters, and spectators watched her go.

After the proceedings, Marshal Hilliard gave Professor Wood the handleless hatchet for testing.

CHAPTER 19

Lizzie's supporters rallied around her, many speaking to reporters. Reverend Jubb was particularly vocal and direct. "Believe in Lizzie's innocence? Indeed I do, absolutely, and I think her incarceration at the hands of the trial justice a travesty on justice. I would think that common decency would have caused Judge Blaisdell to step aside, after having once given judgment so far as to order the issuing of a warrant."

Witness Dr. Handy, whose daughter was also a friend of Lizzie's, said, "I often wonder why Bridget Sullivan was not also arrested as well as Lizzie. There was as much ground for the arrest of one as another. Bridget Sullivan may know something about this murder, and she may also be telling things to save herself."

Bridget left Fall River after the preliminary hearing. She told Officer Harrington, "I did not like the way the papers spoke of me, and said I was in New Bedford jail. And I got a postal card from the court, requesting me to call for my witness fees, that was addressed to New Bedford jail. I did not like this, so I thought I would show them I would not stay any longer."

She took work in a private home in New Bedford.

. . .

Since Abby had been killed before her husband, her assets passed to him and then his daughters. Or at least they would unless Lizzie was convicted of his murder, in which case Emma would inherit everything.

Half of Sarah Whitehead's house, which had been in Abby's name and which had caused such discord in the Borden family, belonged to the Borden sisters. Sarah and her family had no right to it if the sisters chose to sell to another party.

With Andrew's substantial estate, the Borden sisters would each be independently wealthy without the Whitehead house. Reverend Buck counseled the sisters to offer the deed to Sarah Whitehead for a token amount. This, he said, was the Christian thing to do. Jennings and Adams felt the gesture would help the sisters' position with the public; the lawyers would make sure the generous act was known.

The sisters consented, and the gift was aptly reported in *The New York Times*.

Lizzie stayed, again, at the Taunton Jail while she waited for the grand jury decision on formal charges. The decision was not expected until late November at the earliest. She would wait in jail for at least two months.

While everyone else waited the papers and the town rehashed old news, rumor, and innuendo. Lizzie had meals brought up from the nearby hotel and corresponded with friends and supporters. She wrote to Mrs. Annie Lindsey, even commenting on the prison mouser:

> "My dear Annie,
>
> The wind is blowing outside a gale but never a blast inside. Everything is as calm and placid as a summer sea; even to the large white and yellow cat who is lying under the radiator, as sound asleep as if he was dead. He is the quietest boy I ever saw but is lots of company for me...
>
> Yours with love, L.A.B."

On Lizzie's behalf, her lawyers declined all requests for interviews, except one. The *New York Recorder* was granted an exclusive. The reporter, Mrs. Kate Swan McGuirk, was a woman Lizzie knew a little, from a time when they had both worked at the same charity.

Jennings and Adams selected this one interview with this one reporter because of assurances that it would be a sympathetic account of Lizzie's perspective. In the absence of other news this was an opportunity to present Lizzie's case to the world.

Mrs. McGuirk met Lizzie in her cell.

> 'I know I am innocent and I have made up my mind that, no matter what happens, I will try to bear it bravely and make the best of it.' The speaker was a woman. The words came slowly, and her eyes filled with tears that did not fall before they were wiped away. The woman was Lizzie Borden, who had been accused of the murder of her father, and personally has been made to appear in the eyes of the public as a monster.
>
> I was anxious to see if this girl, with whom I was associated several years ago in the work of the Fall River Fruit and Flower Mission, had changed her character and become a monster since the days when she used to load up the plates of vigorous young newsboys and poor children at the annual turkey dinner.
>
> I sought her in the Taunton jail and found her unchanged, except that she showed traces of the great trial she has just been through. Her face was thinner, her mouth had a patient look, as if she had been schooling herself to expect and to bear any treatment, however unpleasant, and her eyes were red from the long nights of weeping.
>
> 'How do you get along here, Miss Borden?' I asked.
>
> 'To tell the truth, I am afraid it is beginning to tell on my health. This lack of fresh air and exercise is hard for me. I have always been out of doors a great deal, and that makes it harder. I cannot sleep nights now, and nothing they give me will produce sleep. If it were not for my friends, I should break down, but as long as they stand by me I can bear it.
>
> 'The hardest thing for me to stand here is the night, when there is no light. They will not allow me to have a candle to read by, and to sit in the dark all evening is very hard; but I do not want any favors that are against the rules. Mr. Wright and his wife are very kind to me

and try to make it easier to bear, but of course, they must do their duty.'

Mrs. McGuirk provided ample space for Lizzie's statements.

'There is one thing which hurts me very much. They say I don't show any grief. Certainly I don't in public. I never did reveal my feelings and I cannot change my nature now. They say I don't cry. They should see me when I am alone, or sometimes with my friends. It hurts me to think people say so about me. I have tried very hard to be brave and womanly through it all. If people would only do me justice, that is all I ask, but it seems as if every word I have uttered has been distorted and such a false construction placed on it that I am bewildered. I can't understand it.'

There was not a trace of anger in her tones—simply a pitiful expression," closed Mrs. McGuirk. "She recovered herself with an effort and we said 'goodbye.'

The published report was everything Jennings had hoped. Many papers covered the interview. The new narrative held. But not for long.

Lizzie read the papers every day, and was known to clip articles about her case, including her interview with Mrs. McGuirk. She also received letters from supporters.

Then a different sort of letter arrived at the jail for Lizzie.

"Westport Sep. 20, 1892.

To Miss Lizzie, with friendly greetings.

I am very anxious to meet you, and as I cannot presume upon your presence without your permission, will you be so kind as to appoint a day for me to visit you as soon as convenient. I can come any day or hour.

Please do not deny this one request. Believe me you have my deepest sympathy and constant prayer.

I am sincerely yours, Curtis I. Piece"

The police began an investigation of Mr. Piece, an itinerant pastor, and his connection to Lizzie and perhaps, the murders.

Lizzie told Jennings she had met Mr. Curtis Piece once, a decade before, at the house of a friend. He had pursued her with repeated and unwelcome advances since. Jennings responded on Lizzie's behalf:

"Fall River, Mass. September 24, 1892
Mr. Curtis I. Piece
Westport Mass

Dear Sir;

Your letters to Sheriff Wright and to Miss Lizzie A. Borden have been handed to me by the latter.

For your sympathy, as for that of everybody else in her suffering, she is grateful, but she is at a loss to understand why you should presume upon her unfortunate position to open correspondence with her, or write to Sheriff Wright asking for an interview.

She does not want to see you, nor to receive letters from you. She has not, tis true, a father to appeal to, or family to compel you to cease your attempts to force yourself upon her notice, but there are others who can and will supply his place. She has told me of your previous conduct, and I am surprised that any man should attempt to renew it under present circumstances.

Yours truly, Andrew J. Jennings"

The Fall River police found no connection between Mr. Piece and the murders. He was not in town at the time of the murders. Curtis Piece did not write again.

Twenty-four-year-old reporter Henry G. Trickey, who specialized in murder cases, had found himself a Borden scoop.

Edwin McHenry, a private detective who had been employed by the Fall River Police for a short time after the Borden murders and still had connections in the department, offered new information to Trickey and his paper, the *Boston Globe.*

In exchange for $400, McHenry provided exclusive details of dozens of previously unreported witnesses and their statements that would soon be made public. The *Globe* ran the story on the tenth of October:

"LIZZIE BORDEN'S SECRET. Mr. Borden Discovered It and Hot Words Followed. Startling Testimony of Twenty-five New Witnesses. Emma Was Kicked During that Quarrel — Family Discord and Murder."

The report named individual witnesses, none of whom had testified at the inquest or preliminary hearing.

"Either let us know what his name is or take the door on Saturday!" Mr. Borden was heard to shout the night before the murders. "I will know the name of the man who got you into trouble!"

One witness saw Lizzie in the guest room window at the time Abby was murdered. Another was prepared to testify that Andrew had told him he planned to write a will which cut out Emma and Lizzie, except a pittance each, leaving the rest to Abby.

Some of the evidence had been obtained when an investigator reportedly hid under Lizzie's bed. From there a fight was overheard and Lizzie seen kicking Emma. John Morse was reported to have suppressed evidence, though the evidence was not specified.

The report not only sold out but was covered by other papers, including the *New York Times*. The *Globe* reprinted it in their late edition.

The next day Adams went to the offices of the *Boston Globe* personally, threatening them with litigation if a retraction and apology were not published. It was soon revealed that no attempt had been made to verify any of the facts prior to publication and none of the named witnesses actually existed. The *Globe* published their apology:

"ABJECT APOLOGY

Globe Begs the Pardon of Lizzie Borden and Morse

To err is human and as newspapers have to be run by men and not by angels, mistakes are inevitable. The Globe feels it a plain duty as an honest newspaper to state that it has been grievously misled in the Lizzie Borden case. It published on Monday a communication that it

> believed to be true evidence. Among all the impositions which newspapers have suffered this was unparalleled in its astonishing completeness and irresistible plausibility. Judging from what we have heard, it impressed our readers as strongly as it did the Globe. Some of this remarkably ingenious and cunningly-contrived story is undoubtedly based on facts, as later developments will show. The Globe believes, however, that much of it is false, and never should have been published. The Globe, being thus misled, has innocently added to the terrible burdens of Miss Lizzie Borden.
>
> So far as lies in our power to repair the wrong we are anxious to do so, and hereby tender her our heartfelt apology for the inhuman reflection upon her honor as a woman and for any injustice the publication inflicted upon her.
>
> The same sincere apology is hereby tendered to John V. Morse and any other persons to whom the publication did an injustice."

Disgraced reporter Henry Trickey fled and hid with relatives out of town.

CHAPTER 20

Knowlton did not want to prosecute the case against Lizzie Borden. In spite of his certainty of her guilt either of murder or involvement, the odds of a conviction against a Victorian Christian lady with an otherwise spotless record and in the absence of direct evidence were small.

State Attorney General Albert Pillsbury had another idea. Based on the police interviews and witness statements, Jennings' statements in court, and Lizzie's behavior, Pillsbury thought that Lizzie Borden was arguably insane, or had been when committing the murders.

Perhaps the prosecution and the defense could make a deal. Lizzie would plead guilty by reason of insanity and spend a predetermined number of years not in prison, but confined to a mental asylum. After, she'd be released to the custody and supervision of her sister.

Jennings "seemed to regard it as some sort of surrender if he consented to anything," Knowlton wrote to Pillsbury. "We can make some investigations into the family matters without him, but it will not be so thorough as it would be if we had his assistance."

Knowlton sent an officer to interview people who had known Morse family members, including Lizzie and Emma's long-deceased mother, Sarah, looking for signs of insanity in that family line. This endeavor became known as the "Sanity Survey."

The grand jury adjourned on November 21 without a decision on an indictment for the Borden murders.

Jennings arrived at the offices of Albert Pillsbury in Boston on November 22, at Pillsbury's request.

Pillsbury and Jennings were both forty-three. Pillsbury had been a prominent and ambitious Boston lawyer and, like Jennings, had served in the Massachusetts House and Senate.

The men knew each other, though not well.

Pillsbury achieved the position of Attorney General in 1891. He was accustomed to getting his way.

"I understand you have heard our proposal, mine and Hosea's," Pillsbury said. "In the coming days or weeks we expect a grand jury indictment against Lizzie Borden for the murders of her parents. We are prepared to prosecute fully. The case against her is not certain, but strong enough, and bolstered by her own inquest testimony."

"Testimony that was not properly taken. We will challenge it at trial," said Jennings.

Pillsbury made a pacifying gesture. "I have heard of your concerns. The inquest was proper under the letter of the law and we will stand by it in court, if it comes to that. It might not."

Jennings waited.

Although they were still investigating, Pillsbury said, "We have reason to believe there is mental instability within the family line."

"The Bordens?" Jennings would not allow any attack, even implied, on his mentor, Andrew.

The focus of concern did not escape Pillsbury's notice. "No, the Morse line. Her birth mother."

Jennings had sometimes considered the same about the Morse line, though he would never speak of it. "Miss Borden is innocent," he said instead. "She deserves an acquittal in court."

"An acquittal is not certain and the trial will be difficult for her, regardless of the outcome," said Pillsbury. "We will be forced to present all of the facts related to the case, including some she and you would prefer not be made public."

Jennings frowned, but Pillsbury could not believe he was surprised at all.

Pillsbury held his hands out as if showing he had no weapons. "We would not do so out of malice, but out of necessity and obligation to the law. She will sit in her place in court and be the subject of scrutiny and criticism in the public eye from which her reputation and standing might never recover. If there is a trial, the Borden name might forever be associated with bloody murder."

Jennings grimaced, which was exactly the reaction Pillsbury had sought.

Jennings said, "I will consult with Adams."

"We would also, of course, need Lizzie to submit to an examination," said Pillsbury.

After Jennings left, Pillsbury sent word:

> "My Dear Knowlton:
>
> Jennings was here today, evidently indisposed to consent at first, but more inclined to before he left, I think. He went away saying that he must see Adams, and that he would let us hear from him as soon as possible.
>
> Yours truly,
>
> Attorney General"

The next day Jennings sent his answer: "Since my talk with you, I have been seriously considering your proposition and have come to the conclusion that I cannot consent to unite with you in the examination proposed. In view of all the circumstances, we could not do anything which suggested a doubt about her innocence. The course proposed would not be wise or expedient on our part."

There ended all discussion regarding an insanity plea.

The day after, on November 24, the police interview notes for the Sanity Survey arrived:

"H. A. Knowlton
District Atty.
New Bedford, Mass.

Sir,

I have interviewed the following persons in reference to the relatives of Lizzie Borden who said as follows:

Capt. James C. Stafford North St. New Bedford: I used to know quite well the mother of Lizzie Borden. Her name was Sarah Morse. Mrs. Morse, the mother of Lizzie Borden, was a very peculiar woman. She had a very bad temper. She was very strong in her likes and dislikes. I never knew or heard of any of the Morses or Bordens was ever insane or anything like it.

Rescom Case 199 Second St. Fall River: I have lived in Fall River fifty-seven years and I know all the Bordens and the Morses well. I used to know Anthony, father of Lizzie's mother. The woman that was murdered use to visit my house. She use to keep her affairs to herself pretty well, but I assure you I have my opinion of Lizzie Borden and I hope they will get more evidence. My wife and I never heard that anyone of them is or ever was insane but I think some of them worse than insane.

D. S. Brigam ex-City Marshal of Fall River: I use to know the Morses never heard of any of them as being insane, but this girl Lizzie Borden is known by a number of people here to be a woman of a bad disposition if they tell what they know.

Geo. A. Patty, Fall River: I did not know much about the history of the Morses. Never heard that any of them is or was ever insane but Lizzie is known to be ugly.

Mrs. Geo. W. Whitehead 45 4th St. Fall River: Sister of Mrs. Borden who was murdered never heard that any of the Morses was insane but ugly.

William Carr, Fall River: For 40 years I know the Bordens better then I know the Morses. The Bordens are peculiar people but I never heard that any of the Bordens or the Morses is or was ever insane.

Respectfully, Moulton Batchelder, District Police"

. . .

Alice's conscience finally swayed her to tell that she'd seen Lizzie burn a dress the Sunday after the murders. A dress with stains on it.

She approached Knowlton and he assured her, with satisfaction, that she'd chosen the only righteous course.

When the grand jury returned to session on December 1, Knowlton presented them with this new testimony. A day later they issued an indictment against Lizzie for both murders.

They also issued an indictment against Henry G. Trickey, *Boston Globe* reporter, possibly for witness tampering related to the Borden case. The exact charges were not made public and never would be. Trickey fled to Canada and was killed when he fell, or threw himself, under a train.

Lizzie, Jennings, and Emma met in Lizzie's cell to discuss her murder trial. Lizzie, agitated but quiet, seemed resigned. "How long until the trial?"

Jennings said, "This is a complex case. It will take time to prepare, on both sides. Most likely the case will commence within two to three months, but we may need to ask for a continuance."

"I prefer this matter be resolved soon," Lizzie said, rubbing her arms. "This dark cell weighs on me."

"Then your defense will accept the earliest trial date that we can properly prepare for. I cannot speak for the prosecution, which may request more time."

Emma nodded. "We trust you to know what is best."

Lizzie said nothing. She seemed more subdued lately to Jennings. Frightened, even.

Fall turned to winter. Lizzie spent the holidays in her dark, damp cell. She'd lost weight, and her visitors also noted a change in her mood. The haughty certainty she'd maintained early on had turned to hopelessness and despair.

Lizzie confided to her friend, Annie:

"My Dear Annie,

I meant to have written long ago, but my head troubles me so much I write very little. I think soon they can take me up the road, to the insane asylum.

We all feel very sober here this week. Mrs. Wright is very ill with pneumonia, both lungs affected.

Do you know I cannot for the life of me see how you and the rest of my friends can be so full of hope over the case. To me, I see nothing but the densest of shadows.

With much love for my loyal friend.

L.A.B."

CHAPTER 21

One day, which otherwise seemed the same as other days to Reverend Buck, he found Lizzie curled on the bed, facing the wall and sobbing.

He sat on the bed next to her. "Miss Lizzie." He touched her back.

She did not turn.

For several minutes they stayed that way.

Reverend Buck began to pray. "Our father in heaven, watch over and guide this girl as she faces unjust trials. Bless her and keep her at your side, so that she may be delivered by your grace. Stay by her side so that she may know peace."

Lizzie still did not turn. "I can't stay here any longer. I've got to leave. I want to go home."

"I understand, child."

"Tell them to let me go."

"I have and will help you as I can, Lizzie. It is only for a little while longer."

"I can't!" she sobbed.

"You can. You are strong in your faith and in Jesus' flock. The Lord will not forsake you."

"He already has."

"Never. And I will not."

She finally turned to face him, tears covering her cheeks.

As long as Buck had known her, Lizzie had been guarded. Now, though, she leaned slightly forward, toward him, and he matched her, embracing in a gentle hug.

"I will not leave you. I will always protect you." He smoothed her hair and she shook with sobs and gasps against his shoulder, as if she had never cried before.

Jennings arrived a few days later with news for Lizzie and Emma, who was visiting. "The prosecution is consulting with John Cummings of Boston. He is a prominent lawyer. I would like to add an additional attorney to our side, someone of equal caliber."

Emma responded without hesitation. "Whatever is necessary to ensure an acquittal, Mr. Jennings. Do you have someone in mind?"

"I will approach Governor Robinson."

Lizzie, incredulous, said, "Massachusetts Governor Robinson?"

"Former, yes. He is an acquaintance of mine and I believe he can be persuaded. He is well liked and can charm the jury and the public."

Emma and Lizzie stared back, stunned.

Jennings went to Robinson's home, the Hale Mansion in Chicopee, to convince Robinson to join.

Fifty-year-old Robinson had acquired a paunch. The press sometimes described him as 'fatherly' those days, an impression Robinson encouraged.

Since leaving the governorship five years before he'd returned to private legal practice. It was profitable work but much less prestigious than the Governorship.

Jennings brought a summary of the allegations and evidence against Lizzie, to discuss. Robinson had seen most of it already in the public reports.

And Jennings needn't have worried about how to convince the governor to consider the case. Robinson nearly grinned at the prospect of taking on the Borden defense, which would test his skills, thrust him back into the limelight, and bring a substantial payday.

But Robinson asked, "Did she do it?" Robinson's one requirement, other than an exorbitant fee, was that he meet Lizzie and be able to make the case for her innocence.

Robinson and Jennings arrived at the jail for the governor's meeting with Lizzie a few days later.

Jennings had not told Lizzie that Robinson needed to be convinced of her innocence, thinking she might not react well to anyone else doubting her.

Lizzie was smaller than Robinson had pictured, based on newspaper accounts of her. She was both shorter in stature and thinner than the fierce woman sometimes depicted, though he knew well how prisoners lost weight. She held a handkerchief as if she'd been crying, but her eyes were dry and her expression guarded. She stood as they entered.

Jennings made the introductions. "Governor Robinson, this is Miss Lizzie Borden."

Robinson nodded and bowed slightly. "How are you keeping together, Miss Lizzie?"

"As best I can." Her voice shook.

The matron brought chairs so that the lawyers and Lizzie could all sit.

Lizzie seemed to Robinson like a frail little bird. He could picture how to play that with a jury.

He took her hand gently, pressing her cold fingers between his. "I'm considering taking on your case, Miss Lizzie, and need to speak with you before deciding."

Lizzie waited and said nothing.

"Attorney Jennings here is certain of your innocence," said Robinson. "You are lucky to have such a strong advocate."

"Yes," said Lizzie, with a small smile for Jennings. "I am grateful."

She did seem sincerely grateful, surprising Jennings, who was accustomed to more caustic responses.

Robinson continued. "I need to hear from you, Miss Lizzie, what happened that terrible day. What were you doing when your father was killed?"

Lizzie seemed to muster her strength, but spoke softly rather than vehemently. "It is as I have always said. I helped him to lay down on the sofa for a nap, then I went out and up in the barn. I found him killed when I came back into the house."

Robinson watched her closely. "And your stepmother?"

Lizzie did not hesitate or falter. "I heard and saw nothing to tell." She looked him in the eye. "I truly know nothing more than I have stated all these months. I do not know and cannot explain what happened, except that I am not responsible."

Robinson touched her arm and said, "Don't you worry, little girl. Everything's going to be all right."

He was thoughtful after he and Jennings left. "I will represent her," he said.

In April, Knowlton wrote to Attorney General Pillsbury:

> "Personally I would like very much to get rid of the trial in this case. I confess, however, I cannot see my way clear to any disposition of the case other than a trial.
>
> "The case has proceeded so far that it does not seem to me we ought to take the responsibility of discharging her without trial, even though there is every reasonable expectation of a verdict of not guilty. Even in my most sanguine moments I have scarcely expected a guilty verdict.
>
> "The situation is this: nothing has developed which satisfies either of us that she is innocent, nor can we escape the conclusion that she must have had some knowledge of the occurrence.
>
> "I cannot see how any other course than setting the case down for trial, and trying it, will satisfy that portion of the public sentiment whether favorable to her or not, which is worthy of being respected."

In May, Lizzie entered a plea of "not guilty". The court scheduled the trial to start in June of 1893.

One observer said she, "looked very well aside from the pallor that was to be expected after her long confinement."

Shortly after her return to the jail, however, Lizzie developed bronchitis. The culprit, reported the papers, was her cold, damp cell.

After a public outcry at her treatment, the sheriff moved her to his own private rooms, to be cared for by his wife and a doctor. Thereafter Lizzie remained in the sheriff's quarters rather than a cell, unlike the other women at the jail.

Once she had recuperated somewhat, Lizzie wrote to her friend Annie. She discouraged the making of plans, even for Christmas time, many months away:

> "My dear Annie
>
> I thank you for your nice long letter and wish I could answer it as it deserves but I am far from well.
>
> My spirits are at ebb tide. I see no ray of light amid the gloom. I try to fill up the waiting time as well as I can, but every day is longer and longer.
>
> I begin to think the tangled threads will never be smoothed out. My friend — do not make any plans for me at Christmas. I do not expect to be free — and if I am, I could not join in any merry making. I do not know that I ever could again. You know my life can never be the same again if I ever come home.
>
> Forgive me for this sober letter, but my heart is heavy and the burden laid upon me seems greater than I can bear.
>
> Sincerely yours,
>
> L.A.B."

Knowlton met with City Marshal Hilliard and Assistant Marshal Fleet at the city station to discuss the trial. Looking through Knowlton's police witness list, Hilliard said, "Everyone will be available and ready. We'll manage shifts around it."

"Good," said Knowlton. "And Mullaly?"

"I spoke to him," said Hilliard. "Told him he must be clear and correct in his testimony." Mullaly was the officer who'd testified at the preliminary hearing that he "hadn't noticed" whether the Bordens' dining room had a dining table in it.

"We must have him as a witness," said Knowlton. "He was the first to question Lizzie on the morning of the murders."

Fleet shrugged. "His recollections were never precise."

"He'll be fine, I think," said Hilliard.

All attempts to find the Jewish peddler Robinsky, who'd written to Emma shortly after the murders about seeing a bloody traveler, had failed. Perhaps fearing the notoriety of the case and sanction for failing to obtain a seller's license, Robinsky had hidden himself. The defense would proceed to trial without Robinsky as a witness, or his bloody traveler.

District Attorneys Knowlton and William H. Moody of the Eastern District would present the case for the prosecution on behalf of Attorney General Pillsbury, who bowed out citing health concerns.

Jennings, Adams, and Robinson would defend.

This would be no battle of provincials, but the best legal actors on both sides.

And in the weeks before the trial, a quiet fight raged between the defense and the prosecution. The case against Lizzie depended in great part on whether the jury could hear her inquest testimony. The defense said they would fight every inch to keep it out of the trial, and the prosecution that they would fight just as hard to get it in.

There was, in fact, a serious problem with the testimony. Since Lizzie had been informed by Mayor Coughlin that the police suspected her and Marshal Hilliard held a warrant for her arrest at the time of the inquest, the testimony might have been improper.

The prosecution agreed to a joint statement with the defense to be presented at trial which conceded that some minor aspects of her testimony were not as they should have been. By making minor concessions, they hoped to avoid any appearance of deliberate impropriety before the court and to protect their ability to present the testimony at trial.

On May 30, while Lizzie Borden waited in the Taunton jail, another axe murder shocked Fall River. Someone killed Bertha Manchester, twenty-two, in her own kitchen. Her father and brother left the house at seven thirty in the morning to make milk deliveries. They returned a few hours later to find Bertha dead and no suspicion of who might have killed her.

The police arrested a laborer from the Manchester farm on June 4, and charged him on June 5, the day Lizzie's trial began.

To some, the evidence was clear. Two such similar murder scenes, within a year of each other, could not be a coincidence. The Manchester axe killer must also be the Borden axe killer.

JUNE, 1893

The court moved Lizzie's trial to nearby New Bedford, Massachusetts, seeking a more objective jury.

Summer heat and humidity arrived again in time for the trial, ten months after the murders. The crowded courtroom sweltered and everyone wiped sweat from their faces with handkerchiefs.

This trial was a sensation not just in Massachusetts and the United States, but across much of the world. Multiple newspaper editions per day reported the events of the trial. Readers who'd not previously known of the case suddenly found it as their front page news. Reporters rehashed evidence, rumors, and speculation for new markets.

Those who had followed the case all along already knew most of the evidence that would be presented at the trial. But this trial would be a battle of legal teams.

Three justices presided: Chief Justice Albert Mason, fifty-seven, Justice Caleb Blodgett, sixty, and Justice Justin Dewey, fifty-six.

Justice Dewey should have recused himself from the case, since he'd been appointed to the bench in 1886 by then Governor Robinson. Dewey did not recuse himself.

Chief Justice Mason had served on the judiciary committee with Robinson in the Massachusetts House of Representatives. Mason did not recuse himself.

At least one of the justices knew Jerome Borden, Andrew's cousin who went to the Borden house the day after the murders to express concerns about protecting the Borden name.

CHAPTER 22

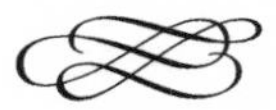

Sheriff Wright escorted Lizzie to court for the first day of the trial. She sat with her legal team: Robinson, Jennings, and Adams. Reverend Buck stayed right next to her, sometimes holding her hand, and other supporters including Mrs. Holmes and Mary Brigham were there, too.

Knowlton and Moody waited at the prosecution table, reviewing extensive notes. The mooing of a cow outside intruded into the room.

Observers scrutinized every detail of Lizzie's behavior and attire, including a loose button on her shoe which worked itself off over the course of the first day.

Friends had sent Lizzie boxes of sweets to boost her mood and Lizzie gained weight over the last weeks of her jail stay, causing reporters to note that her chin was heavy, creating a face better viewed from the side, they said. Seeing her from the front was "less pleasing than the side face."

She wore a black dress with velvet trim and a hat that was "not the style of a city-made hat." She'd brought a black fan to cool herself. Her attorneys wanted her to look the part of the grieving orphan by appearing in unrelieved black, but Lizzie had adorned her hat with a blue feather.

It was reported that Lizzie did not "carry herself well" and was "purely provincial." Others were more sympathetic. "It has been said again and again that this maiden prisoner is a great strong woman, capable of extraordinary physical exertion. It is not so. She is very little, if anything, above average stature. If her arms, which cannot be seen in her puffed sleeves, are large and muscular, they assuredly terminate in very small and ladylike hands."

In spite of the stares and various opinions, Lizzie maintained herself in the courtroom as she consistently did in public—guarded and with a seemingly steel nerve.

Hundreds of potential jurors soon crowded the courthouse. Women were considered too physically and emotionally fragile to serve on juries; a jury of Lizzie's "peers" would be twelve men.

Many potential jurors said that they had already formed an opinion on the case and would not change their minds. They were dismissed. However, finding jurors who hadn't heard anything proved impossible. The court was forced to select jurors who had heard about the case, including newspaper reports and rumors, but swore to the court that they had not reached any conclusions and would decide based only on the evidence presented at trial.

The new jury foreman worked in real estate transactions. Six jurors were farmers, two were manufacturers, and three were mechanics.

The jurors were given a short break to inform their families and businesses that they would be sequestered until completion of their service. Then they were sworn and settled themselves into their seats.

The court clerk read the grand jury indictments, charging that Lizzie "did strike, cut, beat, and bruise" upon the heads of Abby and Andrew Borden, until they were dead. "To each count of which indictment Lizzie Andrew Borden, the prisoner at the bar, has heretofore pleaded and said that she is not guilty. You are now sworn to try the issue. Good men and true, stand together and hearken to your evidence."

Spectators lined up outside the courtroom every day for seats. Like the preliminary hearing, most were there to support Lizzie and included many people she did not know. Some were there merely to be seen.

Someone had moved the cow that had chimed in on the previous day's proceedings to another pasture. Justice Dewey called the court to order.

Thirty-nine year old prosecutor William H. Moody had been a Massachusetts district attorney for three years. He'd graduated Phi Beta Kappa from Harvard University, but the Borden murders were unlike anything he'd ever prosecuted. He was nervous.

Lizzie watched Moody closely as he rose for the prosecution's opening. The courtroom went silent.

"May it please your Honors," he said. "Mr. Foreman and Gentlemen of the Jury. Today a woman of good social position, of hitherto unquestioned character, a member of a Christian church and active in its good works, is at the bar of this court. She is accused of the killings of her father and stepmother, an old man and woman."

Moody gave the background of the family, the layout of the house, and the circumstances surrounding the murders. Then he shared the main points of evidence the prosecution would present against Lizzie.

"Mr. Borden had seen fit to help a relative of Mrs. Borden, causing a change in the relations between the prisoner and Mrs. Borden. Up to that time the prisoner had addressed her stepmother as 'Mother.' From that time she substantially ceased to do so, and held an ill feeling toward the woman. I know of nothing in this case more significant of the feeling between the prisoner and Mrs. Borden than a little incident which occurred not long after the discovery of these homicides. One of the officers said, 'When did you last see your mother?' The prisoner responded, 'She is not my mother. She is my stepmother. My mother is dead.'

"Upon Tuesday night, two nights before the murders, Mr. and Mrs. Borden were taken suddenly ill with a violent retching and vomiting sickness. Mrs. Borden thought they'd been poisoned.

"Then the noon of Wednesday, the very day before these homicides, the prisoner went to a drugstore in Fall River, attempted to buy prussic acid, a dangerous weapon, and was denied.

"The morning of the murders, the prisoner came downstairs and

Mr. Borden goes, leaving only the prisoner, Bridget, and Mrs. Borden in the house.

"There was some talk between Mrs. Borden and Bridget about washing the windows. Mrs. Borden disappeared at this time, and it will appear that she told the prisoner she was going upstairs to put cases upon two pillows—a trifling duty which would take less than a minute. No living person saw Mrs. Borden from that time until her death, except the assailant.

"When Mr. Borden came back, as Bridget let him in she had some difficulty in unloosing the locks. The prisoner, from the hall above, made some laugh or exclamation. At that time, gentlemen, Mrs. Borden's body lay within plain view of that hall, dead, probably more than an hour.

"Mr. Borden came in, went first into the dining room. There the prisoner came to him and said, 'Mrs. Borden has gone out; she had a note from somebody who was sick.'

"That, gentlemen, we put to you as a lie, intended for no purpose except to stifle inquiry as to the whereabouts of Mrs. Borden."

A careful observer, watching Lizzie, would have seen her eyes narrow at the accusation.

"She said that she went out into the barn for a piece of iron or tin to fix a screen when Mr. Borden was killed. When she gave a later and more detailed account, she said that she went to the yard, into the loft of the barn, ate some pears up there, and looked over some lead for sinkers.

"Gentlemen, this day, August 4th, 1892, was one of the hottest days of the last summer in this vicinity. The loft of the barn was almost stifling in the intensity of its heat.

"Officer Medley, who came there quite early after the alarm, went up the stairs of the barn. He saw that the floor was thickly covered with dust and no footprints."

This evidence was new to the spectators.

"Now, gentlemen, in the house there was blood spattering, so that spatters of blood would be upon the person or upon the clothing of the assailant. And there has been produced for the inspection of the Commonwealth the clothing said to have been worn by the prisoner on the morning of August fourth."

He placed the dress Lizzie had provided to the police on the table and gestured to it as he spoke. "The prisoner wore a cotton dress that morning. Mrs. Adelaide Churchill says Lizzie had on a light blue ground with a dark blue diamond. And upon being shown that dress," he gestured to the blue silk, "she will say that it is not the dress that the prisoner at the bar had on that morning.

"Upon Saturday night after the murders, Mayor Coughlin of Fall River informed Lizzie Borden that she was under suspicion. On Sunday morning, Miss Alice Russell came into the kitchen and there was the prisoner, burning a light blue cotton dress that was claimed to have paint stains. A considerable search had been made by the officers and they will say that no clothing covered with paint could have escaped their observation if it were not hidden."

A whisper passed through the room. This account of a burned dress was also new.

Moody turned to the prosecutor's table and a black bag on top. He opened it to reveal two skulls — those of Andrew and Abby Borden. The gallery gasped. Lizzie raised her black fan to cover her face, which flushed. Reporters scribbled.

Moody continued. "There is a thing that is unmistakably told by one of the skulls—I think that of Mr. Borden—that the weapon which brought him to his death was three and one half inches on its blade. That is the exact measurement of the blade of a handleless hatchet found in the house and which we'll present to you.

"No one was seen to escape from any side of that house nor to enter that house on the morning of August fourth. The Commonwealth will prove that from the time when Mrs. Borden left the dining room to go upstairs for that momentary errand, up to the time when the prisoner came downstairs an hour later, there was no other human being except the prisoner present; that these killings were the acts of a person who must have had a familiar knowledge of the interior of the premises and of the whereabouts and the habits of those who were in occupation of them."

He gestured to Lizzie, who seemed to be resting with her eyes closed. "We shall also prove that this prisoner made contradictory statements about her whereabouts.

"Now, gentlemen, if, when the end comes, considering all these circumstances, you are led irresistibly to the conclusion of her guilt, we ask you in your verdict to declare the truth. By so doing, and only by so doing, shall you make true deliverance of the great issue which has been committed to your keeping."

Lizzie appeared to have dozed off in the intense heat of the courtroom. Only when an officer tried to wake her did anyone realize she was unconscious. A gasp went through the room and spectators stood and leaned to get a better look at her, sunk down in her seat. Reverend Buck frantically fanned her with papers while someone fetched a glass of water.

She regained herself only after a few tense minutes.

The *Fall River Daily Globe* reported that news to an eager public: "Lizzie Borden, the sphinx of coolness, who has so often been accused of never manifesting a feminine feeling, had fainted."

During a recess, the jury went to Second Street to see the Borden house and property, the murder rooms, and the locks on all the doors.

CHAPTER 23

The prosecution's case lasted eight of the eleven and one half days of the trial. Witnesses, including Second Street neighbors and those who had seen Mr. Borden the morning of the murders, repeated their testimony from the inquest and preliminary hearing.

Witnesses also testified to contention between Lizzie and Abby, that the relations between the daughters and Abby were never the same after Andrew bought and put the deed for Abby's sister's house in Abby's name.

While answering questions she'd answered in previous hearings, Bridget also told of the poor quality food at the Borden house. Lizzie, still pale and weak, exchanged smiles and a few little laughs with Bridget at this characteristic of Borden life and the shock learning of it created in the courtroom.

Prosecutor Moody questioned Bridget about the day of the murders. "Up to the time when someone called you in your room, did you hear any noise?"

"No, sir."

"Are you able to hear the opening or closing of the screen door from your bedroom?"

"Yes, sir. If anybody goes in or out and is careless and slams the door, I can hear it in my room."

"What next occurred as you were lying upon the bed?"

"Miss Lizzie hollered, 'Maggie, come down! I said, 'What is the matter?' She says, 'Come down quick; father's dead. Somebody come in and killed him.'"

Defense Attorney Robinson asked Bridget, "It was a pleasant family to be in?"

"I don't know how the family was; I got along all right."

"Never saw any quarreling or anything of that kind?"

"No, sir."

"There was not, so far as you knew, any trouble that morning?"

"No, sir, I did not see any trouble."

Moody asked neighbor Adelaide Churchill, "Will you describe the dress that Lizzie had on while you were there?"

"It was cotton, and it had a light blue and white ground work with a dark navy blue diamond printed on it."

He showed her the dress in evidence. "Was that the dress?"

"I did not see her with it on that morning," Adelaide said.

On cross-examination by Robinson, Adelaide recounted what Lizzie said about whether any Portuguese farmhands could have been involved in the crimes. "They asked about a Portuguese that worked for her father, and Lizzie said, 'He isn't a Portuguese, he is a Swede.'"

"She corrected that right on the spot?" Robinson turned to see that the jury was listening.

"Yes, sir."

He also asked about Lizzie's appearance the morning of the murders. "Did you see any blood on her dress?"

"No, sir."

"You were right over her fanning her?"

"Yes, sir, stood in front of her."

"On her hands? Her face?"

"No, sir."

"Or any disarrangement of her hair?"

"No, sir."

Alice Russell testified publicly for the first time about the burned dress. "I went into the kitchen, and I saw Miss Lizzie at the stove. She had a skirt in her hand, and her sister said, 'What are you going to do?' and Lizzie said, 'I am going to burn this old thing up. It is covered with paint.'"

The story of the burned dress had not leaked to the press. They, and the public, heard it for the first time at the trial. Everyone, including a red-faced Lizzie, listened closely. Alice's eyes stayed on Moody. She never looked at Lizzie.

"I said to her, 'I wouldn't let anybody see me do that, Lizzie.' She didn't make any answer," Alice continued.

"Miss Russell, give us a description of the dress that she burned?"

"It was a cheap cotton Bedford cord. Light-blue ground with a dark figure."

Although barely perceptible in the courtroom, a shift happened. Some of Lizzie's strongest supporters and friends began, for the first time, to question.

Deputy Marshal John Fleet sat upright and calm as he gave his testimony. His large, thick mustache animated his words.

He said he'd been a Fall River police officer for twelve years and Assistant City Marshal for seven.

He recounted his arrival and actions at the Borden house on the day of the murders. "I went into the room where Miss Lizzie Borden was, sitting down on a lounge with Reverend Mr. Buck. I asked her if she had any idea who could have killed her father and mother. She said, 'She is not my mother, sir; she is my stepmother; my mother died when I was a child.'"

"Will you describe what you did and said the second time you spoke to Miss Borden?"

"I went to Lizzie's door, rapped on the door. Dr. Bowen came to it and asked what was wanted. I told him that we had come to search the room. He told me to wait. He opened the door again and said—."

"Had he shut it in the meantime?"

"He had; he closed the door. He opened the door again and said that Lizzie wanted to know if it was absolutely necessary for us to search that room. He closed the door again and said something to Miss Borden, and finally opened the door and admitted us. We proceeded to search.

"While the search was still going on I said to Lizzie, 'You said this morning that you was up in the barn for half an hour.' She says, 'I don't say a half an hour, I say twenty minutes to half an hour.' 'Well, we will call it twenty minutes, then,' I say. She says, 'I say from twenty minutes to half an hour, sir.'"

Moody also asked about the hatchets and axes found in the cellar.

Fleet said, "When I got down there Officer Mullaly had two axes and two hatchets on the cellar floor."

"Are those the ones to which you refer?" asked Moody, showing the evidence.

"These seem to be."

"Did you find another axe or hatchet?"

"Yes, I found in a box in the middle cellar on a shelf, the head of a hatchet."

Moody asked, "Was there anything else in the box except the head of the hatchet?"

"Yes, there were other tools—I can't think just what they were now, but there were other small tools in there, pieces of iron."

"Mr. Fleet, will you describe the appearance of that hatchet?"

"The hatchet was covered with a heavy dust of fine white ashes upon the blade of the hatchet, upon both sides."

"Did you notice anything with reference to the condition of the other tools in respect of dust or ashes?"

"I did. There was dust upon them."

"The same as upon this?"

"No, sir. The dust on the other tools was lighter and finer than the dust upon that hatchet."

"Mr. Fleet, did you observe anything with reference to the point of breaking of the hatchet?"

"Only that this was apparently a new break."

"What did you do with that hatchet, Mr. Fleet?"

"I put it back in the box."

Robinson solicited from Fleet that when he'd asked Lizzie whether Bridget or John might have been involved in the murders, she'd said she didn't think they did. "Was it when you were talking with her in her room that she said she did not believe that Maggie, or the servant, had anything to do with it?"

"She did, yes."

"And Mr. Morse?"

"And Mr. Morse couldn't, she said."

"Your name is Michael Mullaly?" asked Moody after Mullaly was sworn.

"Yes, sir."

"You are a police officer of Fall River, are you?"

"Yes, sir."

"And have been how long?"

"Something over fifteen years."

"And your position in the force is what?"

"Patrolman."

"When you were at the Borden house, did you show Assistant Marshal Fleet anything related to the hatchets found in the house?"

"I showed him a box where Bridget had taken them from."

"What did he do after you showed him the box?"

"He took a hatchet out of there."

"Can you tell what sort of hatchet he took out?"

Mullaly pointed to handleless hatchet. "The handle was broken and it was covered with dust or ashes, or something like that. It looked fresh, as if just broken."

Robinson asked, on cross-examination, "Nothing else was taken out of it while you were there?"

"Nothing but the hatchet and parts of the handle."

"Well, that was the wood in the eye, wasn't it?"

"Yes. Then there was another piece."

"Another piece of what?"

"Handle."

Robinson felt a surge of energy. The exchange also had the full attention of the prosecution, though the jurors and spectators did not perhaps yet understand the implications of Mullaly's statement.

"What? Where is it, the handle?"

"I don't know."

"Was it a piece of that same handle?"

"It was a piece that corresponded with that." Mullaly gestured toward the hatchet head.

"The rest of the handle?"

"Yes, sir."

"Did you see it taken out?"

"I did."

"Who took it out?" Robinson felt the thrill of the kill.

"Mr. Fleet took it out."

"Did Mr. Fleet put that back, too?"

"He did."

Robinson turned to the prosecutors. "Have you that handle here, gentlemen?"

Knowlton stood to respond. "No."

"You haven't it in your possession, may I ask?"

"Never had it."

"The government does not know where it is?"

"This is the first time I ever heard of it," Knowlton said, frowning.

The prosecution recalled Assistant Marshal Fleet, who knew immediately it meant a problem, but not what. He only knew that Mullaly had been testifying.

Robinson said, "Mr. Fleet, returning to the subject we had under discussion this morning, about what you found in that box by the chimney."

"Yes, sir."

"Will you state again what you found there at the time you looked in?"

"I found a hatchet head, the handle broken off, together with some other tools in there and the iron that was inside there. I don't know just what it was."

Robinson showed him the handleless hatchet. "Was this what you found?"

"Yes, sir."

"Did you find anything else, except old tools?"

"No, sir."

"Sure about that?"

"Yes, sir."

"Who was with you at that time?"

"Michael Mullaly."

"Anybody else?"

"Not that I recall." Fleet's sinking feeling deepened.

"And that was all you found in the box at that time, except some old tools which you did not take out at all. Is that right?"

"That is all we found in connection with that hatchet."

"You did not find the handle, the broken piece, not at all?"

"No, sir." Fleet saw the problem, the inconsistency that must have been introduced in Mullaly's testimony and which called into question the accuracy of statements made by the Fall River Police, under oath, at a murder trial. He could do nothing but continue to answer.

Robinson said, "Did Mr. Mullaly take it out of the box?"

"Not that I know of."

"You looked in so that you could have seen it if it was in there?"

"Yes, sir."

"You have no doubt about that, have you at all, that you did not find the other piece of the handle that fitted on there?"

"No, sir."

"You would have seen it if it had been, wouldn't you?"

"Yes, sir, it seems to me I should."

Robinson cultivated a look of seriousness, rather than a grin, as he returned to his seat.

Officer Medley had been out of town looking for Robinsky, the peddler, during the preliminary hearing, and had not previously testified in the case.

He described retrieving the handleless hatchet head on Monday, August 8. "I went into a cellar next to the wash cellar, and in there while searching I found a small hatchet head. It was in a box."

"What was there in that box beside the handleless hatchet?"

"It seemed to me like old rubbish and one or two tools, I have forgotten just what they were. And some nails, I think."

"Did you take it from the box?"

"I did."

"What did you do with it?"

"I put it in a paper and showed it, I think, to some other officer, I cannot say just now who, and carried it to the City Marshal's office."

"Did you find any handle or anything having the appearance of a handle to this hatchet, except the piece that was in the eye of the hatchet?"

"No, sir."

Medley had also searched the barn after questioning Lizzie the morning of the murders, finding the barn door latched but not locked. "I went upstairs until part of my body was above the level of the floor. I stooped down low to see if I could discern any marks on the floor of the barn having been made there. I didn't see any, and I reached out my hand and made an impression on the barn floor."

Moody said, "Describe what there was on the floor."

"Seemed to be accumulated hay dust and other dust."

"How distinctly could you see the marks which you made?"

"I could see them quite distinctly when I looked for them."

"Go on and describe anything else which you did."

"I stepped up and took four or five steps on the barn floor. Stooping down and casting my eye on a level with the barn floor, I could see them plainly."

"Did you see any other footsteps in that dust than those which you made yourself?"

"No, sir."

"Did you notice what the temperature was in the loft?"

"I know it was hot, very hot."

. . .

The weekend newspaper summaries of the trial to date were not complementary to the prosecution.

The Woonsocket *Reporter* in Rhode Island said, "After a week's testimony on the part of the prosecution in the Borden murder trial, the indications are that the accused young woman will never be convicted. The defense, if the layman can judge, has much the best of the case so far, for there has been no direct evidence fastening the atrocious crime upon the prisoner. Public sentiment already clamors for an acquittal."

CHAPTER 24

It was time for the prosecution to introduce a key piece of evidence, Lizzie's inquest testimony.

Together the prosecution and defense gave the justices their written statement, agreeing to certain facts: that Lizzie had made statements under oath before she was formally arrested, but the mayor had notified her that she was suspected three days before her testimony; that she was duly summoned by a subpoena; that although she was cautioned by Jennings that she need not testify, he was not allowed to be present at the inquest; that she was not given the caution at the inquest itself; and that City Marshal Hilliard held a warrant for her arrest, secretly, at the time of her testimony.

After the bailiff escorted the jury out, Moody addressed the court. "May it please your Honors, the question now under discussion is that of the admissibility of the declarations of the defendant.

"The statute law under which that inquest was held is, as your Honors well know, in chapter 26 of the Public Statutes. It states that the medical examiner, upon view of a body that is found dead by violence, shall notify the court justice, police, or the district attorney. Then, 'the court or trial justice shall thereupon hold an inquest, which may be private, in which case any or all persons, other than those required to be present by the provisions of this chapter, may be excluded.'

"The inquest at which this defendant testified was held in accordance with the law of this Commonwealth. Defendant's counsel asked the privilege of being present at the inquest. The District Attorney and the Court declined that privilege because the law expressly gives them the power to decline it.

"In the case of Teachout v. People, the defendant was informed that he was under suspicion for murder. He was cautioned by the magistrate that he was not required to criminate himself. He appeared at the inquest and testified. It was held by the Court of Appeals that what was said at the inquest was admissible at trial.

"In the case of People v. Mondon, Justice Rapallo said, 'The mere fact that at the time of a witness' examination he was aware that he was suspected will not prevent his being regarded as a witness whose testimony may be afterward used against himself.'

"This important testimony should be admitted by your Honors and submitted to the consideration of the jury."

Moody took his seat.

Defense attorney Robinson rose animatedly, his face flushed. "May it please the Court, the defendant was kept under the constant observation of the police after the murders and all days following until the conclusion of her testimony and arrest.

"The city marshal held a warrant for her arrest during all the time that she testified. For convenience, somebody took care of the prior warrant and a new warrant was issued subsequent to her testimony so that it was in fact an evasion of the law.

"In other words, the practice that was resorted to was to put her really in the custody of the city marshal, keeping her with the hand upon the shoulder—she a woman, could not run—and under those circumstances taking her to that inquest to testify.

"If that is freedom, God save the Commonwealth of Massachusetts! If anything that a defendant does under circumstances like that is voluntary, then compulsory must hereafter be known as voluntary!

"The Constitution of Massachusetts reads, 'No subject shall be compelled to accuse or furnish evidence against himself.' Shall it be attempted by evasion?

"I stand by these rights which are hers by the Constitution, and to depart from their preservation will be peril, not alone to her, but to everybody hereafter who may be placed in a similar position!"

Moody countered, "His argument is magnificent, your Honors, but it is not the law."

The justices returned in the afternoon with their decision. Mason gave the ruling. "We are of opinion that if the accused was at the time of testimony under arrest, charged with the crime in question, statements so made are not voluntary and are inadmissible at the trial. The principle involved cannot be evaded by avoiding the form of arrest if the witness at the time of such testimony is practically in custody. The prisoner at the time of her testimony was, so far as relates to this question, as effectually in custody as if the formal precept had been served. The evidence is excluded." Lizzie's inquest testimony could not be presented in the case against her. Lizzie wept.

The prosecution tried to regain momentum by soliciting testimony on blood evidence found at the house. Medical Examiner Dolan presented the blood-spattered bedspread, as well as boards taken from the house, and his own observations.

Defense attorney Robinson fanned a pale, weepy Lizzie who had not fully regained herself after the fainting spell.

Next the prosecution called Professor Wood.

He described himself as a physician and chemist, as well as a professor of chemistry in the Harvard Medical School since 1876. He had consulted on several hundred previous trial cases.

No evidence of poison was found in the jars of milk from the Borden house or the stomachs of the murdered couple.

The dress that Lizzie provided to the officers had no blood on it, but the white inner skirt contained a small spot which was most likely human blood. He found no blood evidence on Lizzie's stockings or shoes.

The two axes and two hatchets first found in the house contained no blood or other evidence. On the handleless hatchet, Professor Wood also found no blood. The stains were variously rust, varnish, and other unidentifiable reddish spots. The coating on both sides of the hatchet head had been clearly visible to him, though he had not identified the substance.

"Exactly three and a half inches," he said, when asked if he had measured the cutting blade of the handleless hatchet.

Dr. Frank Draper, who had participated in the full autopsies at Oak Grove Cemetery, spoke to the configuration of the murder blade.

Knowlton said, "From an examination of Mr. Borden's skull coupled with the observations of your autopsy, are you able to determine the length of the edge of the instrument which inflicted the wounds?"

"Three inches and one half."

Before Knowlton retrieved the skull, he paused to confer with the defense counsel. Lizzie was allowed to leave the courtroom. Then Knowlton passed Draper Mr. Borden's skull and the handleless hatchet.

"Will you tell us what it is that leads you to that conclusion?" continued Knowlton.

Draper positioned the blade of the handleless hatchet inside the skull, in grooves cut by the murder weapon. The precise fit was important—tools were manufactured in uniform sizes but as they were used and sharpened over time they took on unique cutting signatures.

"It rests against and cuts the surface of the upper portion, but takes in this edge and no more," said Draper, showing the jury how the handleless hatchet fit the grooves perfectly.

The prosecution called druggist Eli Bence. Knowlton had planned the prussic acid as the last testimony in their case, so that it would be prominent in the juror's minds.

Lizzie gave Bence her full attention and an unkind stare.

"What is your full name?" asked Moody.

"Eli Bence."

"What is your occupation?"

"I am a drug clerk for D. R. Smith."

Robinson rose. "May it please your Honors, there is a question here that we consider of vital importance to discuss." He indicated the jury with a tilt of his head.

Bence and the jury were escorted out.

Moody said, "I perhaps ought first to state what the testimony is that we offer. We offer to show that prussic acid is not an article in commercial use, it is a lethal poison, and that upon the third day of August the prisoner asked for ten cents worth of prussic acid, stating that she wished it for the purpose of cleaning capes."

"Perhaps we had better hear the objection," said Mason.

"It appears upon the testimony of Prof. Wood," said Robinson, "that the stomachs of the deceased showed no traces of any poison whatever. So there is shown no connection to the murder."

"Also," he continued, "it cannot be considered here because the offer is on the third of August, and the killing as charged in the indictment was on the fourth. So perhaps I am bound to say that it is not sufficiently near, if it were pertinent."

Many in the courtroom exchanged confused looks.

Moody said, "May it please your Honors, this indictment not only charges that the prisoner killed Mr. and Mrs. Borden, but that she did it with intent. Any act or declaration of this prisoner which is sufficiently near in point of time or significant to her state of mind has bearing and proper weight for consideration by the jury."

The justices retired to consider. The counsel on both sides sat and waited.

At the end of the day the justices gave their decision. The testimony of Eli Bence was not continued, but Justice Mason gave the prosecution the opportunity to establish, with other testimony, that an attempt to buy prussic acid demonstrated an intent to kill Abby and Andrew Borden. If they could do that, Eli Bence could be recalled.

In particular, the prosecution needed to show, with expert testimony, that prussic acid had no innocent non-prescription uses.

The next day Knowlton called three new witnesses.

The first was a New Bedford druggist of twenty years.

Knowlton asked, "In the time that you have been in business, for what purposes have you sold prussic acid other than as a medicine?"

Robinson said, "I object to that."

Knowlton waved a hand, "I will modify the question a little. Have you sold it during that time for any other purpose than upon a prescription of a physician?"

Robinson said, "Wait a moment."

Justice Mason stopped Knowlton. "I do not think the question in that form is competent. The witness is asked about his personal experience, not as an expert in prussic acid."

Knowlton tried again. "In your experience as a druggist, is that drug an article of commerce for any other purpose than as a medicine?"

"Wait a moment. I object," said Robinson.

Knowlton pushed forward. "Or upon a prescription of a physician?"

"I object to that," said Robinson, raising his arm this time.

Knowlton said, "Is the drug called prussic acid sold commercially for any other purpose than upon the prescription of a physician?"

"Wait a moment. I object to that, your Honors," said Robinson.

"Excluded," said Mason, since the druggist was not an established expert in all uses of prussic acid.

Knowlton tried again, "Have you ever had in your experience a call for prussic acid for any other than upon the prescription of a physician?"

"That I object to," said Robinson.

"It is excluded," said Mason.

Knowlton paused to consider. "Do you know of any use to which prussic acid is put other than the purposes of a medicine?"

"Not that I know of; no, sir."

That was the only question and answer regarding prussic acid allowed.

Knowlton called a man in the business of hats, caps, furs, and furnishings. "Have you any knowledge of the effects of prussic acid upon furs?" asked Knowlton.

"Not at all, sir."

Knowlton attempted to solicit other, more direct statements that prussic acid was never used with furs, but Robinson objected again, on the grounds that the witness could not know all ways of caring for furs.

The witness was excused without answering.

From an analytic chemist, Knowlton obtained only the information that airborne prussic acid caused headaches and nausea.

Finally, Knowlton recalled Medical Examiner Dolan. "Are you acquainted with the drug called prussic acid?" asked Knowlton.

"Yes, sir."

"And what about the poisonous effects of the vapor of prussic acid?"

"The most poisonous that we have."

"Has it come within your scope as a physician to study the effects and properties of it?"

"It has, yes, sir."

"And its capacity for use other than as medicine?"

"Yes, sir. I should qualify that statement—it has also come to me in my position as a medical examiner to know its qualities."

That was the extent of Dolan's testimony regarding prussic acid, since he also could not testify to whether prussic acid was used on capes. The prosecution had no more preliminary witnesses regarding prussic acid.

Justice Mason ruled. "The preliminary questions are not included." The Justices prohibited the inclusion of any evidence that Lizzie had tried to buy prussic acid the day before the murders or any other time, on the grounds that the prosecution had failed to show prussic acid could only be used for criminal purposes.

Many in the courtroom, including the press, wondered if this was in fact how the law worked. Knowlton and Moody could not believe their ears. The jury heard no more of Bence's testimony, or other witnesses, to an attempt to buy poison.

The prosecution had no more witnesses. "The Commonwealth rests," Knowlton said, and sat down.

The defense team relaxed. During the recess, Lizzie and her entourage had a lively conversation. They were nonchalant and even a bit merry.

CHAPTER 25

Jennings presented the defense's opening argument.

"May it please your Honors, Mr. Foreman and Gentlemen of the Jury," he said, and bowed slightly to them. "One of the victims was for many years my client and my personal friend. I want to say right here and now, if I manifest more feeling than perhaps you think necessary in making an opening statement, you will ascribe it to that cause. The counsel, Mr. Foreman and gentlemen, does not cease to be a man when he becomes a lawyer."

Several jurors nodded sympathetically. Lizzie sat, waiting.

"Fact and fiction have furnished many extraordinary examples of crime that have shocked the feelings and staggered the reason of men, but I think no one of them has ever surpassed in its mystery the case that you are now considering. The brutal character of the wounds is only equaled by the audacity of the time and the place chosen.

"This young woman who was arrested had apparently led an honorable, spotless life; she was a member of the church; she was interested in church matters; she was connected with various organizations for charitable work; she was ever ready to help in any good deed; and yet for some reason or other the government in its investigation seemed to fasten the crime upon her.

"I say this is a mysterious case. But you are not sitting there, Mr. Foreman and gentlemen, to answer the question how this deed could have been committed, or who committed it. That is not the issue at all.

"The issue is a simple and direct one. The Commonwealth has charged that Lizzie Andrew Borden, in a certain way, at a certain time, killed Andrew Jackson Borden and Abby Durfee Borden with malice aforethought. And that, and that alone, is the question that you are to answer. Or, to put it in its other form, have they satisfied you beyond a reasonable doubt that she did it?

"And what is a reasonable doubt? Well, I saw a definition, and it struck me it was a very good one. A reasonable doubt is a doubt for which you can give a reason. If you can conceive of any other hypothesis that will make it possible or probable that somebody else might have done this deed, then you have got a reasonable doubt.

"I want to say right here, Mr. Foreman and gentlemen, that there is not one particle of direct evidence in this case against Lizzie Andrew Borden. Our books are filled with cases where the accused has evidently been proven, by circumstantial evidence, to have committed the crime. Subsequent investigations or confessions have shown that he did not.

"Have they furnished the proof that the law requires, that Lizzie Andrew Borden did it, and that there is absolutely no opportunity for anybody else?

"The attempt has been made here to surround this house, completely close it in. You have heard witnesses, nearby in the neighborhood, who saw and heard nothing.

"Mr. Foreman and gentlemen, I want to call to your attention right here that there has not been a living soul put on the stand here to testify that they saw Andrew J. Borden come down street from his house that morning. Was it any easier for him to be unseen than it would be for somebody escaping from this house if they walked quietly away?

"But we shall show you, in addition to that, that there were other strange people about that house; people who have not been located or identified.

"And we shall show you that people were up and around and in that barn before Officer Medley opened the door. We shall satisfy you that

Miss Lizzie did go out to that barn, and was out there when this deed was committed, so far as Mr. Borden was concerned.

"And the Government's testimony and claim, so far as I have been able to understand it, is that whoever killed Abby Durfee Borden killed Andrew J. Borden. Even if they furnish you with a motive on her part to kill the stepmother they have shown you absolutely none to kill the father.

"As to the burning of this dress, we shall show you that it did have paint upon it. That soon after it was made this was got upon it, and that dress was soiled and useless and was not the dress she had on the morning of the murder.

"And so, Mr. Foreman and gentlemen, from the fact that there is no direct evidence in this case, with an opportunity for others to do the deed, we shall ask whether they have shown that she killed. See whether the government have satisfied you beyond a reasonable doubt that she did kill her stepmother, Abby Durfee Borden, and her loved and loving father, Andrew Jackson Borden."

Jennings bowed slightly to the jury and the justices, and took his seat.

Lizzie wept. It seemed that after ten months, her emotions had burst through. *The Boston Herald*, having observed Lizzie in multiple hearings, characterized her: "She had learned to brace herself against adversity and unkindness, but mercy and active friendliness were so new that she broke down before them."

The defense presented witnesses from the preliminary hearing and new ones they'd found in the nine months since.

Their first witness, John Grouard, housepainter, said that Lizzie had stained a dress with a dark brown when he painted the Borden house in May of 1892.

Charles Gifford and Uriah Kirby saw a man sleeping on the steps of a house near the Bordens' on the night before the murders.

Dr. Benjamin Handy told again of the man he saw near the Borden house at about nine and again at ten thirty that morning.

Mrs. Delia Manley and her sister Mrs. Sara Hart saw a man leaning on the Borden front gatepost at about 9:45 a.m. on the morning of the murders.

Mark Chase saw an unfamiliar box buggy in front of the Borden house around eleven the morning of the murders. "It was standing right by a tree right front of Mr. Borden's fence," he said. The driver was unfamiliar, but was a man with a brown hat and black cloak.

Jerome Borden, Andrew's cousin, testified that the Borden house front door did not always latch. "I walked up the steps, and took hold of the doorknob, and turned it, and pushed the door open," he said of his visit the day after the murders. As he left the witness stand, Jerome acknowledged the justices with a nod.

Alfred Clarkson said he went into the upper part of the barn at about 11:40. There were three other men up there when he got there, whom he did not know. His estimation of the time made it before Officer Medley's search of the barn.

Everett Brown and Thomas Barlow, teenage friends, also went in the barn. "It was cooler up in the barn than it was outdoors," said Thomas. Their accounts put their visit before Officer Medley.

Jennings asked Emma about the little gold ring Andrew always wore on his smallest finger. "Did your father wear a ring, Miss Emma?"

"Yes, sir."

"Was or was not that the only article of jewelry which he wore?"

"The only article."

"Do you know from whom he received the ring?"

"My sister Lizzie."

"How long before his death?"

"I can't tell you accurately."

"Do you know whether previously to his wearing it she had worn it?"

"Yes, sir."

"Did he constantly wear it after it was given to him?"

"Always."

Jennings asked about the dresses in the house. "Have you an inventory from your recollection, Miss Emma, of the dresses that were in the clothes closet on Saturday afternoon, the time of the search?"

"I have."

"How many dresses were there?"

"Somewhere about eighteen or nineteen."

"And whose were those dresses?"

"All of them belonged to my sister and I except one that belonged to Mrs. Borden."

"Do you know of a Bedford cord dress which your sister had at that time?"

"I do."

"Won't you describe the dress?"

"It was a blue cotton Bedford cord, very light blue ground with a darker figure."

"And do you know when she had that dress made?"

"The first week in May."

"What kind of material was it as to cost?"

"Very cheap."

"Do you know anything about her getting any paint on it at that time?"

"Yes, she did, along the front and on one side toward the bottom. I think within two weeks."

"Where was that dress, if you know, on the Saturday after the murders?"

"I saw it hanging in the clothes press over the front entry, I think about nine o'clock in the evening."

"How came you to see it at that time?"

"I went in to hang up the dress that I had been wearing during the day, and there was no vacant nail. I searched round to find a nail, and noticed this dress."

"Did you say anything to your sister then about that dress?"

"I did. I said, 'You have not destroyed that old dress yet. Why don't you?'"

"Did she say anything in reply?"

"I don't remember."

"What was the condition of that dress?"

"It was very dirty, very much soiled, and badly faded."

"Was this material of which this dress was made in a condition to be made over for anything else?"

"It could not possibly be used for anything else."

"Why?"

"Because it was not only soiled, but so badly faded. It was a shade that in washing that would be completely ruined, the effect of it."

Knowlton asked Emma about contention in the family. "Did your stepmother have relatives in Fall River?"

"Yes, sir. Half sister. Mrs. Whitehead."

"Did Mrs. Whitehead own the whole of her house?"

"No, sir."

"Who owned the rest of it?"

"Mrs. Borden."

"And how did your stepmother come into possession of it?"

"My father bought it and gave it to her."

"Did that make some trouble in the family?"

"Yes. Between my father and Mrs. Borden, and my sister and I."

"Did it make any trouble between your stepmother and Lizzie and you?"

"Yes, sir."

"Did you find fault with it?"

"Yes, sir."

"Did your father, after the fault finding, give you some money?"

"Yes, sir."

"How much?"

"He gave us grandfather's house on Ferry Street."

"Were the relations between you and Lizzie and your stepmother as cordial after that occurrence of the house that you have spoken of as they were before?"

"Between my sister and Mrs. Borden they were."

"They were entirely the same?"

"I think so."

"Were they so on your part?"

"I think not."

"Wasn't it about at that time that Lizzie ceased to call her 'Mother'?"

"I don't remember."

"Do you say that the relations between your stepmother and your sister Lizzie were cordial?"

"The last two or three years they were very."

"Notwithstanding that she never used the term 'Mother'?"

"Yes, sir."

Knowlton checked his notes, and read from them. "At the inquest, I asked you, 'Do you mean they were entirely cordial between your stepmother and your sister Lizzie?' Answer: 'No.'"

"Well, I shall have to recall it, for I think they were."

"Do you remember giving that answer?"

"No, sir. I don't say I didn't say it, if you say I did. I don't remember saying it."

"Whether you said it or not, do you say that is true, that the relations were not entirely cordial between your sister Lizzie and your stepmother?"

"I think they were for the last three years."

"Now I will read you this question and answer: 'Can you tell me the cause of the lack of cordiality between you and your mother, or was it not any specific thing?' Answer: 'Well, we felt that she was not interested in us, and at one time father gave her some property, and we felt that we ought to have some too; and he afterwards gave us some.' Do you remember that?"

"No, sir."

"I will read another question: 'That, however, did not heal the breach, whatever breach there was? The giving the property to you did not entirely heal the feeling?' Answer: 'No, sir.'"

"It didn't, not with me, but it did with my sister after."

"Do you remember making any such distinction in your answer to that question?"

"I don't remember the question nor the answer."

Knowlton moved on. "Miss Borden, when there was anything to be done with the guest chamber, whose duty was it usually to take care of that?"

"Usually I did."

"Did Miss Lizzie have any particular duties about the housework?"

"She did anything that she cared to do."

"She had no particular duty assigned her?"

"No, I don't think of any."

"Did you keep other items in that dress closet? Did any of the members of your family have waterproofs?"

"Yes, we all had them."

"What kind were they?"

"Mrs. Borden's was a gossamer, rubber."

"That is, you mean rubber on the outside?"

"Yes, sir. And black."

"Where was that hanging?"

"I think she kept it in the little press at the foot of the front stairs."

"Did Miss Lizzie have one too?"

"Yes, sir."

"Where did she keep hers?"

"In the clothes press at the top of the stairs."

"And you had one too?"

"Mine was gossamer."

"Did you have yours with you in Fairhaven?"

"I did."

Mrs. Dr. Phebe Bowen, who lived across the street and had been over the morning of the murders, testified that Lizzie had looked pale and faint. Otherwise, Phebe saw no blood and nothing unusual in Lizzie's appearance.

When shown the dress that Lizzie had provided to police, Phebe confirmed it was the dress Lizzie wore that morning.

The defense rested.

CHAPTER 26

The Honorable George D. Robinson, former governor and all-around charmer, was in his element as he stood to address the jury for the closing argument on behalf of the defendant.

The jurors settled into their seats as if for a show and he intended to give them one. He'd use his wit and persuasion and bring them along to his way of seeing the only reasonable course as returning a "not guilty" verdict.

"May it please your Honors, Mr. Foreman and gentlemen: One of the most dastardly and diabolical of crimes that was ever committed in Massachusetts was perpetrated in August, 1892, in the city of Fall River."

He met each juror's eyes in turn as he spoke. Some sat higher at the recognition.

"The terrors of the murder scenes no language can portray. And so we are challenged at once, at the outset, to find somebody that is equal to that enormity, whose heart is blackened with depravity. A maniac or a fiend."

Robinson first focused on the jury and then directed his attention to the gallery, where he received several agreeing nods.

"Inspection of the victims disclosed that Mrs. Borden had been slain by the use of some sharp and terrible instrument, inflicting upon her head eighteen blows; and below stairs was Mr. Borden's dead and mutilated body, with eleven strokes upon the head."

"They were well directed blows. They were not the result of blundering. It was not the careless, sudden, untrained doing of somebody who had been unfamiliar with such implements.

"You must conclude at the outset that such acts as those are morally and physically impossible for this young woman defendant. To foully murder her stepmother and then go straight away and slay her own father, is a wreck of human morals."

The newspaper reporters wrote furiously to capture every word. Lizzie sniffed into her handkerchief.

"The case was brought to the District Attorney by the Fall River police. I have not time to go into any sarcasm or denunciation of those gentlemen. Policemen are human. And you do not get the greatest ability in the world inside a policeman's coat." He shrugged. "You must only call upon him for such service as he can render."

He walked to the jury and stood directly in front of them. "Who are you twelve men, and how come you here? Selected out of one hundred fifty that were drawn from the body of this county.

"Who are you? Men. Bristol County men. Men with hearts and men with heads and men with souls and men with rights. You come here because, in answer to the demand, you feel that you must render this great service, unpleasant and trying as it may be, exhaustive as are its labors.

"You are out of families, you come from firesides, you recognize the bond that unites. Now bring your hearts and your homes and your intellects here, and let us talk to you as men, not as unmeaning things.

"The clerk swore you to the performance of your duty, and perhaps you did not hear that oath so closely as I did. But I heard him say, 'You shall well and truly try and true deliverance make between the Commonwealth and the defendant, whom you shall have in charge.'

"In no case except a capital case is the oath framed in that way: 'whom you shall have in charge.' And Lizzie Andrew Borden, from the day when we opened this trial until this hour, has been in your charge, gentlemen. That is the oath you took.

"The Commonwealth says, 'We intrust her to you.' Now that is your duty. She is a free, intelligent, thinking, innocent woman, in your charge.

"If the little sparrow does not fall unnoticed to the ground, indeed, in God's great providence, this woman has not been alone in this courtroom, but ever shielded by His providence from above, and by the sympathy and watchful care of those who have her to look after.

"You are trying a capital case, a case that involves her human life, and calls for the imposition of but one penalty, that she shall walk to her death. You are then to say, I will critically consider this question, and I will make no mistake, because if I do, no power on earth or in Heaven can right the wrong.

"Gentlemen, it is not your business to unravel the mystery. You are simply and solely here to say, 'Is this woman defendant guilty?' You must leave out rumors, reports, and statements which you have heard before the trial commenced. You must leave out of your minds now, absolutely, every single thing that the learned gentleman who opened this case, Mr. Moody, said that he was going to prove, unless he has actually proved it.

"Mr. Moody said that the Government was going to prove that this defendant was preparing a dangerous weapon on the day before the murders. You heard him say that.

"They have not proved it, have they? You have heard some discussion that we have had at the bar because, in order that there should be no prejudice, you have been asked to step aside, and many of those things which have been offered in good faith have not been proved because the Court has said they are not proper to be proved in this case.

"Then he said that they were going to show you that the defendant had contradicted herself under oath about these occurrences. Well, there is another question which went to the Court and the Court said: That is not proper in this case. You cannot show that.

"So you will leave those things out, Gentlemen. No poison in this case, no prussic acid, no preparation of a weapon by this woman, no contradictory statement made by her under oath.

"Now there is absolutely no direct evidence against Miss Borden, the defendant. Nobody saw or heard anything or experienced anything that connects her with the tragedies. And the murders did not tell any tales on her, either. There was no blood on her, and blood speaks out, although it is voiceless. Not a spot from her hair to her feet, on dress or person anywhere. Think of it!

"Yes, there was one drop of blood on the white skirt, as big as the head of the smallest pin, says Prof. Wood, and that is every particle of blood that was found upon her clothing.

"Now what reason is there for saying that this defendant is guilty?

"In the first place, they say she was in the house in the forenoon. Well, that may look to you like a very wrong place for her to be in. But it is her own home.

"She is shown to have been upstairs to her room, the Government says, and she must have seen the dead body of Mrs. Borden, as she went up and down the stairs.

"Now we are talking of a time with regard to Miss Lizzie when nothing had happened, when everything was all right. People do not go searching and squinting and playing the detective and all that, to begin with. She didn't see it, and she might, therefore she is the criminal?

"Now she told about the note, they say, and that is evidence of guilt. She told about Mrs. Borden having a note.

"Listen to what Mrs. Churchill says about Bridget telling her of Mrs. Borden having a note: 'She said Mrs. Borden had a note to go and see someone that was sick.' Now that is what Bridget told Mrs. Churchill. You get the idea. Both Bridget and Lizzie had learned from Mrs. Borden that she had had a note. Mrs. Borden had told Bridget.

"Now my friend who opened this case for the Commonwealth said that Lizzie told a lie about that note. He used that word. I submit that that will hardly stand upon his evidence. If he had heard the evidence fully through he would not have uttered that expression, because here you have it proved that Bridget gave the clearest and fullest statement about this matter.

"Now Lizzie told about her visit out to the barn, they say. She told the officers that she went out to the barn; went out in the yard, some twenty or thirty minutes.

"It takes Assistant Marshal Fleet here to tell us about the thirty minutes. You saw him. You saw the set of that mustache and the firmness of those lips and the distinction that he wrought here in the courtroom telling that story.

"And there he was, up in this young woman's room in the afternoon, attended with some other officers, plying her with all sorts of questions in a pretty direct and peremptory way, saying to her, 'You said thirty minutes, and now you say twenty minutes; which way will you have it?' Is that the way for an officer of the law to deal with a woman in her own house? What would you do with a man—I don't care if he had blue on him—that got into your house and was talking to your wife or your daughter in that way?

"Now this man Fleet was troubled, and he was a-scent for a job. He was ferreting out a crime. He had a theory. And so he says, 'You said this morning you were up in the barn for half an hour. Will you say that now?' I think the man was impertinent—I beg your pardon, the defendant thinks he was, thinks he was impertinent. She said, 'I do not say half an hour. I say twenty minutes to half an hour.' 'Well, we will call it twenty minutes, then.'

"Much obliged to him. He was ready to call it twenty minutes, was he? What a favor that was! Now Lizzie has some sense of her own, and she says, 'I say from twenty minutes to half an hour, sir.' He had not awed her into silence. Think about a woman saying something or doing something in the presence of a man who talks that way to her under those circumstances."

Robinson paused, shifting to a new line of argument.

"They say she killed her stepmother because of trouble, but then there is no trouble with her father, and she had a change of purpose, or she had a double purpose—to kill Mrs. Borden because she did not like her, and to kill her father because she liked him but wanted his money. What sort of a compound are you making out of this defendant by any such argument as that?

"Now, says Mr. Fleet, in his emphatic police manner, Miss Lizzie said to him, 'She is not my mother; she is my stepmother.' Perhaps she did. We will assume she said it, but there is nothing criminal about it or nothing that savors of a murderous purpose, is there?

"Sometimes when the children get grown up and they are told about their mother that died long ago, there springs up in the mind of the children a yearning or a longing to know of the parent that they really had. He introduces her as 'My mother,' but the first words after you engage him in conversation are, 'She is not my mother; she is my stepmother. My own mother died long ago.'

"They say that Mrs. Gifford, the cloak maker, says Lizzie said, 'Don't say mother to me. She is a mean good-for-nothing thing.'

"Now I agree with you right off that that is not a good way to talk. I agree with you that Lizzie Borden is not a saint, and, saving your presence, I have some doubts whether all of you are saints."

The jurors chuckled.

"Is there anything bad about this case where a woman like this defendant who speaks out openly and frankly and says right out, 'She is not my mother; she is my stepmother?' She spoke so about the man who was called a Portuguese. What did she say? 'He is not a Portuguese; he is a Swede,' in just the same tone of voice. That is her way of speaking.

Robinson paused to check his notes, then turned back to the jury.

"The father had put in Mrs. Borden's hands a piece of property, and Emma says we did not feel satisfied and we told him so. And Emma says she never felt just right about it afterwards. She says up to the day of the death of Mrs. Borden she had not overlooked it, but she says as to Lizzie there never was any trouble about it after that time. From that time, five years, there is no word of any trouble, or indication of anything except this remark made to Mrs. Gifford.

"Andrew Borden was a man that wore nothing in the way of ornament, of jewelry, but one ring, and that ring was Lizzie's. The old man wore it and it lies buried with him in the cemetery.

"Then they say she burned a dress. Nowadays when rags are not worth anything you have almost to pay a man to take them away from the house, and a common way of getting rid of old things is to put them into the fire and burn them up.

"The Government stakes its case on that dress. The Government says: You gave us up the blue dress that lies before me. That is not the Bedford cord dress. You practically commit a falsehood by giving us that.

"There is a disagreement among the persons who saw what Lizzie had on that morning, some of them saying that she had this very dress, and Mrs. Churchill speaking of it as a lighter blue than that.

"Suppose Lizzie had the Bedford cord on, you say, that morning. That is the present theory. The Government said she had it on up to twelve o'clock.

"The witnesses all say and every single person who has testified says that there was not a particle or spot of blood on it. They say there was no blood on her hands, her face or hair. Now, you have removed all idea that that dress was burned with a wrongful intent because all the witnesses say it was perfectly clear of blood.

"I ask them this: if Lizzie Borden killed her mother at 9:45 o'clock in that morning, and then was ready to come downstairs and greet her father and meet him, having on that blue dress, do you think that is probable, besmeared as she would have been with the blood of the first victim?

"Then of course they are going to say, 'Oh, but she changed her dress, and then when she killed her father she either had that back again or she put on another.' Then she had to put that on again, exposing herself to have her underclothing soiled in that way. And then if she put on another dress, then there were two dresses to burn and dispose of, instead of one.

"I would not wonder if they are going to claim that this woman denuded herself and did not have any dress on at all when she committed either murder!

"Then comes this little innocent-looking fellow called the handleless hatchet, and that is the one on which you think the government is going to stand. They have abandoned the claw hammer, so I will bring it down, somewhat disgraced by its former associations and suspicions."

He frowned disapprovingly at the claw hammer as he moved it to the back of the table. The jury and spectators laughed, and some stretched in their seats for a better view.

He gestured to the other hatchet and axes with handles. "Just as innocent—all four of those, as is the defendant sitting here today: not guilty, all of them. They have been suspected; the police have had them. Dr. Dolan saw blood on them all, found human hair on one; sent off to the professor, and it turned out to be the hair of a cow. Blood on them all; and Professor Wood says there is not a particle of blood on any one of them.

"Well, then they find this little fellow covered all over with ashes, and when the officers went down there and got those four that I have put aside as innocent, they did not take this handleless hatchet. Whether Mr. Mullaly or Mr. Fleet is right about it, there is no handle here now.

"The prosecution says, and they said they would prove to you, that there is exclusive opportunity. They said nobody else could have done it. Emma was gone. Morse was gone. Bridget was outdoors, they said, and later in her room. They said that the defendant was shut up in that house with the two victims and that everybody else was shut out.

"The side screen door was unfastened from about nine o'clock to 10:45 or eleven. If a door wasn't locked, gentlemen, Lizzie wasn't locked in and everybody else wasn't locked out. The assassin could go into various places. It was easy enough for him to go up into that guest chamber and secret himself, to stay there, and when he is in there he comes confronting right onto Mrs. Borden.

"Now what is going to be done? He is there for murder; not to murder her, but to murder Mr. Borden. And he is confronted and surprised. And possibly he is somebody that she knew, somebody that would be identified, and he must strike her down.

"And when he had done his work and Mr. Borden had come in, as he could hear him, he made ready then to come down at the first opportunity. Bridget was upstairs, Lizzie outdoors. And then he could do his work quickly and pass out the same door that he came in, the side door.

"They bring in her neighbors who saw no person pass but also never saw some officers who were there. There was also the testimony of neighbors and passersby who heard strange noises and saw men they did not know around the Borden house. You can see then how everything in this idea of exclusive opportunity falls to the ground, because there was no exclusive opportunity. And you are going to sit down in the jury room and criticize the theory that the government advances, and you will see that it is vulnerable, and you will see that a person can take one of those theories just as well as another.

"It is enough if the Government fails to prove the charge. Then your duty is to find her not guilty. Gentlemen, as you look upon her you will pass your judgment that she is not insane. To find her guilty you must believe she is a fiend.

"With great weariness on your part, but with abundant patience and intelligence and care, you have listened to what I have had to offer. So far as you are concerned it is the last word of the defendant to you. Take it; take care of her as you have and give us promptly your verdict 'not guilty' that she may go home and be Lizzie Andrew Borden of Fall River in that blood stained and wrecked home where she has passed her life so many years."

Robinson nodded to the jurors and the justices before returning to his seat.

"The jury may retire with the officers," said Justice Mason, and the jury wordlessly shuffled out of the room. The reporters flew out to the telegraph stands.

CHAPTER 27

Knowlton had prayed for guidance. He'd seen the easy, relaxed alliance between the jurors and the silver-tongued Robinson. Not only did the jurors believe Lizzie to be innocent after Robinson's closing, they also wanted her to be innocent.

The prosecution's case had been perhaps fatally wounded by the inability to present Lizzie's inquest testimony. And the case had been, Knowlton felt, deliberately sabotaged by the decision of the justices to exclude the prussic acid evidence.

The task now was to bring the jury back to facts, and remind them of bloody murders. Knowlton would convince them that convicting Lizzie Borden was justice under the law and under God. Charisma was never Knowlton's gift, but he had facts and evidence. And Knowlton's words would be the last words in the trial, before the justices gave the case to the jury.

When Knowlton stood to make his arguments, he did not see the friendly, open, relaxed faces the jury had for Robinson. They waited for Knowlton, but without much interest. These jurors were ready for the trial to be over. In their minds, perhaps it already was.

Knowlton cleared his throat and bowed. "May it please your Honors, Mr. Foreman and you, gentlemen of the Jury. In the midst of the largest city of this county, in the midst of a household surrounded by houses and people and civilization, an aged man and woman are suddenly and brutally assassinated.

"We are trying a crime that would have been deemed impossible but for the fact that it was, and are charging with the commission of it a woman whom we would have believed incapable of doing it but for the evidence that it is my duty, my painful duty, to call to your attention."

The jurors watched and waited. Hopefully their attention wasn't just a show for the eager members of the gallery tracking their every move.

"The prisoner is a woman, one of that sex that all high-minded men revere, that all generous men love, that all wise men acknowledge their indebtedness to. It is hard, Mr. Foreman and gentlemen, to conceive that woman can be guilty of crime.

"But I am obliged to say, what strikes the justice of every man to whom I am talking, that while we revere the sex, while we show our courtesies to them, they are human like unto us. If they lack in strength and coarseness and vigor, they make up for it in cunning, in dispatch, in celerity, in ferocity. Their hates are more undying, more unyielding, more persistent.

"Is that an unjust criticism? I do the sex no injustice.

"You have been educated to believe, you are proud to recognize your loyalty, your fealty to the sex. Gentlemen, that consideration has no place under the oath you have taken. We are to find the facts.

"With all sympathy for the woman, in which, believe me, I share with you, let me remind you that you stand not only to deliver that woman but to deliver the community."

Knowlton paused to allow that last sentence to settle into their minds.

"At half past nine, if we are to believe the consensus of this testimony, the assassin met Abby in that room and put an end to her innocent old life.

"Gentlemen, that is a controlling fact in this case. It is the key of the case. Why do I say that? Because the murderer of this man was the murderer of Mrs. Borden. It was the malice against Mrs. Borden that inspired the assassin. It was Mrs. Borden whose life that wicked person sought.

"They were a close-mouthed family. They did not parade their difficulties. Yet, Mr. Foreman, there was a skeleton in the closet of that house.

"That correction of Mr. Fleet at the very moment the poor woman who had reared that girl lay dead within ten feet of her voice was not merely accidental.

"Mrs. Borden was the only mother she had ever known. And then a quarrel—what a quarrel, Mr. Foreman! A man wants to help his wife, his faithful wife who has served him thirty years, wants to buy the interest in a little homestead where her sister lives.

"How wicked to have found fault with it. How petty to have found fault with it. And she repudiated the title that woman should have had from her.

"When Mrs. Gifford spoke to Lizzie, talking about her mother, Lizzie said, 'don't say mother to me—she is a mean, good for nothing old thing.' Nay, that is not all— 'we do not have much to do with her. I stay in my room most of the time.'

"Lizzie had repudiated the title of mother. She had lived with her in hatred. Had the poor woman an enemy in all the world? She had one. Was anybody in the world to be benefited by her taking away? There was one.

"Mr. Foreman, there was nothing in those blows but hatred, and a desire to kill. What sort of blows were they? Some struck here at an angle, badly aimed; some struck in the neck, badly directed.

"The hand that held that weapon was not the hand of masculine strength. It was the hand of a person strong only in hate and desire to kill."

The jurors, the press, and the gallery listened with full attention. It was not light-hearted, as it had been with Robinson. Now they were deadly serious.

"We find, Mr. Foreman, perhaps the most remarkable house that you ever heard of. Everything was locked up. Why, did you notice there was even the barbed wire at the bottom of the fence as well as on the top and on the stringers?

"The outside cellar door was found locked by all the witnesses that examined it. The barn door was locked at night. The dress closet, up at the head of the stairs, was found locked by Mr. Fleet, and every time that he wanted to go in there, Lizzie furnished the keys that unlocked it.

"The front door was locked not only with the spring lock but with the bolt and with the lower lock, all three put together. Then the screen door. Up to the time Bridget went out to wash the windows there had been no room for the assassin to come in.

"If Lizzie Borden was downstairs she was in the passageway of the assassin. If she was upstairs there was nothing that separated her from the murder but the thinness of that door that you saw.

"The dead body tells us another thing. The poor woman was standing when she was struck, and fell with all the force of that two-hundred pounds of flesh, flat and prone and dead on the floor. That jar could not have failed to have been heard all over that house. Why, Bridget tells us that she could hear the screen door from her attic room when it slammed.

"Before Bridget went upstairs to her room Lizzie says to her, 'If you go out, be sure and lock the door, for Mrs. Borden has gone out on a sick call, and I might go out too.' Bridget says, 'Miss Lizzie, who is sick?' naturally enough. Lizzie said, 'I don't know, but she had a note this morning, and it must be in town.' The doorbell never rang that morning at all.

"Almighty Providence directed the course of this world to bring murderers to grief and justice. Little did it occur to Lizzie Borden when she told that lie that there would be eighty thousand witnesses of the falsity of it. Why, Mr. Foreman, do you believe there exists in Fall River anybody so lost to all sense of humanity who would not have rushed forward and state, 'I wrote that'?"

It was nearing the end of the day. Knowlton was not finished with his closing, but wanted to leave the jury with something to consider overnight.

"God forbid that anybody should have committed this murder but somebody did. And when I have found that Abby was killed, not by the strong hand of man, but by the weak and ineffectual blows of woman, when I find that those are the blows of hatred rather than of strength, when I find that she is left alone at the very moment of murder, shut up in that house where every sound went from one end to the other, with the only person in all God's universe who could say she was not her friend, with the only person in the universe who could be benefited by her taking away, and when I find, and as you must find, if you answer your consciences in this case, that the story told about a note coming is as false as the crime itself, I am not responsible, Mr. Foreman, you are not responsible, for the conclusions to which you are driven."

The court adjourned and the public waited for the late editions to learn what had happened.

Court resumed at nine on Tuesday, June 20, 1893, the thirteenth and final day of the trial. Jury, spectators, and press waited in eager anticipation of Knowlton's final statements, and then the verdict.

"May it please your Honors, Mr. Foreman and gentlemen of the jury," said Knowlton. "I congratulate you that the end of this hard season is drawing nigh."

"I wish to explain the position of the Commonwealth with respect to motive," he said. "We are called upon to prove that the thing was done, and our duty stops there. We are not called upon to prove why it was done.

"But the malice was all before this act. The ingratitude, the poisoning, the hate, the stabbing of the mind, which is worse than the stabbing of the body, had gone on under that roof for many, many months.

"There may be something in this case which saves us from the idea that Lizzie Andrew Borden planned to kill her father. I hope she did not. But Lizzie Andrew Borden never came down those stairs. It was not the daughter of Andrew J. Borden that came down those stairs, but a murderess, transformed from all the thirty-two years of an honest life.

"Nay, Mr. Foreman, that was not all. She came down to meet that stern old man, the one man in all this universe who would know who killed his wife. She had not thought of that. She had gone on with stealth and cunning, but she had forgotten the hereafter. There wouldn't be any question of what he would know of the reason that woman lay in death. He knew who couldn't tolerate the woman's presence, and she did not dare to let him live.

"Mr. Borden returned from his errands. He came in and down came Lizzie from the very place where Mrs. Borden lay dead, and told him what we cannot believe to be true about where his wife was. That would keep the old man silent for a time, but it would not last.

"The old gentleman goes into the sitting room and sits down. Lizzie suggests to him, with the spirit in which Judas kissed his master, that it would be well for him to lie down upon the sofa and rest. Bridget goes upstairs to take her little rest. Again she was alone with her victim. In what may be safely said to be less than twenty minutes, she calls Bridget downstairs and tells her that her father is killed.

"Assistant Marshal Fleet came there as much dreaming that Miss Borden had anything to do with this crime as his own chief did, but as was his duty he came to her room to get the correct story of all this tragedy.

"When he went into her room to talk with her she was not alone. Mr. Fleet came in, and politely, as you may believe, courteously, he talked with her about that important question of where she was when this thing happened.

"He asked her if she knew anything about the murders. She said that she did not, she went up in the barn. She said after she had been up there about half an hour she came down again, went into the house, and found her father lying on the lounge.

"Mr. Foreman and gentlemen, I assert that the story is simply incredible. The story is absurd. It is not within the bounds of reasonable possibilities. But it was necessary that she should be in the loft. It was the only place where she could put herself and not have known what took place.

"Among the early men that came there was the keen-eyed Medley. He went upstairs in the barn and found no clue that she had been there. Other men went in the barn. But Medley went there first, because he was the one that found the door shut, and the others found it open.

"Of course the question arises to everyone's lips, how could she have avoided the spattering of her dress with blood if she was the author of these crimes.

"As to the first crime it is scarcely necessary to attempt to answer the question. In the solitude of that house with ample fire in the stove, with ample wit of woman, all the evidence of that crime could have been concealed. But as to the second murder, the question is one of more difficulty. I cannot answer it. You cannot answer it. You have neither the craft of the assassin nor the cunning and deftness of the sex.

"When the officers had completed their search and in good faith asked her to produce the dress she was wearing that morning they were fooled with that garment." He gestured at the dress in evidence. "This dress is a silk dress and dark blue, a dress which is not a cheap dress, a dress which would not be worn in ironing by any prudent woman.

"That clear eyed, intelligent, honest daughter of one of Fall River's most honored citizens, Adelaide Churchill, said, 'I did not see her with it on that morning.'

"Still I have not answered the question, how could it be that it didn't get covered with blood? Did it occur to you how remarkable it is that the coat which the old man took off, instead of being hung up, as a prudent old man would have hung it, was folded up underneath his cushion?

"Some attempt might well have been made to cover up that dress. A woman's cunning can devise that. She had had one experience. She had found how blood spurted from hatchet wounds.

"That morning dress had been good enough to keep through May, through June, through July, through the first week in August. Of all times in the world it should be selected on the Lord's day to destroy a dress, and within twelve hours of the time that Lizzie was told that formal accusation was being made against her."

He picked up the handleless hatchet.

"Gentlemen of the jury, do you imagine for a moment, conceding that the officers conspired to lug into the case a hatchet that was faked—if I may use a vulgar word—that they could have had the extraordinary luck to have produced a hatchet which, when applied to those wounds by the hand of science, was found to fit them exactly?"

"They took that hatchet to the police station. It lay there unnoticed, because they supposed there was in the hands of the expert in Boston a hatchet with blood and hairs. But the first hatchets came down from Boston, and we produced the evidence that they were out of the case.

"Then Hilliard said, of course, as was the business of an honest and impartial detective, 'See what about this hatchet.'

"Would an assassin carry away the bloody weapon with which this thing was done? He never would have gone into the streets, armed with the evidence that would convict him. It would have been left at the scene. There is found in the cellar a hatchet which answers every requirement of this case, where no outside assassin would have concealed it. Prof. Wood said that the instrument could have been cleaned. And he is as honest an expert as there is in the State of Massachusetts."

He gestured toward Lizzie.

"Tell me that this woman was physically incapable of that deed?

"We find a murdered woman that had no enemies in all this world excepting the daughter that had repudiated her.

"We find a woman that was killed at half past nine when it passes the bound of human credulity to believe that it could have been done without Lizzie Borden's knowledge, her presence, her sight, her hearing. We find a house guarded by night and by day so that no assassin could find lodgment in it. She had fifteen minutes to kill her Father, which is a long time, and then called Bridget down.

"I submit these facts to you with the confidence that you are men of courage and truth, and shall deal with them with the courage that befits sons of Massachusetts.

"Rise, gentlemen, to the altitude of your duty. Act as you would be reported to act when you stand before the Great White Throne at the last day. What shall be your reward? The ineffable consciousness of duty done. Only he who hears the voice of his inner consciousness—it is the voice of God himself, saying to him, 'Well done, good and faithful servant,'—can enter into the reward and lay hold of eternal life."

Knowlton bowed to the jury. He felt that he'd done as well as possible and that they had a chance at conviction.

Lizzie, for her part, had listened intently as Knowlton spoke but after, turned away as if barely interested.

. . .

Chief Justice Mason said, "Lizzie Andrew Borden: It is your privilege to add any word which you may desire to say in person to the jury. You now have that opportunity."

Lizzie and her counsel rose. "I am innocent," she said, her voice strong. "I leave it to my counsel to speak for me."

The most junior justice on the panel, Justice Dewey, gave the instructions to the jury regarding the law and their responsibilities.

He began by explaining that justices could not tell jurors how to interpret the evidence and arguments presented. The justices could help the jurors understand the law, but that was all. He instructed the jury that Lizzie must be assumed to be innocent unless the prosecution had proven her guilty and to determine guilt or innocence on each killing separately.

Those instructions were the responsibility of the justices to provide to the jury. What Dewey did next, though, was later called judicial misconduct.

First, he told the jurors that, if they found Lizzie's character to be good enough, that might be sufficient in itself to acquit. "You have the right to take into consideration her character such as is admitted or apparent," he said. "It may raise a reasonable doubt of a defendant's guilt even in the face of strongly incriminating circumstances. What shall be its effect here rests in your reasonable discretion."

Next he challenged the assertion that inherited wealth could be sufficient motive for the murders. "Unless the child be destitute of natural affection, will the desire to come into possession of the inheritance be likely to constitute an active, efficient inducement for the child to take the parent's life?"

About the testimony of Mrs. Gifford, the seamstress, that Lizzie had called her stepmother "a mean, good-for-nothing thing," he said, "Remember that it is the language of a young woman. What, according to common observation, is the habit of young women in the use of language? Is it not rather that of intense expression?"

Neither of the other justices interceded. The prosecution shifted uncomfortably in their seats but did not speak. The defense sat stone-faced. The gallery and jury were silent.

"Now you observe, gentlemen," continued Dewey, seemingly oblivious to the mood in the room, "that the Government submits this case to you upon circumstantial evidence. No witness testifies to seeing the defendant in the act of doing the crime charged."

He then suggested that the experts who testified for the prosecution were biased and that their evidence was based on opinion rather than expertise. "I think I may say to you that expert testimony constitutes a class of evidence which the law requires you to subject to careful scrutiny. They sometimes manifest a strong bias or partisan spirit in favor of the party employing them."

Finally, he gave the case to the jury. "And now, gentlemen, the case is committed into your hands. The tragedy which has given rise to this investigation deeply excited public attention and feeling. The press has administered to this excitement by publishing without moderation rumors and reports of all kinds. This makes it difficult to secure a trial free from prejudice."

The irony escaped Dewey.

"Seeking only for the truth, you will lift the case above the range of passion and prejudice and excited feeling, into the clear atmosphere of reason and law."

Justice Dewey had embarked on a second closing for the defense, essentially instructing the jurors to acquit. Even many on Lizzie's side were shocked. Prosecutors Knowlton and Moody tried not to show it in the courtroom, to the jury and the press, but after Justice Dewey's instructions they both felt they'd lost.

The jurors left to consider their decisions.

CHAPTER 28

The jury stayed out an hour, though they'd agreed in the first ten minutes and waited only because they did not want it to appear that they'd decided without debate. Which they had.

"At no time during the trial has the prisoner's almost supernatural courage so appalled the spectators as at this sublime moment of her entry into the courtroom to hear her doom," declared the *Fall River Herald*, as Lizzie returned, head held high, to hear the verdict.

As the jury re-entered the courtroom, their faces betrayed their feelings and before the justices could read the individual charges and ask for the verdicts, the jury foreman exclaimed, "Not guilty!"

Spectators in the gallery burst into cheers and waved handkerchiefs. Lizzie collapsed to her seat, her hands on the rail.

"Thank God," said Jennings, near to tears as he shook Adams' hand.

The justices made small efforts to regain order but they too showed relief and pleasure at the verdict.

Only the prosecution looked glum. It seemed a satisfying end for almost everyone.

An editorial in *The Boston Herald* proclaimed, "The verdict of the jury in the Lizzie Borden case is simply a confirmation of the opinions entertained by those who followed the evidence submitted by the prosecution and witnessed the effect upon it of a vigorous cross-examination. The government was obliged to prove guilt beyond a reasonable doubt, and this it failed to do."

A *New York Times* editorial read:

> "It will be a certain relief to every right-minded man or woman who has followed the case to learn that the jury at New Bedford has not only acquitted Miss LIZZIE BORDEN of the atrocious crime with which she was charged, but has done so with a promptness that was very significant.
>
> The acquittal of this most unfortunate and cruelly persecuted woman was, by its promptness, in effect, a condemnation of the police authorities of Fall River and of the legal officers who secured the indictment and have conducted the trial.
>
> It was a declaration, not only that the prisoner was guiltless, but that there never was any serious reason to suppose that she was guilty. She has escaped the awful fate with which she was threatened, but the long imprisonment she has undergone, the intolerable suspense and anguish inflicted upon her, the outrageous injury to her feelings as a woman and as a daughter, are shareable directly to the police and legal authorities.
>
> That she should have been subjected to these is a shame to Massachusetts which the good sense of the jury only in part removes."

In the Justices' chamber, Lizzie gave a brief audience to the press. She cried and beamed and basked in their enthusiastic attention and congratulations.

She and Emma took the train back to Fall River but did not go to the Second Street house. Instead, they went to family friend Mrs. Holmes' house for a reception, where friends and loyal supporters had been invited to share their congratulations. The group was smaller than expected. Many friends chose not to attend. Lizzie seemed not to notice.

Newspaper drawings of Lizzie that had appeared throughout the case were brought out and examined, and some laughed at for their roughness and poor likenesses. Lizzie laughed and breathed relaxed sighs. She seemed to enjoy the attention and triumphant celebration. She said she was, "the happiest woman in the world."

"What are your first plans, Lizzie, now that you are free?" asked Mrs. Holmes.

Lizzie began to answer but Emma interrupted. "We'll be living reserved lives. We do not want to draw attention." Lizzie glared at Emma but said nothing.

The sisters stayed overnight at the Holmes house, and returned to Second Street the next day. No large crowd gathered as when Lizzie was last home, ten months before. But reporters loitered and passersby peered into the house, making it necessary to keep the windows and shutters closed and avoid going out.

Lizzie had plenty to do right away in the house, though. Hundreds of letters arrived from members of the public, most congratulating her on the acquittal.

The Second Street house was the sisters' own house now, a safe haven, but Lizzie had other plans.

Two days later, Lizzie went on a day trip to Taunton to personally thank Sheriff and Mrs. Wright for their kindness during her stay at the jail.

Lizzie also made a package for prosecutor Moody. In it were clippings, crime scene photographs, and recent headlines announcing her acquittal in bold. Her letter to him read, "souvenirs of an interesting occasion."

Then one evening she snuck away from Second Street, bound for Newport, Rhode Island. She had borrowed a house from a friend where she hoped to have a peaceful recovery from her ordeal, surrounded by quiet and good friends.

Those around the Borden sisters, their closest friends and supporters, were so elated at the acquittal that it seemed the verdict pleased everyone. The loudest voices shouted that, finally, the justice system corrected its immense mistake.

Lizzie and Emma could have been forgiven for believing that

everyone agreed. On trips into town, people sometimes poured out of buildings when they heard Lizzie Borden was there. They congratulated her and shook her hand, much to Lizzie's delight. She smiled and entertained anyone who wished to congratulate her.

However, many who'd at first believed her innocent had begun to limit their contact with her. Her letters went unanswered, or with long waits between responses. Alice Russell no longer associated with either sister and she, like many former friends, went on with her life as if Lizzie and Emma were not still there, in Fall River, up the road.

And the burst of celebration in some quarters only temporarily overshadowed others, where they'd always been certain of her guilt. The acquittal drove resentment. This was an injustice that could not now be corrected.

Still others made a business of it. While Lizzie sat in jail, awaiting trial, a tourist trade began for visitors to ride past the murder house on Second Street. Money continued to be made.

A few Sundays after her acquittal, Lizzie attended service at her Central Congregational Church. The Holmes' escorted her. Many stared as she entered and sat in the Borden pew. Some who were nearby moved away.

So soon after the acquittal, it seemed those things were temporary and would pass. Instead, most everyone, regardless of their stance on Lizzie's innocence or guilt, saw her now in a new way. They watched her and waited, some just to see what she would do next and some for what they felt would be an inevitable confession or slip that would betray her guilt.

Governor Robinson's bill, in the amount of $25,000, sent Lizzie into a rage. A house with land on Fall River's fashionable Hill cost less than half that. But the Borden sisters paid it.

With the trial complete, the authorities released the evidence, including the Borden parents' skulls, to Jennings. The parents' bodies were exhumed, their skulls reunited, and reburied.

The other evidence, such as the bloody guest bedroom bedspread and clips of the parents' hair, was of little interest to the daughters. They left it all with Jennings.

The public learned that it was Governor Robinson who had appointed Judge Dewey to the bench. And it was Judge Dewey who had issued the charge to the jury which so lacked impartiality that esteemed lawyers publicly called for his removal from the bench.

Those on Lizzie's side believed that the evidence was still in her favor and the jury would have acquitted regardless of Dewey's instructions.

Those who felt she was guilty solidified their idea that the trial was rigged. Resentment and anger were directed primarily at Lizzie Borden.

Independently wealthy John Morse appeared at the County Clerk's office to collect his witness fees. When asked his place of residence, for calculation of travel expenses, John said he lived in Iowa at the time of his testimony.

The clerk pressed for his local residence by asking where he had his laundry done. John replied, "Don't have any done; when one shirt is soiled I throw it away and buy another."

Soon after, John moved back to Hastings, Iowa.

Three weeks after the acquittal the Borden jurors posed for a photograph together in their finest suits. It marked their work and time in the spotlight. One juror sent Lizzie a copy. She kept it, and sent a personal thank you letter to each member of the jury.

Bridget left Fall River forever.

A rumor spread through town that not only did Bridget suddenly have enough money for a trip back to Ireland, she also bought a farm there.

. . .

In August, the *Fall River Globe*, which had always been on the side of Lizzie's guilt, began a new tradition. Each year on the anniversary, they provided front page coverage memorializing the Borden murders. The reports included sarcastic speculation on the ongoing search for the killer.

The Fall River Tragedy: A History of the Borden Murders was published in September by Edwin H. Porter, a *Fall River Daily Globe* reporter who had covered the Borden case in detail. His book collected his reports on the murders and reflected his certainty in Lizzie's guilt. As she had done with newspaper accounts covering her, Lizzie read every page. She kept it in her collection.

The sisters split their father's estate equally, after legal expenses, with enough left for each to live well for the rest of their lives. But if they married, they could lose control of their money and their choices.

Business manager Charles Cook saw to the details and guided the sisters through the process of setting up their accounts and holdings.

Jennings had grown tired of the Borden sisters and Lizzie in particular. He'd discharged his debt to Andrew with relief, by achieving an acquittal, and looked forward to the end of their dealings.

Lizzie's will prevailed and she and Emma purchased a house together on the French Street area of the Hill, where the affluent lived. The press covered the day she and Emma moved to their new home in September, three months after the acquittal.

The new house, built in 1887, had fourteen rooms with quarters for two live-in maids, a cook, and a coachman. It was 4,000 square feet and had modern luxuries, including gas lighting, multiple bathrooms, and a bathtub. A small wooded area behind the house became Lizzie's outside escape. She appreciated the outside ever more after her dark, damp cell.

The price, around $13,000, was high for the property. Some people thought the sisters had overpaid and that they would not do well managing money on their own without a father or other male supervisor.

Newspapers treated the news of the purchase as if everyone in Fall River and all over New England should care. Many did.

Emma thought the new house was overly large and indulgent. Lizzie delighted in it. Lizzie had the largest bedroom and her own library. She secretly planned to someday host parties so bright they lit the neighborhood. Emma took one of the smaller rooms.

Most of the Second Street furniture remained behind to furnish the house as a rental. Lizzie did not care for the old, heavy, dated furniture from their parents' home. Instead, Lizzie added all new decor to their new house.

Gawkers in the street in front of the new house, hoping to catch a glimpse, dampened her optimistic mood, but otherwise, it had finally arrived — Lizzie's new life.

In October, Lizzie traveled to the Chicago World's Fair with Reverend Buck's daughter Alice and distant cousin Caroline Borden. The ladies feigned ignorance of the murders when people recognized the Borden name in Chicago.

The Fair was called the Columbia Exposition in celebration of four hundred years since Columbus sailed to the new world, and the affair spread over six hundred ninety acres. Twenty-seven million people visited that year from around the world.

The three ladies saw wonders they had never imagined but which would soon be common, including elevators, zippers, the Ferris wheel, and voice recordings.

They visited The Women's Building, which was designed by fourteen female architects specifically for the fair. It housed galleries of women's art and an assembly hall and general gathering place for women and those who supported their causes. During the fair The Women's Building hosted speakers from all over the world. For Lizzie, this was proof that the world moved forward and things had changed, even if it took longer to reach Fall River.

After they left and the fair closed, the organizers demolished most of the exhibition buildings, including The Women's Building. It was never meant to stay.

CHAPTER 29

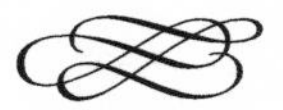

1894

Children chanted outside the store as Lizzie shopped. They'd seen her step from her carriage, cross a few feet of pavement and enter the store, but it had been enough to start the taunting. Soon there was a little chorus, dancing and singing:

> "Lizzie Borden took an axe,
> Gave her mother forty whacks,
> When she saw what she had done,
> She gave her father forty-one."

She didn't blame them. Children behaved as they were taught and allowed. Their parents were at fault.

A year after the acquittal, Lizzie had expected such things to begin to die down. Instead, they were as fervent as ever.

The salesman guided her to the rear of the store. "Children...," he apologized.

“Yes,” said Lizzie. Did he secretly feel the same as those little ones? She could not read anyone anymore.

Since the acquittal, some friends and acquaintances had made friendly gestures toward Lizzie and Emma, only to reveal their true motives later by trying to get a quote or some gossip. Lizzie and Emma were of one mind on that matter, at least. Neither had a word to say about the murders or the trial.

Their vigilance was not rewarded. Emma seemed to have the same friends she’d always had — quiet, well-behaved women who kept to themselves. Lizzie, who wanted to expand her acquaintances, found herself with fewer and fewer friends she could trust.

But she could finally travel and attend the theater at her leisure. She did not go far, generally Boston or New York, registering under false names to avoid scrutiny. It rarely worked. Her image had been printed in so many newspapers and her story followed by so many people that she could not, truly, remain anonymous. Once someone recognized her, news spread and then nothing stopped it.

While some avoided her and whispered behind their hands, others seemed entirely at ease with Miss Lizzie, the acquitted murderess.

The theatrical community acknowledged Lizzie and sometimes invited her backstage after performances when she’d been spotted in the audience. They treated her as if she were one of their own celebrated artists, and she began to believe that perhaps infamy was not always a burden. It opened doors, though not the doors Emma would have thought proper.

Lizzie loved the theater crowd. They were brave and carefree souls who, for the first time in her life, seemed to delight in her company. Still, she was shy and reserved and mostly kept to herself.

Hosea Knowlton and his family left Fall River. He succeeded Albert Pillsbury as Massachusetts Attorney General. Andrew Jennings, Lizzie’s defense counsel, replaced Knowlton as District Attorney.

1896

In February, defense attorney Governor George Dexter Robinson died at the age of 62. The Borden case remained his most prominent case in his later years, though he practiced until his death.

Bridget Sullivan, age 31, moved to Montana where her childhood friend Minnie had settled. Bridget took work as a domestic.

1897

Police issued a warrant again for the arrest of Lizzie A. Borden, four years after her acquittal. This time for theft.

A visiting friend of Lizzie's had admired two small porcelain plates on display in her home. Lizzie, always generous, gave the plates to the friend. Some time later, the friend damaged one and took it for repairs to Tilden-Thurber Co., the Providence, Rhode Island shop whose mark appeared on the back.

The shopkeepers immediately recognized the plate as one of a set that had been stolen years before. The police were summoned, statements taken, and soon after, a warrant sworn out for Lizzie's arrest. Emma and Lizzie again imposed on Andrew Jennings for help.

Jennings believed, after speaking with Lizzie, that she had stolen the plates. She evaded and said she could certainly have afforded to buy them. He had the feeling she'd stolen just to do it.

He arranged with the shopkeepers for the charges to be dropped in exchange for restitution far exceeding the value of the plates. The warrant rescinded, Lizzie was free from further risk of prosecution in the matter.

After completing the work, Jennings swore to his son, "I will have nothing to do with that woman from here on."

Later that year Lizzie bought the property at 5 French Street, the neighbor just to the east of their home. The house there was moved, leaving the lot empty as an extension of the Borden property.

1899

Reverend Buck had made a practice of visiting the Borden sisters. He'd gotten especially close to Emma by then, and by the same measures, less so with Lizzie. Lizzie no longer needed counseling, it seemed.

When he retired in April, Buck said he'd no longer be making calls but invited the sisters to visit him at his home, any time they needed a friend.

The Borden sisters hired a new coachman, a Mr. Joseph Tetrault. He was a handsome man, previously a barber. Joe moved into the house and cared for the carriage and horses, and drove the sisters whenever either went out.

Miss Lizzie took frequent carriage rides. Since people were inclined to stare and make rude comments when Lizzie appeared in public, she'd begun delegating errands instead of going out.

She became fond, instead, of long carriage rides around and outside of town. The fresh air and space away from Emma, who was so inclined to criticize, both appealed.

Joe was a charmer, popular with the ladies, and stepped up from barber to his new position as coachman to a wealthy household. Working for the Borden sisters also gave him a notoriety which he welcomed. Though always careful not to endanger his position by gossiping, he talked about his work when he was about town in his personal time, making a point to defend Lizzie. All in all, the position suited him just fine.

On the long carriage rides when he drove Miss Lizzie wherever her fancy directed, the two often chatted. He found her kind and considerate, with a delightful, easy laugh. Soon they'd established what he felt was a sincere friendship, within certain boundaries. He often shared the gossip from town with her, which she heard so little of herself otherwise.

Months into his tenure Miss Lizzie presented him with a gift — a gold watch chain with a horse's head in onyx. The gift stunned Joe. The easy job left him feeling overpaid for light duties. It was not the first gift

Joe had received from a woman, but he had not expected it from Miss Lizzie, who was his senior.

"Thank you very kindly, Miss Lizzie," he said. "I am always at your service."

"I mean it to thank you for your company as well as your kindnesses," she said. "It's helpful to me to be able to get out in the fresh air, and I so enjoy our chats."

"Always, Miss Lizzie, and happy to be so," he said. He gave her his most winning smile and, if he was not mistaken, she blushed.

In the following months and years, Lizzie bought other expensive gifts for Joe.

CHAPTER 30

1901

Queen Victoria's sixty-four-year reign ended with her death in 1901. Her passing, coinciding with the birth of the new century, seemed to herald change.

The Borden sisters had always belonged more to the rules and requirements of their father's generation than their own, having lived so long under his domain. In the eight years since the acquittal, during which they had much more freedom and independence, they'd continued to live much as if still under their father's eye.

The twentieth century, perhaps, would be their time.

1902

Emma had tried not to raise her voice this time, but Lizzie was so trying. "Of course I have fired him!"

Lizzie, forty-two, felt no restrictions on shouting back louder in her own home. "You had no right! How dare you!"

Fifty-one-year-old Emma tried to shush her. The servants had surely heard.

"Oh, Emma. No one cares."

"You ought to care, Lizzie. Just as you ought to have behaved better with Mr. Tetrault."

"I am grown, Emma."

"Well he's gone and it's done." Lizzie fumed. "Will you not behave properly, Lizzie?"

Lizzie spat her response. "Not if it means living as you do."

Emma lowered her voice. "But you dallied with the coachman."

Lizzie laughed. She seemed surprised, and perhaps impressed, with herself. "And if I did dally?"

"It is *our* name you slight. I have sacrificed, always, for you."

Curiosity replaced Lizzie's anger. "What did you sacrifice for me?"

Emma's eyes flashed in a rare moment of true rage. Her voice shook. "It is all I have ever done, watch out for and care for you, Lizzie. Since Mother died when you were a baby, I have been your mother. And you thank me by behaving in ways that do not let us have peace!"

Lizzie stared back, stunned, as Emma seethed. Lizzie considered before responding, her own anger faded away. "I don't think you're protecting me, Emma, and I am long past needing a mother."

Emma seemed not to have heard her. "Mr. Tetrault is gone. You are not to see him again."

Lizzie, her old coolness back, watched Emma go.

Emma wrote to Reverend Buck for advice. He remained a friend and confidant of the Borden sisters at seventy-seven, though much more so with Emma than Lizzie. Emma visited Buck a few days before he passed. He was, she said, her, "best friend in the world." He counseled Emma that some things were not to be born, and that Emma should stand firm in her morals. If necessary, she must leave the house.

She did not, but spent less time at French Street and more time visiting out-of-town friends.

Former prosecutor Hosea Knowlton died shortly before Christmas, age fifty-five. Newspapers commemorated his death with a Borden trial rehash.

1903

The last leg of actress Nance O'Neil's world tour did not go well.

She was twenty-eight and had been a traveling star for five years. An Oakland, California native, Nance made her life on the stage. She debuted in San Francisco at nineteen, in 1893, the year of Lizzie's acquittal.

Nance and the theater company which she now led had received accolades in Australia and Egypt. The reception in London, where they had their own stars, was more tempered. The company took financial losses, abandoned planned future performances, and escaped instead to Boston and to what they hoped would be more favorable and profitable venues.

1904

Nance's efforts in Boston and surrounding areas were well-received artistically, though she and the company still privately struggled financially from the canceled London schedule's unmet obligations.

On one of her many Boston visits, Lizzie saw Nance perform and sent the actress flowers and a note of appreciation. Nance would later claim that she'd never heard of Lizzie Borden or the famous murders until a friend educated her.

A few days after sending the note, Lizzie went to Nance's Boston apartment, on invitation for tea. The dark wallpaper and ornate flowers matched Lizzie's own French Street house.

The actress, five inches taller than Lizzie, wore a stylish but immodest dress plunging low at the neckline. In the past Lizzie's collars would have reached her chin but she'd progressed to lower collars, still on her neck.

Lizzie could not help being awed by the glamorous, acclaimed, and confident actress. Boston loved Nance. Audiences threw flowers onto the stage for her many encores. It was a fame so different from Lizzie's.

Nance seemed not the least uncomfortable as she invited Lizzie to sit. "I'm so glad you wrote, Miss Borden." Nance graced Lizzie with a charming smile and her full attention.

Lizzie was forty-four and fourteen years Nance's senior. But her hand shook as she lifted her china cup. "Of course I had to write. I was so moved by your performance, as was everyone who attended, I'm sure you could tell."

"That's lovely of you," said Nance, sipping her own tea. "What brought you to Boston?"

"Oh, your performance! I'm a great fan of the theater."

"I hope it was worth your trip, then." Nance did not allow the conversation to wane. "Would you like to hear some of the traveling escapades of our little company, that we don't usually share?" She gave Lizzie a conspiratorial eye.

Lizzie leaned forward in her seat. "Oh yes!" she said, a little too loud.

Nance, world-weary from traveling, rehearsals, and performances, roused at the potential of a friendship with a famous murderess. Or not murderess. The reputation was enough. Nance's tales, usually saved for journalists and parties, found Lizzie to be an attentive listener. Nance began to like this gentle, soft-spoken, and wealthy woman.

Nance and Lizzie made a good start to an acquaintanceship during their tea and then grew it to a friendship through the spring and summer. They met frequently in Boston during that time and were seen in public together. They made an odd pair at lunches in town, the statuesque, confident actress and the smaller, quiet, graying woman of infamy who seemed to belong to the last century in her manners and not-quite-stylish clothes.

One of Nance's skills, cultivated over a decade of performances, was an intense, undivided focus. Lizzie felt seen and heard for the first time, and that she would not be disparaged for not behaving as she should. She spoke with Nance about many things, though never of the murders, except to share her heartbreak at the way people had and still judged her.

"I thought," Lizzie told Nance, "that once I was acquitted at trial, the truth would will out. Instead, I fear I will never escape this shadow."

Nance shrugged. "People will talk. Choose not to care." Lizzie could not imagine how she could cease to care what others thought, the way Nance seemed to with such ease.

At Nance's shows and parties, Lizzie was welcomed with enthusiasm and for the first time in her life felt an easier comfort with others. She realized she was not nearly as wild as some in the theater company were, no matter that the papers had sometimes lately characterized her 'wild ways.' It seemed Lizzie was held to a higher standard.

Nance was especially kind to Lizzie and took care that her gentle guest was treated well by the others. Lizzie made friendships with others in that group, though none as closely as with Nance.

One day, Nance said, "I don't think you're Lizzie Borden, actually. Lizzie is a common name. You're quite uncommon. You're not Lizzie Borden." Nance's given name was Gertrude Lamson; stage names were expected. "Choose to become someone new and change your name to something more suitable. Dorothy? Evelyn? Constance? Chastity?" Nance never feared to tease.

Lizzie laughed her light, easy laugh. "None of those, please." She considered for a moment and then said, "Lizbeth?"

"Very nice."

Once she'd thought about it, Lizzie decided both that she did like the name and that she'd already been creating her new self for some time. Perhaps she could find a way to live without concern for the harassment and rejection which seemed they would never end.

Poor Nance was herself harassed by some expensive legal matters related to the theater company and unfulfilled obligations. Lizzie helped, in spite of the large amount. Ricca, a friend in the company, also imposed on Lizzie for a loan of $50.

Lizzie began asking others to call her Lizbeth Andrews Borden instead of Lizzie Andrew Borden.

The *Fall River Globe*'s annual recollection of the Borden murders arrived on their front page, right on schedule for the August fourth anniversary. For the 1904 edition, the sarcasm was especially pointed:

"A DOZEN YEARS

SINCE THE BORDENS WERE BRUTALLY BUTCHERED,
and yet the Horrible Crime is Unpunished.
Perhaps Murderer or Murderess, May be in the City —
Who Can Tell?"

In October, Nance came to Fall River with her company to perform two plays, *Magda* and *Fires of St. John*. Lizbeth attended multiple performances and hosted a lavish party for the company at the French Street house. She hired musicians and rented palm plants. The lights lit up the neighborhood.

Emma was out of town.

Lizbeth finally heard word of Joe Tetrault, through her maid. He was back in Fall River and had taken up barbershop work again. Lizbeth sent him a note. Soon, he was back as coachman.

1905

Nance O'Neil took her leisure at the French Street house in May. It was a subdued visit. Exhausted from her schedule, Nance still engaged Lizbeth with her free, brash spirit and ease.

After Nance left, Emma barely spoke to Lizbeth. It seemed that Lizbeth had finally gone too far with all of the unsuitable guests in their home. The idea of having gone too far with Emma did not bother Lizbeth at all.

"Lizzie Borden Left by Sister," *The Boston Sunday Herald* reported on June 3. "After repeated disagreements, Lizzie A. Borden and her sister, Emma Borden, have parted company. Several days ago Miss Emma packed up her belongings, called a moving wagon and shook the dust of the French Street home, where they have lived together ever since the acquittal in the famous murder trial, from her feet. The tongue of gossip has been wagging tremendously, even for Fall River, which is saying a great deal. All sorts of reasons for the quarrel between the sisters have been afloat, but the best founded ones involve the name of Miss Nance O'Neil, the actress, and also that of Miss Lizzie's coachman, Joseph Tetrault.

"It is nothing new to learn that the sisters have not agreed. Miss Emma was sedate and retiring, Miss Lizzie was fond of good times and jolly company. When they moved from the Second Street establishment, where the murders occurred, to the handsome residence on French Street, rumors of disagreement continued to escape from the neighborhood. When the moving van backed up, a few days ago, the gossip fairly poured out."

Soon after Emma's departure the Borden sisters reached an agreement through their lawyers. It specified that the house remain mutually owned and in equal halves by both Lizbeth and Emma. On the death of either, their portion should transfer to the surviving sister.

The sisters signed the contract separately and did not meet in person.

In celebration of the successful resolution of Nance's legal matters, Lizbeth paid for a week-long house party at Nance's new house in Tyngsboro for the touring company and other guests who came and went throughout the week.

There was, at times, alcohol and morphine and general debauchery. Lizbeth kept her distance from those. Some of the revelers wanted Lizbeth to recount her tales. "Tell us about the *murders*."

Lizbeth had no interest in becoming the entertainment, and was already in a sour mood: Nance kept putting Lizbeth off over repayment of Lizbeth's money, even though Nance had somehow found the funds to buy the Tyngsboro house the year before, in 1904.

Ricca, likewise, was sadly unable to say when she could repay her dear and generous friend Lizbeth.

Lizbeth bought the plot of land across the road from the French Street house, so that she owned four nearby plots and properties, all empty.

Bridget Sullivan, age 39, married John Sullivan in Anaconda, Montana.

1906

Nance's last performance in Fall River was in January, after which the touring company would move west into the United States. That had always been the plan.

Lizbeth's letters and demands regarding the loaned money went unanswered. Lizbeth did not attend the performance.

1907

Lizbeth was forty-eight when Joe left the second time, this time to Providence, Rhode Island. He'd been her coachman for three more years, but it wasn't enough for him.

Lizbeth would not have minded the scandal of marrying her coachman, but she would never marry. And she was not so naive these days to believe that Joe had no interest in her money, or that he could resist spending it.

In time she hired Mr. Ernest Terry to drive her on outings in her new automobile, one of the first in Fall River. Mr. Terry, a respectable man, became a friend she could talk to.

1908

Lizbeth gave the French Street house a name. Wealthy and fashionable Gilded Age families christened their palatial estates with names like "The Breakers" and "Biltmore Estate." Lizbeth had her chosen name carved into the concrete steps leading to the front door.

Some thought it gauche, naming a house as if it were an estate. Now Lizzie Borden was taking on airs, they said. Lizbeth felt she had earned the privilege and chosen a good name: "Maplecroft."

CHAPTER 31

1912

John Morse never married and had no children.

He lived in Iowa from 1893 until his death on March 1, 1912, at age 78, leaving an estate worth more than $23,000. His will directed that his estate be split between his nieces and nephews "except those named Borden, who are not in need of it."

1913

In April, twenty years after Lizbeth's acquittal, Emma gave an interview to the *Boston Sunday Post*. She'd heard that Lizzie planned to give an interview and wanted to make sure her own views were heard.

Fall River and the world had never yet failed to be interested in the affairs of the Borden sisters.

Emma dressed for mourning, as she had ever since the deaths of their parents.

"For 20 years the Bordens have maintained a sphinx-like attitude toward the treatment accorded the acquitted woman by the world in general and Fall River in particular," wrote journalist Edwin Maguire. "Doors of old time family friends were closed to her following her trial on the charge of murdering Andrew J. Borden, one of the city's wealthiest citizens and his second wife. The frigidity of an Arctic temperature displaced the pleasantries she had formerly known from her life-long friends.

"Eight years ago Emma Borden quit the spacious mansion in the French Street section of the exclusive 'hill district' where she and Lizzie Borden were residing. Since Emma Borden's departure they have never met or communicated with each other."

Emma was sixty-two with white hair and kidney problems. "The happenings at the French Street house that caused me to leave," she said, "I must refuse to talk about. I did not go until conditions became absolutely unbearable. Then, before taking action, I consulted the Rev Buck, who had for years been the family spiritual advisor. After carefully listening to my story he said it was imperative that I should make my home elsewhere. I do not expect ever to set foot in the place where she lives."

Emma also shared something of the commitment she had to her younger sister.

"I did my duty at the time of the trial, and I am still going to do it in defending my sister even though circumstances have separated us. The vision of my dear mother always is bright in my mind. I want to feel that when Mother and I meet in the hereafter, she will tell me that I was faithful to her trust and that I looked after 'Baby Lizzie' to the best of my ability."

When asked whether Lizzie could have committed the murders, Emma said, "Time and again she has avowed her innocence to me and I believe her. The axe, or whatever it was that figured in the killing, has never been found. If Lizzie did the deed she never could have hidden the weapon so well."

The reporter asked whether her sister was not queer, implying that perhaps Lizzie's strangeness itself could have allowed her to commit an otherwise incomprehensible crime.

"Queer?" Emma responded. "Yes, Lizzie was queer, but guilty on that terrible charge made against her—no—emphatically, no."

. . .

Lizbeth's friend Helen Leighton came to see her at Maplecroft in October.

Fifty-three-year-old Lizbeth had created a refuge in and around Maplecroft, since she no longer traveled as much.

Bird feeders peppered the backyard and her squirrels were curious and friendly. The woods and empty properties surrounding the house, all owned by Lizbeth, buffered the house and distanced it from unkind eyes.

Lizbeth lived there with her Boston terriers, cat, and a full time staff of four. She adored her staff, often engaging them in conversations about their lives and families, as if those families were her own. Lizbeth sent thoughtful gifts to their younger and ill relatives.

Helen had brought another woman, Gertrude Baker, a local schoolteacher, this time. The women wanted Lizbeth's help.

With the introduction of motor cars, the need for horses quickly and greatly diminished. Many horses, especially draft horses, were killed for food or abandoned to starve. The ladies' idea was to create the Fall River Animal Rescue League. Helen, a nurse, would be President, and knowing of Lizbeth's affection for animals, thought that perhaps Lizbeth would help them with founding contributions.

She was right.

Gertrude, who had not previously known Lizbeth, was amazed at the gentle nature of the woman. Gertrude had, without thinking, expected the woman to behave outrageously.

Lizbeth kept her word and made a large donation to the new Animal Rescue League. She also hosted a fundraising party at Maplecroft to raise funds for the new endeavor.

Some of the guests watched Lizbeth.

Lizbeth recalled how people, and Lizbeth herself, had watched Nance with a blissful adoration.

This was not that.

1920-1927

The long years and the perpetual scrutiny had drained Lizbeth. She shared her feelings with friend Amanda Thelen:

> "June 10, 1923
>
> Dear Manda, I have not been well and am going away for a little while to try and rest my nerves.
>
> When I feel more like myself I'll be glad to see you and will let you know. I hope all goes well with you and yours.
>
> Your friend,
>
> L.A. Borden"

In October, 1923, Andrew Jennings died at the age of 74 and was buried in Oak Grove Cemetery with so many other Fall Riverites.

In the attic of Jennings' home, in a hip-bath tub, he left behind extensive journals, notes, and the physical evidence related to the Borden case and the defense of Lizzie Borden. These included clipped hair from both Andrew and Abby's heads and the blood-spattered guest bedspread.

The journals had been compiled by Jennings and Arthur Sherman Phillips, a young member of the defense team, and contained extensive notes on interviews and information related to the case. Not all of it had been presented in court.

For decades after Jennings' death, no one realized what the tub contained.

As it was for all of her life, Lizbeth had a few close friends.

After the trial so many she considered friends had shunned her or fallen silently away. Others who were unwavering in their support, including Marianna Holmes, had died. But she'd built some new friendships, and close ones, that would remain true to her last days.

Helen was steadfast, and Lizbeth felt assured that her other friends and household staff did genuinely care for her. And she had her Boston terriers and cat, Blackie.

Lizbeth's world grew gradually smaller in her sixties until it existed mostly at Maplecroft.

Some children liked the old lady down the street who gave out cookies if you went to her door. Some egged her windows and put honey on the doorknobs instead. They didn't know her or why many in town exchanged knowing looks about her, the ghoul called Lizzie Borden, but they knew to taunt her and to run away. Don't let her catch you.

Lizbeth went on trips, though less often than before. More often she went for rides in one of her fine motor cars with Mr. Terry, to get air and see the changing Fall River. She'd discovered that dogs delighted in taking drives in motor cars as much as she did.

She came to understand that those long ago afternoons in the carriage with Joe, where she hid behind dark curtains so people would not gawk, were some of the best times in her life. All those years ago, after the acquittal, she'd thought that she was beginning to live.

In February of 1926, sixty-five-year-old Lizbeth was admitted to Truesdale Hospital in Fall River on the advice of her doctor, Dr. Annie Campbell MacRae.

She stayed under an alias: Miss Mary Smith Borden. The hospital administration agreed to the alias to protect both Lizbeth and the privacy of their other patients from the disruption that would have been caused if Fall River's most famous resident was known to be there.

She spent weeks in the hospital, recovering from gallbladder removal. The newspapers discovered her in spite of the alias.

"Personals: Miss Lizbeth A. Borden, 306 French Street, is ill at the Truesdale."

"Local Lines: The condition of Miss Borden, who underwent an operation at the Truesdale, is reported as being satisfactory to her physicians."

People made a point to walk past her room.

Later that year, while still convalescing at home, Lizbeth bought the property at 3 French Street, second to the east from Maplecroft.

Lizbeth owned five neighboring plots around Maplecroft.

Emma's doctor said she would live for some time longer, but her activities would be severely constrained.

Emma did not reach out to Lizzie. Instead, she purchased a house in Newmarket, New Hampshire, and deeded it to a caregiver on the condition that the woman care for Emma until her death.

Emma and Lizzie had not spoken or corresponded directly since 1905.

Helen held Lizbeth's hand as she sat at Lizbeth's bedside.

Lizbeth had never fully recovered from the gallbladder surgery and now she struggled for breath as she slept, desperately ill with pneumonia.

Helen imagined Emma would want to know and should be summoned, except that Helen did not know where Emma was or even if she was still alive. Perhaps Emma would see Lizbeth's death noted in the papers and return to Fall River.

In Lizbeth's later years she was always kind and still managed to laugh sometimes. She also confessed to being bitterly unhappy. The tragedy and the sorrow of the murders and everything that happened during and after was always present in her, like a darkness that never cleared.

Lizbeth died on June 1, 1927, of a heart attack caused by pneumonia.

That same day, in New Hampshire, Emma fell and broke her hip.

Many newspapers covered Lizbeth's death, including the *New Bedford Sunday Standard*: "TOOK 35-YEAR HOPE TO GRAVE. Lizzie Borden Lived in Expectation of Proving to Skeptical World She Never Killed Kin."

The Morning Mercury out of New Bedford had details of Lizbeth's will. "LIZZIE BORDEN LEAVES $30,000 TO ANIMAL RESCUE LEAGUE."

She had actually given $30,000 in cash and also stock, totaling more than $50,000. Her will told of her love for animals. "I have been fond of animals and their need is great and there are so few who care for them."

She left her household staff, including Mr. Terry, $3,000 each. She also gave property and cash to his wife and children.

She left Helen Leighton three diamond rings, a mahogany desk, first choice of the furniture in Maplecroft, and a part ownership of the A.J. Borden building, total value $36,000.

Lizbeth remembered other friends, some from childhood.

Emma received nothing from Lizbeth's will. "I have not given to my sister, Emma L. Borden, anything, as she has her share of her father's estate and is supposed to have enough to make her comfortable."

No one thought it wise to inform Emma of Lizbeth's death as Emma's health deteriorated precipitously. In her muddled sleep she sometimes whispered reassurances to Baby Lizzie.

On June 10, 1927, nine days after her sister, Emma followed.

Like Lizbeth, Emma left many charitable bequests, remembered friends, and also left a sum to the City of Fall River for maintenance of the family burial plot. She supported the Ninth Street Day Nursery of Fall River, the Salvation Army, Rescue Mission, Children's Home, and Women's Union of Fall River.

Emma's will also remembered the promise the sisters had made to each other, and left Emma's half of Maplecroft to "my sister, Lizzie A. Borden." Lizbeth's estate did not receive ownership, however, since she'd predeceased her sister.

The sisters were buried next to each other in the Borden plot in Oak Grove Cemetery, next to their parents. Lizzie had never legally changed her name to Lizbeth, but her headstone read "LIZBETH."

1948

Seventy-seven-year-old Bridget Sullivan was ill and feared she was close to her end. She summoned her friend Minnie Green, who had been a girlhood friend of Bridget's in Ireland, and who lived nearby.

Bridget asked Minnie to hurry, saying that she had some secret to confess before she passed. Minnie rushed to Bridget's bedside.

On the first day of Minnie's visit, Bridget swore her to secrecy and told her that she, Bridget, had worked for a family named Borden. Minnie had never heard of the Borden murders.

Bridget said that she had liked the daughter, Lizzie, and sympathized with her when there were conflicts in the household. At the trial, Bridget said, she had helped Lizzie by not revealing everything.

Bridget didn't have the strength to say more that night.

The next day, however, Bridget was much improved and refused to continue her tale.

Bridget Sullivan died in Montana, on March 25, 1948, age 82. Her husband, John, had predeceased her by many years. They had no children; Bridget left her small estate to three nieces who knew nothing of Bridget's time serving in the Borden household or of Bridget's involvement in the trial. All they knew was that sometimes, briefly, Aunt Bridget had mentioned having worked for a woman named Lizzie Borden.

Bridget's will and personal effects contained no memoirs or notes regarding the Borden family or Bridget's involvement, or not, in murder.

With Bridget's death, all those who were directly involved the day of the murders were gone. It had been fifty-six years, but there was more to the story still to tell.

CHAPTER 32

1863: TWENTY-NINE YEARS BEFORE THE MURDERS

At dusk Sarah Morse Borden called her eldest daughter into her bedroom for the last time.

Sarah had been dying for weeks. At first she'd believed, even while she grew more pale and exhausted, that she could recover. Soon she realized there was no help for her.

Twelve-year-old Emma arrived in the bedroom with red eyes and a sniffling nose. All those weeks Sarah had assured Emma that it was not so serious. At first Emma believed, too. But Emma knew well how many women died in childbirth or from poorly understood "women's problems." Relatives, neighbors, and friends had all died. No married woman of childbearing age was safe.

Emma did not know that Sarah was dying from a choice which left her hemorrhaging. That Sarah chose because she would not risk dying in childbirth and leaving Emma and two-year-old Lizzie. Now she was leaving them anyway.

Emma sat on her mother's bed, near but not touching her mother, who was so pale and thin. Sarah worked for every breath as she took

Emma's hand. "It's all right," Sarah said, though it wasn't. "Women like us must be strong and not show our feelings to the world, but we can cry here, together."

Emma crawled onto the bed to curl up next to her mother. They rocked and cried. Emma already missed her mother's presence and strength in the house.

In the past, people in town had judged Sarah as too pushy, emotional, and overbearing. Sarah wasn't such a good wife, they said. Mrs. Andrew Borden would do better to hold her tongue and defer to her husband, but Emma needed her mother's strong will.

On her deathbed, Sarah sought something from Emma. "You must make a promise to me, Emma, that you will watch over Baby Lizzie."

"I will," Emma said through sobs. "I promise." Emma was glad she'd said it, because her mother looked so relieved. In truth, Emma had never stood strong for anything and did not know how she would mother Lizzie after their own mother was gone.

"Bring me a paper for a letter," Sarah said. "When I seal it up and give it to you, take it yourself to the post office. Do not show it to your father or let him know."

Sarah spent what little energy she had writing the letter. She did not know if the letter would be of any good, but she tried, and Emma did as her mother said.

Two-year-old Lizzie Andrew, her father's namesake and his favorite, understood nothing of her mother's illness and death.

It wasn't proper for a household with children to be without a caregiver. After Sarah died, Andrew's sister Lurana, whose only child had died at age nine, offered to move into the house and care for the girls until he found a new wife. He declined.

John Morse and his brother-in-law, Andrew Borden, both lived frugally and proudly pinched their pennies, though Andrew was rigid and unforgiving while John cared more about others.

At twenty-nine years of age, John lived a bachelor's life on his farm out west, not married, with no children, and in that way naive in many matters.

He learned of his sister's death by way of a telegram from Andrew. It stated only that she had passed and was buried in a family plot in Oak Grove Cemetery.

More than a week later John received a letter from Sarah herself, sent a few days before her death and of which Andrew had not seemed aware.

> "Dearest John,
>
> The doctor consoles me that my illness will not resolve, and there is nothing to be done. I am exhausted from the ordeal. Only my fear of leaving Emma and Baby Lizzie has sustained me.
>
> This is my final wish and request of you, my blood and theirs: come back to Fall River. Come back and watch over them and protect them, in my stead.
>
> With all my love and hopes, Sarah"

John could not understand her meaning. John's life was in the west and their own father would keep watch over the girls.

John thought, perhaps, that the illness had deprived Sarah of some sense. He kept the letter, though, and thought that he might, after things were more settled with his farm, return to Fall River for at least a visit.

Though he was a Fall River Borden, Andrew J. Borden came from humble beginnings. His own father was unsuccessful and worked as a fishmonger. When he was still a boy, Andrew swore he would do better.

By the time his first wife died, Andrew had shown himself to be an astute and reliable co-owner and manager at Borden & Almy, a furniture and funeral supply firm in Fall River.

Andrew had also begun to build what would become a substantial portfolio of commercial and residential real estate holdings. By 1863, the name Andrew J. Borden was known as that of an honest and precise man, though not perhaps one sought after as a friend.

Andrew attended to his businesses while at the Borden house their live-in maid took care of the cooking and cleaning. Emma had the care of Lizzie.

1865

Abby Durfee Gray did not love Andrew Borden, but she was marrying him anyway.

He seemed a cold but proper man, an acquaintance from church. At thirty-eight, Abby had no other prospects and likely never would.

The proposal from such a wealthy and respected man was a surprise and a blessing for Abby and her family. They struggled financially.

By accepting his proposal, Abby would never again be at risk of losing her home or of not having enough to eat. She might not like the man much, but she would, at least, be safe. And perhaps she could help the rest of her family, if he ever shared his wealth.

For his part, Andrew gained a wife to run his household, raise his daughters, and perform wifely duties.

Abby was surprised the first time she saw the Borden house on Ferry Street. The humble house was not what she would have imagined as the house of a man of so much reputed wealth. Andrew was known to be so tight with money that he hardly ever spent it. On seeing the family home, Abby thought that must be true.

She'd hoped the inside of the house would be happier than the outside, but was disappointed. The dark, close house did not improve her situation much over the house she'd left behind.

Abby greeted her new daughters shyly. Emma, age fourteen, held five-year-old Lizzie's hand as Abby stood at their bedroom door. Emma appeared to be sizing Abby up.

"Hello," Abby said.

The girls stared back. They seemed odd and pale.

Abby expected them to be excited. "I'm to be your new mother," she said, brightly.

Lizzie looked up at Emma. "She's not our mother," Emma said, and shut the door.

. . .

Andrew decided he was pleased with his matchmaking skills. Abby, it seemed to him after a few months, made a better wife than his first, who henpecked and kept him under her eye.

Abby not only rarely asked anything of him, she already knew to hold her tongue and not participate in discussions of business, money, or politics. Andrew hadn't needed to teach her. And she did not pay much attention to his activities. She left him to himself.

Abby also felt the marriage worked. She and her new husband were both business-like in their approach to the partnership.

The two stepdaughters, however, made Abby's new home an unpleasant place. Emma insisted on calling her Abby instead of Mother and Lizzie learned to dislike Abby from Emma. The girls did not warm to her.

At least Abby had enough to eat.

Sometimes, when Abby went to market to buy sweet bread on the maid's day off, Andrew told her to take one of the girls with her.

Lizzie rarely spoke in those days, but sometimes, as Abby and Emma were leaving, Lizzie asked Abby in her quiet, shy, five-year-old voice, to go to market, too.

Abby did not need both girls with her at the market. "Your father wants you to stay," she'd say.

Emma never said anything in those moments, but her eyes showed she knew.

Andrew would take Lizzie's hand as they watched the other two leave. Once they were alone in the quiet house and he took her to her room with him, Andrew would tell her not to make noise or be upset. It was better, he said, not to feel.

After a while that was true.

1870

Although Abby had been in the house for five years, Emma still did most of the caregiving for Lizzie, age ten. The arrangement suited Abby fine.

Abby managed the housework and the Borden girl, and left

everyone else to themselves. The girls' hatred of Abby, though, seemed to grow no matter how nicely she spoke to them.

1872

Andrew was shopping for a new house. He wanted a property within walking distance of downtown. The house at 92 Second Street was built in 1844 and was two apartments. It was also a short walk to his businesses, and Andrew determined to buy the house if he could get it for the price he wanted.

It was also, coincidentally, one house to the north of a house owned by his elderly uncle, Lodowick. In that house in 1848, Lodowick's wife, Eliza, had drowned their two youngest children in the cistern and then slit her own throat with Lodowick's razor.

Andrew, neither sentimental nor superstitious, was not bothered by living next door to a murder house.

Emma, twenty-one-years-old, and Lizzie, twelve-years-old, made do as they could with the awkward bedroom situation in the new house. The two bedrooms for the girls were connected, with the only entry to the smaller bedroom through the larger.

Emma had that larger, south-facing room and Lizzie the smaller, north room. The door connecting directly from their parents' room was locked when they moved in.

The family ate supper together that night, as they always did. That was one of Andrew's rules. Before the meal they always prayed with gratitude for all that they had. That was also one of his rules.

1876

John returned to Fall River and lived at the Borden house for a year, when Emma was twenty-six and Lizzie sixteen.

He'd corresponded with Emma over the years, and also with Andrew and had meant to return sooner.

The Bordens learned well the power of John's own frugality — he did not bathe, wash his hair, or have his clothes washed. Those were his habits and he did not change them even while living in the Borden house, where their girl did the laundry.

John had not forgotten the letter from his sister. He stayed with the family and watched.

1877

Seventeen-year-old Lizzie decided she did not want to finish high school. She'd tired of it.

She had a simple gold ring of her own, paid for with Father's money. One afternoon when Father came home from work and no one else was around, Lizzie said, "Do you see the ring, Father?" She stretched her arm out to show it to him on her left hand ring finger.

"Yes." He held her hand lightly and turned it to see the ring better in the light from the window.

"It's so special to me, I want you to have it," Lizzie said.

"Oh?" he said. "It was for you."

"Which is why I want you to have it, because I'm your favorite."

"Yes," he said.

He eased the ring off her finger and placed it on the smallest finger on his own left hand.

Later, Lizzie did not ask for permission to leave school. She announced her decision at supper. Abby started to speak but Andrew cut off the conversation before it started. He said he did not want an argument and to let the matter lie.

From then on Lizzie spent her days at home. She never attended school again.

Andrew sold his portion of the Borden, Almy & Company and retired at age fifty-six from that day-to-day work. Instead, he held positions on corporate boards and banks, and managed his investments. His achievements were such that about town they recognized him as a wealthy, successful, and respectable man.

1880

At twenty-nine years old, Emma was a confirmed spinster but Lizzie, twenty, attended balls and parties.

Lizzie had never had the social panache of other wealthy Fall River families' daughters. Her directness chased many an ambitious gentleman away, who could not afford an uncouth wife.

If she had grown up in the almost daily social events as other young ladies did, rather than in a modest house in the business part of town, she might have learned, in time.

Andrew and Abby's marriage didn't blossom into love, but Andrew still felt that this marriage succeeded more than his first.

The house began to feel like two families, as if it was two apartments again, this time with Andrew and Abby in the back of the house and Emma and Lizzie in the front. Though she'd been their stepmother for fifteen years, Emma and Lizzie treated Abby and her relatives almost as strangers.

1885

By the time Lizzie was twenty-five, she was, like her older sister, considered a spinster.

Lizzie had not tried to find a husband, but she'd enjoyed the parties and picnics and other events. Now it seemed her season had passed. Hostesses no longer invited her to their affairs with such frequency and the Borden house had never hosted any such events.

Emma had never cared for parties, preferring quiet visits with a friend or two, and so Lizzie had barely noticed when invitations ceased to arrive for Emma.

With the end of invitations for Lizzie, though, she realized this was the end of most possibilities to marry. Once the option faded she wondered if she wouldn't rather have a husband and run her own household with her own family.

She saw her married friends in town and how differently they were treated. They were "missus" while Lizzie was still a "girl."

She began to suspect that her future life would be very much as it had been, in the same house, the same days, never changing, her life not mattering to anyone, even herself.

At supper Father tried to engage her in conversation but she barely replied. She could not explain why but suddenly she could not stand the sight of him.

Lizzie met Reverend Buck and, with his encouragement and guidance, became active in the Central Congregational Church's charities. She left the house more and made more friends.

1887

Abby had a problem. Her half sister, Sarah Whitehead, found herself in a desperate circumstance.

Sarah's husband, George Whitehead, provided poor support to Sarah and their children. The Whiteheads owned half of a house. The other half was owned by Sarah's mother, Jane Gray. Jane needed to move but the Whiteheads could not afford to buy Jane's half of the house and as a result the entire house was set to be sold. The Whiteheads would be without a home.

Sarah was younger than Lizzie and had been more like a daughter than sister to Abby. Abby often walked the five blocks to the Whitehead residence to visit her sister, taking whatever gifts and money she could scrape together.

By May of 1887, Abby had been a faithful, frugal, and discrete wife to Andrew for more than twenty years. When he pinched on the household budgets, she made do as she must and did not complain. She did not ask for anything for herself, and she always took Andrew's side in disagreements with his daughters. This she felt was both her obligation as a wife and prudent.

She'd always made sure to stay on his good side, and now she intended to get something in return. Something she desperately needed.

Abby also knew to keep the matter away from the ears of her stepdaughters, so she waited until both were out of the house to approach him.

"Andrew," she said. "I need your help."

He looked up from his mail in surprise. She rarely brought up serious topics of discussion with him.

"Sarah and her family will lose their home, unless someone can purchase my stepmother Jane's half of the house."

"That is George's problem. He ought to better support his family."

"Not everyone is as gifted in business as you are, Andrew. He does what he can but has not the intelligence to do more. Poor Sarah does her best for herself and the children. I have not asked for much, all these years. What rules you made, I have followed."

"Yes," he said. Naturally it should be so.

"But I'm asking you for this. Please buy Jane's half of the house, so that Sarah and her family will not lose their home. You could add the property to your others. It's a good place, and would make a good investment."

Andrew watched Abby as she made this plea. Unlike his daughters, she truly had not asked for much of anything at all in twenty-two years that had led to a much more peaceful life for Andrew in his second marriage, at least as far as matters with his wife were concerned.

"I will consider it," he said, and returned to his mail.

"Thank you," she said and let out the breath she'd been holding.

Relief emanated from Abby because of that one concession. On consideration, Andrew decided he would in fact buy the property, if a good price could be reached.

When he told Abby, she hugged him, such was her delight and relief. He found himself grinning back, a tad.

He even decided to put the deed in Abby's name so that when he died, the property would stay with Abby and then Sarah. He was sixty-four in 1887, and could not reasonably expect to live much longer. The house would be part of Abby's portion of his estate.

Word of the transaction eventually reached the ears of Emma and Lizzie, who were livid.

1889

A new girl, Bridget Sullivan, twenty-two, came to work at the Borden house. She replaced their previous girl, Maggie. Abby hoped she would work out. They had a hard time keeping girls.

1890

Andrew gave Lizzie an extravagant gift for her thirtieth birthday: a European tour. Emma had not had one herself. The tour, traditionally a gift to a young lady before she married, allowed the girl to see the classical world and build her trousseau. It was less common for a woman of thirty.

The trip included six young ladies plus mature aunts as chaperones. They began with a steamer ship from America and over nineteen weeks visited sites in England, Scotland, France, Germany, Switzerland, and Italy.

Lizzie finally felt that she was with her own social class, the class to which she'd always rightly belonged. The one black mark on the trip: Lizzie lacked the money to acquire the clothes, art, furniture, and antiques her fellow travelers bought and shipped home. Lizzie had no extravagant funds to draw on and no need to prepare for married life and motherhood.

She'd had some of her own money at the start of the trip but quickly exhausted it and wired home for more. The answer, a firm "no" burned Lizzie ever more as the tour continued and she repeatedly feigned discretion as the limit on her purchases. The other ladies were kind enough to not comment on it, but Lizzie knew they knew.

Lizzie also knew this trip was a temporary escape for her rather than anticipation of a new life, as it was for others. On the ship home she confided to a friend. "I regret," she said, "the necessity of returning after I've had such a happy summer. The home I'm returning to is such an unhappy home."

Back at the house Emma sympathized and offered to switch rooms so that Lizzie had the larger, sunnier room. Lizzie put her bed in the corner, blocking the door from her parents' room.

. . .

Mr. Alfred Johnson, farmer at the Bordens' Swansea farm, brought the milk and eggs and, on that day, he would also chop wood for the house.

He was well known at the house and Bridget let him in. Although the Bordens did not care to maintain tools in good condition, he found a hatchet with a sharper edge.

The snow on the ground and on the wood pile did not hinder his work; the wood had not frozen. As the sun rose it warmed him and the yard and melted the snow into pools of clear water. The hatchet cut well enough but next time, he told himself, he would remember to bring an axe which he maintained himself and kept sharp.

Bridget brought him breakfast after the family ate. As was so often at the Borden house, he could not be sure what the meal was, but it was hot and he ate it fine.

After breakfast he finished with the wood pile and left, back to Swansea.

The next morning Bridget saw that he'd left the hatchet out. It rested on the edge of the walkway, in a small pool of water which soaked into the wood just below the head. She wiped it dry and put it in a box in the cellar with other tools. She did not realize that the ash wood handle was especially vulnerable to mold and weakness from water.

Bridget told Abby she would be leaving the Borden house. It was not that the work was difficult but the contentiousness in the house and between the family members bothered her too much.

Abby gave Bridget a raise out of her own allowance and also made sure Bridget's work in the house wasn't so hard.

1891

On June 24, a year before the murders, Andrew Borden reported a daylight robbery in his home to the police. Not only had his desk been ransacked and valuable property stolen in broad daylight, but it had happened while both of his daughters and the maid were at home.

Apparently the thief or thieves had crept up the back stairs and used a nail to pick the lock. The intruder had escaped without detection.

Andrew determined to see the responsible party brought to justice. Although the police had few clues to work from and little hope of making an arrest, Andrew insisted that they try.

An officer canvassed the neighborhood. He spoke with everyone who could be found who had been nearby, including the Borden daughters and Bridget. No one could account for how an intruder could have gotten into and out of the house undetected.

After a week, Andrew told the police to drop the matter, that it had been resolved.

CHAPTER 33

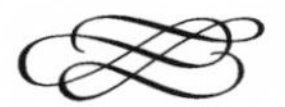

SPRING 1892

Mrs. Hanna Gifford measured Miss Lizzie for a new cloak and mentioned Mrs. Borden, calling her Lizzie's "Mother," and Lizzie called Abby, "a mean, good-for-nothing thing."

Around the same time, Bridget threatened to quit again and got another raise for her efforts.

The dressmaker, Mrs. Raymond, came to the Borden house for three weeks in May and the ladies of the house made new dresses. Shortly after, Lizzie picked a drab brown paint with brownish-green trim for the house, which stained the new Bedford cord with the blue diamond pattern.

AUGUST 1892

Emma and Lizzie had both been away from home for a week, though they were visiting different friends.

Lizzie went to Emma at the Brownell's, and the two spoke privately.

"It cannot wait any longer," said Lizzie, who had been festering for days. "If Father is giving away one of the Swansea farms, what will stop him from giving other properties, and money?" Andrew had stated his intention regarding the farm shortly before the daughters left. "He cares so much for his name and reputation. He will choose that legacy as a benefactor and leave us with nothing."

"You exaggerate."

"Oh? When has he cared what we need? When does he give to us unless we made him, with fight and difficulty? He will choose a grander name in town over us."

"That is why he would not leave us destitute, because of what people would say. He will make sure we have enough."

"How much is enough? Enough to live without living, as we do now? To eat poor food, do nothing, and be reminded to be grateful for what little we get? He gives us enough to keep people from talking, no more. We have earned more."

Lizzie caught Emma's eye. Emma looked away.

"At least we must find out what is true, about his plans," said Lizzie.

"I will write to Uncle John."

"Uncle John has always been closer to Father than us, his own blood!"

"You're wrong, Lizzie. He will help. He will find out Father's plans."

"And then?"

"And then, we can speak to Father if need be. Perhaps there will be no need at all."

Lizzie sighed. "I'm going home. I will see what I can find out myself."

"I don't think that you should go, being angry." But Emma didn't bother to argue further, with Lizzie in that mood. Instead, Emma sent the letter to John and considered returning to Fall River herself.

Lizzie returned home. Andrew and Abby greeted her without enthusiasm.

On Monday, August 1, Lizzie waited until Father was alone in the sitting room, reading the newspaper. She calmed her temper and did not equivocate. "Father, Emma and I are concerned. You've said you'll be making bequests. We are not sure what will be left for our care when you are gone."

He scrutinized her briefly. "I have always given to you girls. You have your own money. What has happened to what I gave you and Emma a few weeks ago when I bought Grandfather's house back?"

"We still have it," Lizzie said, "but it is not enough for us to live on and sustain ourselves, if you do not protect us in your estate."

He did not look up. "That house brings a rental income, if you and your sister had cared to take responsibility for managing it."

That house was old and in constant need of repair; it made little to no profit, but Lizzie did not mention that. "We are not businessmen, as you are, Father."

"I made the money and do with it as I choose. I will decide what is for you."

Lizzie left him to his reading.

In South Dartmouth, outside Fall River, John received Emma's letter. This was not the first time she's shared concerns regarding their father's plans for his estate and his daughter's livelihoods, who had no other means.

Emma and Lizzie were John's blood. He had not forgotten Sarah's dying request that he watch out for them, and protect them. All these years he'd kept it in mind.

John sent word back to Emma that he would go to the house that week, and asked what she thought should be done.

Tuesday, August 2 was a typical day in the Borden house, for the most part. Andrew left as usual at nine. Lizzie got up after nine and Bridget served her at a separate breakfast.

After, Bridget went down to the cellar to finish the week's laundry, and then fried fresh swordfish for lunch. Abby did light housework.

In the afternoon Bridget went to the baker's for bread and bought rolls instead when they were out. Alone in the kitchen, Lizzie used the time to lace the family's milk with rat poison.

At supper that night, unusually, Lizzie ate with her parents. The family had the last of the swordfish, reheated after sitting out on the stove all day, along with the baker's bread and sweet cakes. They also had milk, though a careful observer would have noticed that Lizzie only sipped hers.

That night the Borden parents were violently ill and Abby was at Dr. Bowen's door across the street at 7:45 the next morning, pale, sweating, and agitated. Dr. Bowen assured her it was only "summer sickness."

Abby never complained about Andrew's skinflint ways. But her friends and relatives knew the Bordens lived poorly in spite of Andrew's wealth and she hated that even the family doctor knew, and that he used it to dismiss her concerns.

At ten thirty that Wednesday morning Lizzie quietly left the house through the front door. She walked to Smith's drug store two blocks away and asked for ten cents worth of prussic acid for a seal-skin cap. Druggist Eli Bence refused and she returned home.

Shortly after one thirty Uncle John Morse arrived at the house, unexpectedly, having come on the train. He said he came regarding the hiring of a manager for Andrew's Swansea farm.

Abby served him a meal of mutton stew and fruit. After he ate, John joined the Borden parents in the sitting room.

"Forgive us if we are not good hosts today," said Abby. "We were very ill last night, and not so much better today."

"Oh?" said John.

"The whole household was taken ill," said Abby. "Lizzie and ourselves. We think we are poisoned."

"Poisoned!"

"It was not poison," Andrew said with a stern look to his wife.

"How is Lizzie?" asked John.

Abby straightened her skirt. "She said earlier she was only a little sick. She has not come down all day today."

John glanced up at the ceiling and Lizzie's room, directly above, but heard nothing. "We can go this afternoon to meet the man I've found who might take charge of your farm," John said to Andrew.

"I'm too tired today. Go without me."

John left in late afternoon. He had supper at a relative's house and then went to Andrew's farm in Swansea.

Lizzie ate supper with her parents that evening. They all ate light, and barely spoke. Lizzie thought her parents looked ill, but not like they were dying. She left in the evening and walked to Alice Russell's for a visit.

John returned to the Borden house about 8:45 to spend the night. He chatted in the sitting room with Mr. and Mrs. Borden, about the hired man for the farm and nothing else of consequence.

After nine, when Lizzie got home, she went straight up to her room, though she could hear the voices of her father and John. Lizzie laid awake in her room that night, in the dark. The light breeze coming in her windows did not cool the room.

The windows to the sitting room directly below were also open, and after Abby went to bed, Andrew and John stayed.

"I am old and have determined that it's time to dispose of some of my assets," said Andrew. "The Swansea farm will go to the old ladies' home, as we discussed before. I am deciding on additional gifts."

"I do not mean to pry, but what of Emma and Lizzie?"

Andrew frowned. "That is not your concern. I have always made sure they were taken care of."

John and Andrew each went to bed, John to the guest bedroom. It was hot and he pondered long into the night.

Bridget was in the kitchen by 6:15 on the morning of Thursday, August 4. She took ash from the stove and got wood and coal from the cellar.

Andrew and Abby Borden and John Morse had their breakfast of unrefrigerated mutton, johnny cakes, and bananas. When they were done Bridget served herself in the kitchen, and drank the last of Tuesday's milk.

Abby had planned to go to her half-sister Sarah Whitehead's that morning, to watch their youngest while the rest of the family was out of town. Instead she'd sent word that she was ill and could not go.

Lizzie stayed in bed, listening, before she got up. She heard Father, Abby, and John talking in the sitting room. She watched out Emma's window until John left. Then she went down and greeted her father in the sitting room as he read the *Providence Journal*.

He said he was not well and might not go down street that morning.

Lizzie knew Father well enough to be sure that, in spite of being ill, he would make all efforts to work that day. If he did go, he'd likely be back early.

Abby dusted in the dining room. Lizzie went into the kitchen.

"Would you like me to get you breakfast, Miss Lizzie?" asked Bridget.

Lizzie smelled the same mutton stew from the day before. "No, I'm not hungry."

"Mrs. Borden has me to wash the first floor windows inside," Bridget said. "If you decide you want something, I'll be about." A moment later Bridget ran out to the yard to vomit. Lizzie got a cookie and sat at the kitchen table with a magazine.

When Bridget returned, she set about gathering tools to wash the windows. With the pail and brush from the cellar, Bridget went out the side door to the barn and Lizzie heard her filling the pail from the barn faucet.

Abby stepped into the kitchen to speak to Lizzie. "We have another guest coming on Monday. The guest bedding needs changing."

The white sheets and pillowcases would definitely be dirty after John slept there. "I'll not be doing it," said Lizzie.

Abby frowned. Lizzie, she thought, will tax me until the day I die. "Emma does all the work in that room only because you will not. It is both of your responsibility."

"I'm unwell today," said Lizzie.

Abby went up to the guest bedroom herself.

Bridget walked past the kitchen windows on her way to the Kelly fence at the south of the Borden yard. There she met the Kelly girl. Bridget, Lizzie knew, would not be quick about chatting.

In that instant, a tiny moment she'd both known and not know was coming, Lizzie chose. She'd thought about it so many times, she already knew what to do. She hurried down the cellar stairs, to a back storage room. As she went back up and through the house, past the front door, she bolted it. Then she stopped for something in the small front coat closet.

Abby glanced up as Lizzie climbed the stairs with a garment over her arm. Lizzie looked out the stairwell window to Bridget, still at the Kelly fence.

Abby attended to the pillows, facing the wall, when Lizzie came in and closed the slatted blinds on the front two windows.

Abby had almost finished smoothing the bedspread when she turned her attention to her stepdaughter. "What are you up to?" she said.

Lizzie had put on Abby's black waterproof cloak, fastened at the throat. Abby began to ask Lizzie again what she was up to but stopped. The hair on the back of Abby's neck stood up when she saw her stepdaughter of twenty-seven years in front of her, grinning.

Lizzie brought her right arm out from behind her back. In it was a hatchet. It took Abby a second to understand and start to react. She did not call out or scream.

Lizzie drew her arm up and back. The first blow struck Abby on the left side of her head, near her temple. It glanced off her skull and slipped inside the flesh on the side of Abby's scalp. Lizzie struck again, this time driving the blade into Abby's head.

Abby gasped and raised her arms to her head. She spun around to flee, perhaps over the bed, but before she could there was another impact on the back and right of her head. She felt a white hot and crushing pain as she heard, both outside and inside her head, the hatchet break through her skull and into her brain.

Abby fell forward with a thud, her elbows to the sides and her arms trapped underneath. The dresser and mirror shook, and the floor shook through more than the guest bedroom in the thin-walled, thin-floored house, if anyone else were in it to hear.

Abby did not move as Lizzie stepped forward and straddled her body, with a foot on either side of Abby's hips. Lizzie struck again. Four, five.

Abby's head shook with each impact, and crushed in at the top and right side.

Six, seven, eight, nine.

Some strikes missed their mark and sunk into the tissue on Abby's upper back, shoulders, and neck.

Ten, eleven, twelve, thirteen.

Surprisingly little blood sprayed out with each strike or when she drew the hatchet back. Though it ran freely out of Abby's head and neck, it did not splatter much from the blade as Lizzie raised and lowered it.

Fourteen, fifteen, sixteen.

Lizzie had only half believed she would do it.

The quiet house.

Seventeen, eighteen.

Lizzie stopped. It wasn't that she'd exhausted her rage. She'd not felt rageful. Or much of anything. And she did not know that the reason there was so little blood spatter and so little blood on herself was her own doing. Tuesday's arsenic poisoning had caused anemia in both Andrew and Abby, and their blood was thin. Abby's blood spattered in a fine mist that was harder to see than large globs.

Lizzie looked for signs of breathing, and saw none.

The hatchet dripped softly onto the rug near Abby's head, where blood had already pooled, and Lizzie laid the hatchet there, with the handle resting against Abby's shoulder.

Lizzie was blood spattered, but not dripping, as she walked back to her room. She wiped her hands and face and Abby's black waterproof with a cloth she used for her monthly illness, and dropped it into the pail she kept for those items. Another cloth cleaned up the rest.

She soaked and scrubbed the few tiny blood spots off her light blue Bedford cord dress with a wet cloth. Such thin fabric in a hot house. No one would notice the wet spots before they dried.

There didn't appear to be blood drops leading into or in her room. She used another cloth, dipped first in water from the wash basin, to clean the bits of blood she had missed from her head, arms, and hands. She cleaned carefully around her nails, but neglected to check her black shoes and stockings.

Bridget, still at the south fence, chatted with the Kelly girl as Lizzie crept down to put Abby's cloak back in the closet at the base of the stairs.

Nothing remained but to wait. Lizzie sat on her bed with her feet hanging off and listened. Bridget came into the kitchen from the side door and left again. The sound of Bridget splashing water outside drifted up.

Lizzie had imagined this, or something like it, many times. Now she felt oddly settled, and a little excited. Was this glee?

Bridget came in again, and started cleaning in the sitting room.

Lizzie noticed the clock. It was almost ten thirty. Her sense of time was off. Somehow, nearly an hour had passed since Abby had been alive, and Lizzie felt fear for the first time. She shouldn't have stayed in her room so long, so close to the guest room.

Maybe it was all right. Bridget was outside most of the time and wouldn't know when Lizzie had been upstairs or down.

A noise at the front door, of someone trying to get in, drew her attention. Lizzie went to the top of the stairs to look. Bridget struggled with the stuck bolt on the front door. She yanked repeatedly but the door did not open. "Pshaw!" Bridget said in frustration.

Lizzie heard the cursed exclamation from Bridget, and at that same moment she realized she'd been right. Father was home early, before the family would gather for the noon meal. This one morning, if she could sort out how, she'd solve it all for herself and Emma.

Lizzie laughed.

CHAPTER 34

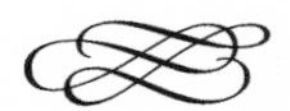

Bridget opened the door and Andrew came in, pale, with hunched shoulders. Lizzie heard his strained breathing even from where she stood at the top of the stairs.

He did not seem to notice Lizzie. She followed him into the dining room, where he hung up his Prince Albert coat, as he always did on returning home. He set down the mail from the post office. He had a small box, but kept it in his hands. Lizzie asked about mail for her. He said there wasn't any. She told him Abby had a note, about someone sick, and had gone out.

He got his key and went up the back stairs to his room.

Bridget washed windows in the sitting room.

Lizzie searched the papers in the dining room. In the pocket of his Prince Albert coat, a rolled sheet had notes about bequests. They were written in Father's own hand, with scratched out changes. He'd not given these to his lawyer, Jennings, yet.

Lizzie tossed the rolled paper into the stove fire. She went up to her room for handkerchiefs, and took them to the dining room.

Bridget started cleaning the dining room windows.

Andrew came down, sat in the sitting room, and told Lizzie he wasn't feeling well. He laid down across the sofa, his head resting on a pillow on the armrest, and went to sleep.

Lizzie watched him for a minute, following his breathing. Then she went to the dining room where Bridget cleaned the windows. Lizzie spoke softly, so as not to disturb Father. "There's a sale at Sargeants for dress goods this afternoon at eight cents a yard."

"I will have one at that price," Bridget said. Bridget finished in the dining room and went back to the kitchen. "I'm not well today. I'm going up to my room for a nap before dinner."

"I hope you feel better," said Lizzie lightly. She smiled, a little.

Bridget returned her water pail and other supplies to the cellar, and climbed to the attic.

Lizzie watched Father, listening for sounds of Bridget coming back down. The house was silent except for his labored breathing.

She'd crept out of the sitting room and up the front stairs, retrieved the hatchet and the napkin pail, and brought them down to the dining room.

If she moved quickly now, she realized, she would have help masking sounds, in this house where noise spread so easily.

In the dining room she got Father's black Prince Albert coat and put it on backwards, so that it covered her whole front. The raised collar reached over her chin. Father was much taller than Lizzie; his coat fell well below the arm of the sofa and below her knees.

When she stood behind the dining room door jamb, her right arm easily reached around to strike from behind and above.

She had experience now, and knew how much force to use.

She aimed and waited. Father's ragged breath.

The City Hall clock struck once as it began to mark eleven o'clock. Lizzie struck in rhythm with the strikes of the bell.

Her first was true and crushed into Father's skull. He gave a small twitch, a gasp or a groan. His hands tensed and then relaxed.

Lizzie had the feel and range of the hatchet. She could almost aim without looking. She struck him again from behind the doorway as she snuck around.

As with Abby, not much blood sprayed. What spatter there was hit the sofa, the wall behind, and the kitchen and parlor doors on either ends.

Twice more and the left eye socket collapsed, his eyeball split and popping out of the socket. That did not disturb her. Instead, she felt relief. She sighed as tension she hadn't known she held left her body.

Two more and Lizzie looked. The left side of Father's face and head were crushed. Bone chips scattered around.

Five more times, each with more strength.

A gash gaped all through from his cheek, into his nose, and down to his chin.

On the eleventh strike, her strongest yet, the hatchet head penetrated fully inside Father's skull, scoring deep grooves inside as it wedged in place. She pulled back, but the long ago wound in the hatchet handle gave way. The hatchet head snapped off and stuck inside.

She felt a touch of not anger or fear, but frustration, because she hadn't wanted to be done. The act itself distressed as much as folding laundry.

But she was done. She stood for a moment, looking, listening, breathing, and taking in the silence and the peace in the house.

She carefully removed the black Prince Albert coat and used it to wipe her hands and the hatchet head, after wrenching it out of the skull.

Making sure not to get blood on her dress, she folded the coat and, lifting the head and pillow, slid it underneath.

Almost no blood had landed on Lizzie. The wall and coat shielded her. She'd felt only a little as it hit her face and head.

She took the pail along and threw the broken handle into the kitchen stove fire as she went. She could have thrown the hatchet head as well, but the kitchen stove was too close to where she was known to have been and the metal head would not burn.

In the cellar, she left the napkin pail and splashed water from the cellar sink over her face and hair. The August heat would dry both quickly, or the water would be confused with the normal oily state of skin and hair.

She rinsed the hatchet head as well as she could, but some blood in the grains of the wood and in the joint where the handle met the head did not rinse off.

Using coal ash from the furnace she scrubbed more of the blood off of the hatchet head. Then she poured vinegar and baking soda over the hatchet head. She let it foam and scrubbed with the laundry brush, repeated, then rinsed it clean.

She hurried. It seemed she had time, but she couldn't be sure.

She scrubbed her hands and under her nails and used a white cloth to wipe her face and hair. Not a spec of blood appeared on it. It had all been a surprisingly clean affair.

In the wood room she returned the hatchet head to the box where she'd gotten it. Once in the box, however, it looked conspicuously fresh compared to the dusty tools. When she patted on more coal ash, it looked almost like dust. Not quite, but perhaps close enough to avoid notice. And so long as she could get back upstairs before Bridget came down, no one would match Lizzie with this hatchet head in the cellar, even if they should look there.

Up the stairs she flew, to the kitchen. Even in the sunlight, she saw no spots on her dress.

The house was quiet. She took a few moments to think if she'd forgotten anything. She peered into the sitting room, to the body. When she could think of nothing more to do, Lizzie went to the foot of the back stairs, off the kitchen, and called up to Bridget in the attic. "Maggie! Maggie!"

Bridget had been resting, not asleep, and had heard the city clock strike eleven. She rose at the shouts and the urgency in Lizzie's voice.

Bridget called from the top of the stairs. "What's the matter?"

"Come down! Quick!" Lizzie shouted back and Bridget did. She'd never heard Lizzie call with such urgency. "Go for Dr. Bowen," said Lizzie. "Father is killed."

Confused, Bridget started for the sitting room to see for herself.

"Oh, Maggie, don't go in," said Lizzie. "Go over. I have got to have the doctor." Bridget ran across the street to Dr. Bowen's, who wasn't home, and then darted back, seen by Mrs. Churchill.

In the Borden kitchen, Lizzie was still near the side door. "Miss Lizzie, where was you?"

"I was out in the backyard and heard a groan and came in and the screen door was wide open," said Lizzie, and sent Bridget off to get Alice Russell.

Lizzie stayed in the kitchen, facing out through the screen door, making a show of being upset. It was finished, both. She and Emma could finally have lives they chose for themselves.

Around noon, with a house of police, neighbors, and friends, Lizzie tried to show a fatigued acquiescence at Dr. Bowen's suggestion that she retire upstairs, to avoid further strain. Actually, the last thing she wanted was to remain downstairs. Alice escorted her up to her room.

Once there, Lizzie said, "Alice, will you tell Dr. Bowen that when it is necessary for an undertaker I want Winward?"

When Alice went to let Bowen know, Lizzie changed the Bedford cord shirtwaist for a pink wrapper with a red ribbon at the waist. Lizzie locked the Bedford cord in Emma's trunk.

In her room she would be protected by her entourage of supporters. First, Alice Russell and Reverend Buck, then Mrs. Holmes and Dr. Bowen.

She sat on the lounge as officers asked questions which were easy enough for Lizzie to answer. She hadn't seen or heard anything, she said. Her friends busied themselves comforting her.

The evening of the murders, Alice and Lizzie went down to the cellar. They emptied their slop pails by the light of the kerosene lamp.

After Alice settled into bed in the parents' room, Lizzie went back down alone. She knew the officers outside could see her through the windows, so she feigned activity at the laundry sink but, instead, she looked for something.

There was no pail of bloody napkins. Someone, the police, must have taken it. They'd not believed her account of its contents. She might be caught.

. . .

On the morning of Friday, August 5, after Emma and Alice had gone downstairs, Lizzie moved the dress from the trunk in Emma's room to the dress closet. She'd thought carefully, while watching the officers search the dress closet the day before, about how to hide it better. She hid the dress inside one of the more expensive, darker dresses of thicker fabric.

Lizzie and Emma spoke to Bridget that morning and asked her to keep some details of the Borden family, things Bridget had seen in their home, quiet.

If she could refrain from sharing those unless forced by the police or prosecution, that would be better, they said, for everyone involved. And perhaps there would be some money from the estate for Bridget, too.

On Saturday, Lizzie suspected that the police were waiting for the family to depart to the cemetery so they could conduct yet another search, without the family present. She'd barely eaten for two days, and the cheap Bedford cord fit under her black mourning dress. She wore it out of the house, to the cemetery, back, and all afternoon.

From Jennings she learned that experts could find blood even on cleaned fabric, so she gave him and Hilliard a different dress that day.

On Sunday, she burned the Bedford cord dress.

After the Borden sisters' deaths, people mourned the tragic lives of all the Bordens and made pilgrimages to the Borden family plot in Oak Grove Cemetery.

Some said that the problem with Lizzie was not that she was a murderer, though many thought she was. The problem was that she was a difficult woman who hadn't behaved as she should. She was odd. She spoke directly, sometimes forcefully, and held to her own views. Later, she'd made friends with the wrong kinds of people and even had affairs, some believed.

She'd not been heartbroken over the loss of her parents. She was the daughter of one of Fall River's great men, and should have behaved in ways consistent with that position. Then, they said, she'd have been accepted and loved.

But that was never true.

People, even Emma, saw who they wanted to see. Perhaps they always would, long after she was gone.

No one knew her. She struggled all her life to know herself.

In the end, her life wasn't what Lizbeth had hoped for or wanted. Much of the time she was, as her friend Helen had seen, bitter, disappointed, and heartbroken.

But Lizbeth had also managed, in spite of it all, to create her own freedom and peace. In all those years of mistakes and missteps she'd found herself.

It began with the murders, those acts that had never bothered her. She'd learned so well, when she was a child, how not to feel.

PRIMARY CHARACTERS

These are the primary individuals involved in the Borden story. See the Historical Notes for information on minor characters not included or not named in *Killing the Bordens*.

Adams, Melvin O. Defense attorney for Lizzie Borden.

Bence, Eli. Fall River druggist (pharmacist).

Blaisdell, Josiah. Justice who presided over the Borden murder inquest and preliminary hearing considering the guilt of Lizzie Borden for murder.

Blodget, Caleb. One of three justices presiding over the trial of Lizzie Borden for murder.

Borden, Abby Durfee, born 1828. Murdered August 4, 1892.

Borden, Andrew Jackson, born 1822. Murdered August 4, 1892.

Borden, Emma Lenora, born 1851. Daughter of murdered couple.

Borden, Lizzie Andrew, born 1860. Daughter of murdered couple.

Borden, Sarah Morse. First wife of Andrew Borden. Birth mother of Emma and Lizzie Borden.

Bowen, Phebe. Wife of Dr. Seabury Bowen, the Borden family doctor. Phebe was in the Borden house after the discovery of the bodies.

Bowen, Seabury. Borden family doctor who lived across the street and helped in the house after discovery of the murders.

Brigham, Mary. Friend of Lizzie Borden's.

Buck, Reverend Edwin. Reverend from Lizzie's church.

Churchill, Adelaide Buffinton. Borden neighbor.

Coughlin, John. Fall River mayor in 1892.

Doherty, Patrick. Fall River police officer; early officer at the murder scenes.

Dolan, William. Bristol County Medical Examiner for Borden Murders.

Fleet, John. Fall River Assistant City Marshall. Fleet was the lead officer responsible for the investigation at the Borden house on the day of the murders.

Harrington, Philip. Fall River police officer who investigated at the house and in town on the day of the murders.

Hilliard, Rufus B. Fall River City Marshall, in charge of the Fall River Police and the Borden murder investigation.

Holmes, Marianna. Mother of two of Lizzie's childhood friends.

Jennings, Andrew. Friend of Andrew Borden and attorney for Lizzie Borden.

Knowlton, Hosea. District Attorney for Suffolk County.

Medley, William. Fall River police officer; one of the first officers on scene at the Borden house.

Moody, William Henry. Prosecutor at the Borden murder trial.

Morse, John V. Brother of Sarah Morse Borden and uncle to Emma and Lizzie Borden.

Mullaly, Michael. Fall River police officer. One of the first officers on scene at the Borden house.

O'Neil, Nance. Actress and friend of Lizzie Borden.

Reagan, Hanna. Fall River Central Police Station matron.

Robinson, George Dexter. Attorney for Lizzie Borden.

Russell, Alice. Borden family friend.

Sawyer, Charles. Borden family neighbor; stood guard at the Borden house side door.

Sullivan, Bridget, Borden family live-in maid, referred to at the time as the "Borden girl", and called "Maggie" by the Borden sisters.

BORDEN HOUSE FLOOR PLANS

These floor plans are also available at www.ccreewriter.com.

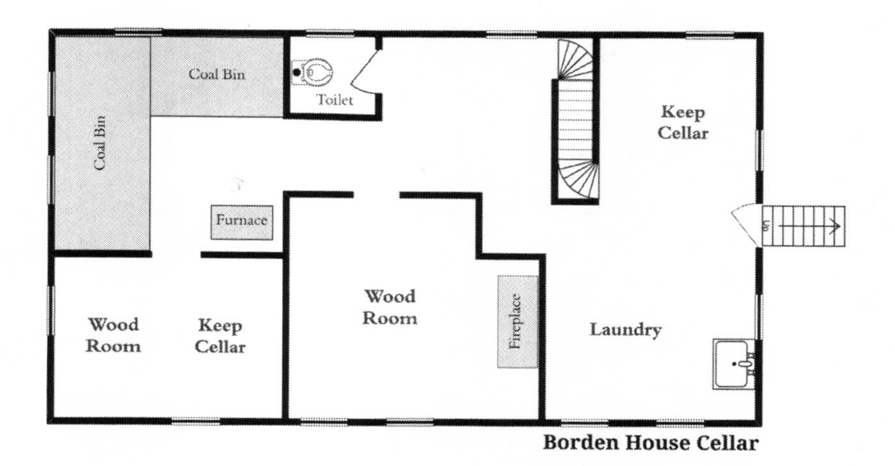

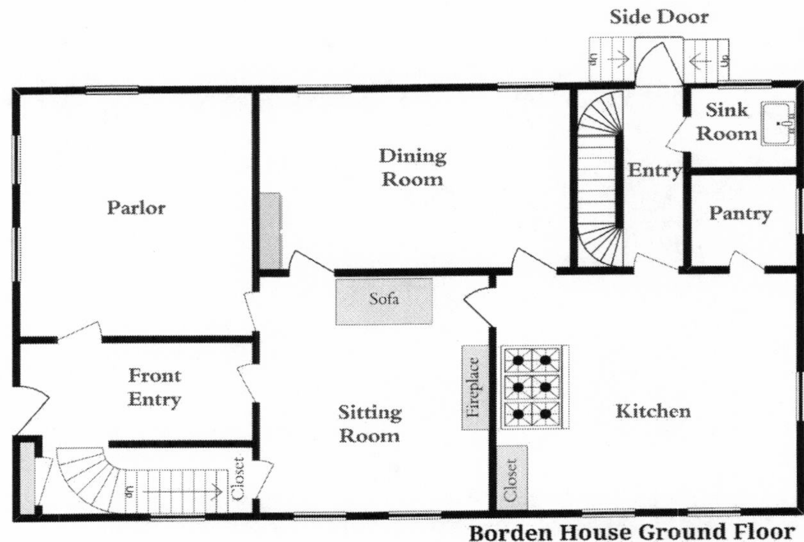

Borden House Ground Floor

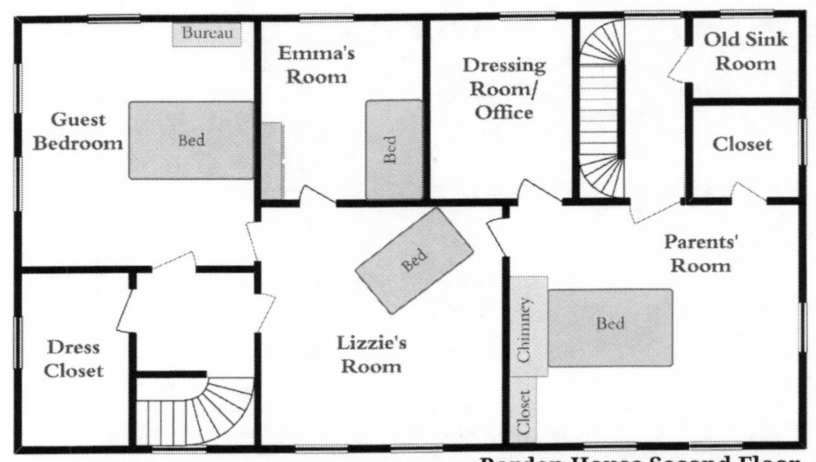

Borden House Second Floor

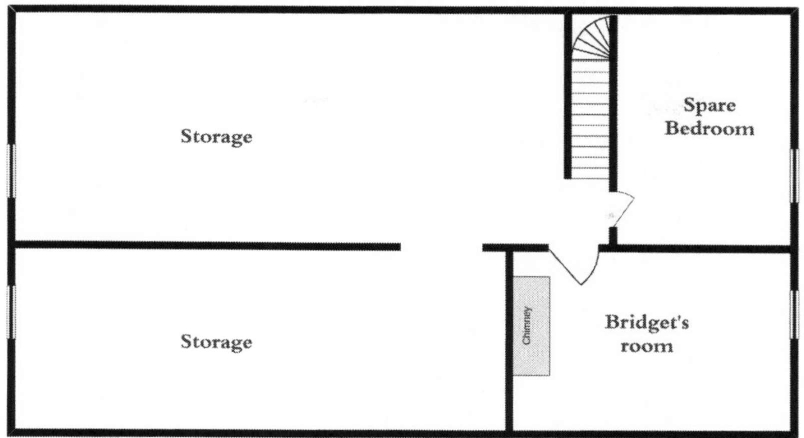
Storage
Spare
Bedroom
Storage
Chimney
Bridget's
room
Borden House Attic

HISTORICAL NOTES

The article on the cover ("Husband and Wife Murdered in Daylight") is from *The New York Herald* and is abridged.

Prussic acid is an older name for hydrogen cyanide.

There have been Lizzie Borden clubs and fan clubs since at least 1893.

The house where Abby and Andrew Borden were murdered still exists and is now The Historic Lizzie Borden House, a bed and breakfast and museum. For details and to book tours or rooms, see https://lizzie-borden.com.

Maplecroft still exists and has been restored to the style and decor of the time Lizzie and Emma lived there. It is sometimes available for tours.

Crime scene photos of both bodies are available online.

Historical notes after this point contain spoilers. Read only after finishing the book.

Not everyone known to have been involved in the Borden case is named or mentioned in this book. More than fifty individuals were in and around the Borden house on the day of the murders. Some had more minor or tangential involvement.

There were more than thirty officers involved in the investigation, including Hilliard, Fleet, Mullaly, Doherty, Harrington, and Medley.

Medley checked John Morse's alibi for the time of the murders.

Officer George Allen was the first officer on scene.

Officer Frank Wixon is the officer who climbed over the back fence to speak to neighbors.

Other officers in and around the Borden house that day or involved in the investigation include Buffinton, Chace, Connors, Desmond, Devine, Dexter, Dowty, Dyson, Edson, Feeney, Ferguson, Gillon (Gillam?), Hurley, Hyde, Linnehan, Mahoney, Mayall, McCarthy, Minnehan, Perron, Quigley, Reagan, Riley, Seaver, Shea, and Wilson.

Medical doctors who were at the Borden house or assisted with the Borden autopsies include Bowen, Cone, Coughlin, Dedrick, Dolan, Draper, Dutra, Gunning, Learned, Leary, Peckham, and Tourtellot.

A doctor's wife who entertained a friend next door to the Borden's the morning of the murders was Mary Caroline Kelly.

The newspaper seller who called the police (and his friends at Fall River newspapers) the morning of the murders was John Cunningham. He called from Gorman's paint shop.

The crime scene photographer was John Walsh.

Charles Bryant opened the Borden chimneys after the murders, looking for hiding places and hidden items.

John Maher, a safecracker, opened Mr. Borden's safe looking for a will.

There were two properties behind the Borden house. One was Dr. Chagnon's, and one was Crowe's, where men worked at stonecutting the day of the murders.

George A. Pettee, a former tenant of the house before it was owned by the Bordens, happened to be in the neighborhood on the day of the murders and also went into the house and the crime scenes.

There were many reporters at the Borden house on the day of the murders, including John Manning and Walter Stevens.

See other sources listed in the Bibliography for additional information, including an alphabetical listing of individuals related to the case starting on page 511 of *Lizzie Borden: Past & Present*.

The authorities made many mistakes when handling the evidence in the Borden case and handled evidence in ways that were accepted at the time but not by modern standards. These include never locking down the crime scenes, allowing suspects to have access to the evidence in the house, leaving the bodies and other evidence in the house, and not performing full autopsies until a week after the murders, on decomposing bodies.

One odd example of how the police and medical examiner mishandled evidence that is not otherwise mentioned in this book is a bag of minor-seeming evidence such as the Borden parents' clothes, some of Abby's hair, and blood-stained pillows from the sofa. The police collected those in a bag but left it in the house overnight after the murders, hidden in the cellar. The next day it was moved outside and buried in the yard where they could observe if it was disturbed. Only on the Saturday after the murders was the bag dug up and taken to the police station.

Also, how much did Abby actually weigh? This fact is important, because the prosecution argued she weighed so much that Lizzie couldn't have failed to hear her body fall as she was killed, wherever Lizzie was in the house.

Dr. Dolan, medical examiner, testified that Abby's height was "five feet three inches" and "I should think she weighed about two-hundred pounds."

The crime scene photos are still available, and are discoverable online. Abby carried extra weight but it's hard to believe from the photos taken on the day of her death that she was both five feet, three inches and two-hundred pounds. In fact Dolan and other investigators did not have the ability to accurately weight Abby after her death, Dr. Dolan made a guess at Abby's weight, but her weight was presented as two-hundred pounds at the trial and that "fact" used in arguments.

In spite of the prosecution's assertion that the day of the murders was one of the hottest days that summer, it was not. The recorded high that day in Fall River was 83 degrees.

Bridget Sullivan's inquest transcript has been lost since shortly after the trial in 1893. Prosecutor Knowlton described her preliminary hearing testimony as essentially the same as her inquest testimony; her preliminary hearing testimony was used in place of her inquest testimony in this book.

The June 1891 daylight robbery at the Borden house was never solved. Some believe the culprit was Lizzie, that Mr. Borden realized it was her, that's why he told the police to let the matter drop, and that's why he started leaving his key on the mantle, to show her he knew.

It's unclear what Dr. Bowen burned in the Borden stove the day of the murders. It might have been notes to himself for the telegram he sent to Emma, or it might have been incriminating evidence he'd found in the house.

Lizzie testified at the inquest that she did not know about D. R. Smith's drugstore, where Eli Bence worked, but it was there for fourteen years, two blocks from her home.

There was a specific test for arsenic poisoning available at the time of the Borden murders, called the Marsh test. It doesn't appear from Professor Wood's testimony that he performed the Marsh test on tissues from the Borden bodies.

Justice Dewey's instructions to the jury are an obvious overreach of his obligations and rights as a Justice, and were described as such by contemporary legal observers.

His full statements to the jury encompassed an hour and a half and more than ten thousand words (thirty pages in a print book). It was necessary to trim his statements here. However, the full text is worth reading, and is available in the second part of the trial transcripts, available online. (See the Bibliography).

The Jennings hip bath sat undisturbed in Jennings' attic from his death in 1923 until the house was sold in the 1940s. While preparing to complete the sale the family discovered the contents, which were then preserved by Jennings' daughter, Marion.

Marion was reluctant to discuss or share the contents, or discuss the Borden case at all.

The contents of the hip bath tub were eventually donated to the Fall River Historical society in 2011 by her son, Edward Saunders Waring. After years of painstaking transcription of Jennings' often muddled handwriting and notes, and issues related to the age of the materials, the papers were published in 2021 as *The Jennings Journals*. See https://fallriverhistorical.org/lizzie-borden-collections/hip-bath-collection/.

We don't know what Emma told Jennings that caused Lizzie to accuse Emma of giving her away, assuming Mrs. Reagan's account was accurate. If it was true, the thing Emma told Jennings was possibly that Lizzie had burned a dress the Sunday after the murders.

Samuel Robinsky, the purported Jewish peddler who wrote to Emma about seeing a bloody traveler on the day of the murders, was never found. The contents of his letter were never confirmed nor refuted.

Sarah Morse Borden, Andrew Borden's first wife and birth mother of Emma and Lizzie Borden, died on March 26, 1863 at age 39. Women's health issues were not well understood at the time and her death certificate lists the causes of death, enigmatically, as "uterine congestion" and "disease of spine."

The theory that there was incest in the Borden house is substantiated by circumstantial but not direct evidence. For an overview of the theory, see the *American Heritage* article cited in the Bibliography.

As mentioned in the article, incest was not generally acknowledged at the time and raising an allegation was much more likely to cause harm to the accuser than to stop wrongdoing.

Circumstantial evidence of incest at the Borden house includes the gold ring from Lizzie that Mr. Borden always wore in spite of not wearing a wedding ring, Mr. Borden's refusal to let his sister help in the house in the years between Mrs. Bordens, Lizzie's odd relationship with her father (including the moment observed by Mrs. Holmes when Lizzie kissed her father's rotting corpse on the lips), and a comment made by Florence Cook Brigham to Michael Martins, coauthor of *Parallel Lives,* that Lizzie was "a girl who was 'kept out of circulation' by her father." (pg. 78)

Emma almost certainly lied during her trial testimony in 1893. The stained Bedford cord dress couldn't have been hanging out in the open in the dress closet as she said. Multiple officers searched there and didn't see it.

She swore both that the Bedford cord dress was hardly worn and so faded that the fabric could not be saved for any other purpose.

She also changed her testimony between the inquest and the full trial regarding the relationship between Abby and Lizzie.

Bridget appears to have been honest under oath (even telling the truth about cleaning only six of the ten ground floor windows) but possibly lied when she denied contentiousness in the Borden household or other things she knew about the Borden family.

Former Fall River Marshal Rufus B. Hilliard died from liver cirrhosis and nephritis in 1912. He was 62, and was buried in Oak Grove Cemetery.

Former Fall River Assistant Marshal John Fleet died from heart failure on May 13, 1916.

William H. Moody, co-prosecutor at Lizzie's murder trial, was elected to the U.S. House of Representatives in 1895. He was appointed Secretary of the Navy by President Theodore Roosevelt in 1902. In May of 1904, he took on a new role as United States Attorney General. In December 1906, he became a United States Supreme Court Justice but left after a short service, due to health problems. He died in 1917 at his home in Haverhill, Massachusetts. He was sixty-three.

Dr. Seabury Bowen died of heart disease in Fall River in 1918, at age 77. He'd lived all those years after the murders in the same house, across the street from the house where Abby and Andrew were killed.

On June 15, 1918, the Borden sisters completed sale of the Second Street house to a man named John W. Dunn, who was of no relation. No Borden ever again lived in the Second Street house.

Defense Attorney Melvin O. Adams died in 1920 at age 70.

Former Fall River Medical Examiner William Dolan died in 1922, age 64.

Mrs. Adelaide Churchill died in February, 1926. She was seventy-six, and was buried in Oak Grove Cemetery. She never remarried. Her son lived in the Mayor Buffinton House next door to the Borden house for the rest of his life. The house has since been demolished.

When Lizzie died in 1927, Charles Cook, her longtime business agent, attempted to bill her estate $10,000 for executor services. The probate court determined that the fee was exorbitant, and allowed him half.

Emma's will was contested by cousins who charged that part of her substantial half-million-dollar estate rightly belonged to them. They later dropped the challenge.

On January 21, 1941, Alice Russell died in Fall River at the age of 88. She and the Borden sisters had not been close since Alice testified about the burned dress to the grand jury and at Lizzie's trial. Alice lived a reserved life in Fall River after the Borden trial, and later in life taught sewing in public schools. She never married. Until the end she insisted that she'd told everything she knew about the murders at the trial.

Nance O'Neil died in New Jersey on February 7, 1965, age 90. She'd continued her stage career, married, and briefly been a silent film star. You can learn about her film work online.

FACT AND FICTION

This chapter summarizes the types of fiction and decisions I made when writing *Killing the Bordens,* and contains minor story spoilers.

WHAT, EXACTLY, IS THE AUGUST 4 TIMELINE?

There's debate, all these years later, about what times things happened on the day of the murders. Exactly when did Andrew Borden get home that morning? When did officers first arrive? For *Killing the Bordens* I've generally followed Leonard Rebello's timeline in *Lizzie Borden: Past & Present.*

WHAT PEOPLE WERE THINKING AND FEELING

It's almost impossible to know what individuals were thinking and feeling during the events in the book, except on the rare occasion that they testified to or shared them in another way that's part of the preserved record. Generally speaking, thoughts and feelings attributed to characters in this book are fiction, informed by the facts.

PEOPLE AND EVENTS LEFT OUT

There were many people involved in the story who were excluded in order to prevent overly complicating the core story. Many are mentioned in the historical notes. There were non-material events related to the story that are also not included in the book. The trial transcripts are thousands of pages. Much of the testimony was insignificant and excluded.

ABRIDGING

Almost all of the real events, but especially the legal proceedings, are abridged. The closing arguments in the Borden murder trial are, if unabridged, as long as a book. It was necessary to abridge all of the legal proceedings and most of the moments/scenes so that they fit better in a fictionalized format. While abridging, some phrasing was changed to clarify and smooth transitions. Prosecutor Moody's statements in court were particularly problematic. He spoke in long, run-on sentences that sometimes required multiple rereads to understand. Sometimes I rewrote for phrasing and word choice.

CONSTRUCTED SCENES

I constructed some scenes in the book in order to complete the narrative. For example, we know the gist of Assistant Marshall Fleet's interview of John Morse in the Borden kitchen based on police notes, but not the exact words. Likewise, Lizzie's conversations with her lawyers are not preserved in the historical record and I wrote them for the book. In those cases the scene is based on what's known about events, individuals involved, and circumstances.

EVENTS CHANGED, ADDED, AND SIMPLIFIED

I sometimes changed non-material events and details to simplify the story. For example, Dr. Bowen testified that on the morning of the murders he went from the kitchen to the dining room to the sitting room to see Andrew Borden's body. It's not clear from his testimony why he went the long way around. To simplify the story, I changed that detail such that he enters the sitting room directly from the kitchen.

Also, when Lizzie said she heard a "groan" while out in the yard, she actually said that only to Bridget. However, since Bridget and Lizzie are both suspects, in this book we're not privy to their private conversations, so that comment is included in Chapter 3.

Other parts of the story are not part of the historical record and were added to this book to complete the story. For example, we do not know if Sarah Morse Borden wrote to her brother John before her death.

I took pains to avoid changing material details or major events.

WAS IT TRUE OR NOT?

Some of the Borden history isn't proven, but there's good reason to believe it's true. For example, in *A Private Disgrace*, Victoria Lincoln, who grew up in Fall River and knew Fall Riverites who were alive at the time of the Borden Murders, asserts that Andrew Borden sometimes sold extra eggs from a basket on his way to work at the bank. I made individual decisions about inclusion or exclusion for each based on the source and evidence.

SELECTED BIBLIOGRAPHY

PRIMARY SOURCES

Inquest Upon the Deaths of Andrew J. Borden and Abby D. Borden. Annie M. White, Stenographer. Collection of Fall River Historical Society. (Digitized by Stefani and Kat Koorey)

Preliminary Hearing (Stenographer's Minutes): Commonwealth of Massachusetts vs. Lizzie A. Borden, August 25, 1892-September 1, 1892, Judge Josiah Coleman Blaisdell, presiding, Second District Court, Fall River, MA. Annie M. White, Stenographer. Collection of Fall River Historical Society. (Digitized by Harry Widdows, Stefani Koorey, and Kat Koorey)

Trial of Lizzie Andrew Borden Upon an indictment charging her with the Murder of Abby Durfee Borden and Andrew Jackson Borden Before the Superior Court for the County of Bristol; Mason, C. J. and Blodgett and Dewey, J. J. Presiding. Official Stenographic Report by Frank H. Burt, 1893. (Digitized by Harry Widdows).

The Witness Statements for the Lizzie Borden Murder Case, August 4-October 6, 1892. Collection of Fall River Historical Society. (Digitized by Stefani Koorey).

BOOKS AND ARTICLES

Carlisle, Marcia R. "What Made Lizzie Borden Kill?" *American Heritage* 43, no. 4 (June-July 1992): 66-72. https://www.americanheritage.com/what-made-lizzie-borden-kill

Conforti, Joseph A. *Lizzie Borden on Trial: Murder, Ethnicity, and Gender.* Lawrence: University of Kansas Press, 2015

Dziedzic, Shelley. "Abby's Sisters." Lizzie Borden Warps and Wefts. 2010. https://lizziebordenwarpsandwefts.com/september-muttoneaters-online-the-sisters-of-abby-borden/. Accessed August 20, 2023.

Dziedzic, Shelley. "Lizzie's School Days." Lizzie Borden Warps and Wefts. 2007. https://lizziebordenwarpsandwefts.com/lizzie-bordens-school-days-the-morgan-street-school/. Accessed September 7, 2023.

Kent, David. *Forty Whacks: New Evidence in the Life and Legend of Lizzie Borden.* Emmaus, PA: Yankee Books, 1992.

Kent, David. *The Lizzie Borden Sourcebook.* Boston: Branden Publishing Company, 1992.

Knowlton, Frank W., and Edmund Lester Pearson. *The Knowlton/Pearson Correspondence: 1923-1930.* Fall River, MA: Fall River Historical Society, 1997.

Lincoln, Victoria. *A Private Disgrace: Lizzie Borden by Daylight.* New York: G. P. Putnam's Sons, 1967.

Martins, Michael, and Dennis A. Binette. *Parallel Lives: A Social History of Lizzie A. Borden and Her Fall River.* Fall River, MA: Fall River Historical Society, 2010.

Martins, Michael, and Dennis A. Binette, eds. *The Commonwealth of Massachusetts vs. Lizzie A. Borden: The Knowlton Papers, 1892-1893: A Collection of Previously Unpub-*

lished Letters and Documents from the Files of Prosecuting Attorney Hosea Morrill Knowlton. Fall River, MA: Fall River Historical Society, 1994.

Martins, Michael, Dennis A. Binette, and Stefani Koorey, eds. *The Jennings Journals 1892: The unpublished notes and documents from the files of Lizzie Borden's Defense Attorney, Andrew Jackson Jennings.* Fall River, MA: Fall River Historical Society, 2021.

Miller, Sarah. *The Borden Murders: Lizzie Borden and the Trial of the Century*. New York: Schwartz & Wade, 2014.

Oneill, Therese, *Unmentionable: The Victorian Lady's Guide to Sex, Marriage, and Manners*. New York: Little, Brown and Company, 2016.

Pearson, Edmund. "Legends of Lizzie," The New Yorker, April 22, 1933: 20-22.

Pearson, Edmund Lester, ed. *The Trial of Lizzie Borden*. New York: Doubleday, Doran & Company, 1937.

Porter, Edwin H. *The Fall River Tragedy: A History of the Borden Murders*. Fall River, MA: George R. H. Buffinton, 1893.

Rebello, Leonard. *Lizzie Borden: Past & Present*. Fall River, MA: Al-Zach Press, 1999.

Robertson, Cara. *The Trial of Lizzie Borden: A True Story*. New York: Simon & Schuster, 2019.

Spiering, Frank. *Lizzie*. New York: Random House, 1984.

Widdows, Harry. "Crime in the City: Fall River, 1892." The Hatchet: Journal of Lizzie Borden Studies. August/September, 2007, Volume 4, Issue 3. https://lizzieandrewborden.com/HatchetOnline/crime-in-the-city-fall-river-1892.html. Accessed September 2, 2023.

Wootton, Charles W., and Barbara E. Kemmerer. "The Changing Genderization of Bookkeeping in the United States, 1870-1930." *The Business History Review* Vol. 70, Nov. 4 (Winter, 1996): 541-586.

"The Popular Officer Harrington-an Update." Lizzie Borden Warps and Wefts. 2022. https://lizziebordenwarpsandwefts.com/2022/08/13/the-popular-officer-harrington-an-update/. Accessed September 21, 2023.

"Remembering John Fleet." Lizzie Borden Warps and Wefts. 2010. https://lizziebordenwarpsandwefts.com/2010/05/10/remembering-john-fleet/. Accessed September 21, 2023.

ONLINE

The Fall River Historical Society, https://fallriverhistorical.org/

Lizzie Andrew Borden Virtual Museum and Library, https://lizzieandrewborden.com/.

Lizzie Borden Warps and Wefts, https://lizziebordenwarpsandwefts.com.

The Hatchet: A Journal of Lizzie Borden & Victorian Studies, https://lizzieandrewborden.com/HatchetOnline.

ACKNOWLEDGMENTS

This book could not have been written without the work of thousands of individuals and organizations who've preserved, puzzled over, and contributed to the Borden story. Thank you to the Lizzie Borden experts and aficionados everywhere, especially the Fall River Historical Society, Dennis A. Binette, David Kent, Kat Koorey, Stefani Koorey, Michael Martins, Sarah Miller, Leonard Rebello, Cara Robertson, and Harry Widdows.

Special thanks and all my love to Chris and Tim for your unwavering support and assistance.

Les Rosen, thank you for talking through the story and book, over and over for years, with kindness, patience, and honesty. You are a true friend.

Pamela L. Kelly, thanks for being an enthusiastic, clear-sighted, and wise sounding board. Also, thanks for the title.

Mitul Patel, thank you for being the first person to read the complete book and for providing many suggestions to improve the readability and clarity.

To friends who listened to ideas, read, and gave feedback or advice and support, you're in my heart: Amanda Groe, Caroline Chow, Jake Caldwell, Jim Gummow, Jon Thiem, Laura Hansen, Natalie Bolton, and Rose Boswell.

Elizabeth West, thank you for teaching me to know what I know. I couldn't have gotten here without you.

Made in the USA
Columbia, SC
23 December 2024